MARY

MARY

Mother—Spouse—Servant
Three Days with the Mother of Jesus

A Novel

CHRISTOPHER GRAHAM

XULON PRESS ELITE

Xulon Press Elite
2301 Lucien Way #415
Maitland, FL 32751
407.339.4217
www.xulonpress.com

Printed in the United States of America.

Paperback ISBN-13: 978-1-6628-1353-5
eBook ISBN-13: 978-1-6628-1354-2

Acknowledgements

The inspiration for this project comes from the mothers I have been blessed with in my life. My mother Ann Graham. My Mother-in-law Mary Lee Przybysz. My Grandmothers Anna Zbikowski and Mary Graham. And a close friend Marian Swisher. These women dedicated themselves to the wellbeing of their families and they each had a great dedication to Mary and the rosary.

Thank you, mom, for all the love and help you provided me in my life. I miss you and this story is for you.

I would like to thank my wife Kathy and my children Christopher Graham and Alicia Wray for their love and support shown me as I gathered my thoughts and searched my heart and soul to express the love I have witnessed in my lifetime.

I would like to thank the following people for their encouragement, guidance, and support for this project. They have added depth to the content of the story and deepened my understanding of God, Mary, and the importance of loving one another. Thank you to, Paul Kunzen, Jim Horath, Shelly Hoffman, Sallie Bachar, Greg Gill, Kathy Krohn-Gill. Allan Crevier, Carol Crevier, Chris Lee, and Evelyn Lee.

And Thank you to Kate Ball Photography in Spalding, Lincolnshire, UK for supplying the cover photography.

Table of Contents

CHAPTER 1

Voices and Angels

It was mid-afternoon, and the storm that had lasted for three hours was ending. She turned her head skyward and, looking to heaven, she heard a voice. There was a tremendous amount of noise surrounding her. Men yelling instructions, horses splashing in the mud, people crying out because of the death of her son. But above all the noise, she heard a voice. It was a voice muffled by the sounds of the activities around her. It was a voice she thought she had heard before but could not be sure. Her senses were not as sharp as they should be because of the emotional trauma she was under.

However, she did hear a voice saying, "Hello, Mother. It has taken a long time to get to this place."

She refocused her gaze and looked at the body of her son. He was hanging on a cross with his head buried deep within his chest. He was dead. The reason she was born was no longer breathing. She was alone. The world seemed darker. The light brought into this world through her son was extinguished by the Romans. She felt exposed to the powers of evil for the first time in her life.

She closed her eyes to rest her weary mind and began to pray. She asked God to help her. There was so much more to do. She needed the help of others. She was a widow who had just lost her only child to a brutal death. Crucifixion. How was she going to take care of the body of her child? How would the laws prohibiting the touching of a dead body prevent her from burying her Son before the end of the Sabbath? Where could she find help at this late hour?

The noise around her began to increase. She watched as the Romans removed the body from the cross. A small group of four soldiers walked toward the cross with gloomy looks upon their faces. They were young, strong, and seemed to possess a level of dignity for an undignified duty. They gently removed the cross from its base and then carefully brought it to the ground. The earth upon which the cross was laid was muddy from the storm that rolled through the area with a hard rain. It seemed to recognize this man that just moments ago asked God to accept His spirit. The earth knew this was its Creator and appeared to reach up through the puddles and sweetly embrace the body, gently easing it to its resting place.

The Roman soldiers worked as if in a trance, removing the nails from his hands and feet. They looked with genuine disgust at the crown of thorns that adorned his head and removed this crown of mockery. Each thorn was carefully extracted from the scalp and placed into a pile next to his body. The wounds from the crown were deep and disfigured his face, all distinguishing features gone. The man known as Jesus of Nazareth was no longer recognizable.

The Roman centurion, who arrived after the man was nailed to the cross, dismounted his horse. He looked around to evaluate the situation, then walked over to the woman who was at the foot of the cross surrounded by her friends. He marched with a confident stride, but his face was full of agony and anguish. He motioned for his men to bring the body over to the woman. He looked her in the eyes, eyes red from crying, and said gently in a trembling voice, "Mother, behold the fruit of thy womb. It is done."

She was startled at his words. Then she turned her head and looked directly at the stranger. She stared at the centurion and looked deeply into his eyes. She had seen these eyes before! But they were attached to a different being. These were the eyes of the angel who appeared to her to announce she was to bear a child, a child she would love for all eternity.

How could these eyes be looking at her through the body of a Roman centurion? How could this centurion know about the fruit of her womb? She was stunned, but she was not afraid. She had learned over the years messages and messengers from God can come in many different forms. While she was in great emotional distress, she maintained her eye contact and smiled. Her eyes fell softly on the centurion, and she nodded her head to acknowledge his words.

Suddenly, she again heard the muffled voice. "Hello, Mother. It has taken an eternity to get here, but we have arrived."

Mary, the mother of Jesus of Nazareth, looked around her for the source of this voice. She was unable to locate it, so with a mystified look on her face, Mary turned toward the centurion. He quickly turned his head from the woman and began to scan the area. It appeared that he too had also heard something and was looking for the source.

Mother Mary not seeing anything unusual said in a soft voice, "Centurion, why do you speak of the fruit of my womb? What is your name?"

The centurion refocused his eyes on the woman and responded calmly, "I am Gabriel, Mother. I am here to serve you. These men who have removed your son from the cross are assigned to me. We are here to assist in the preparation of placing the body of your son into its tomb. It appears you have friends with much influence. Joseph of Arimathea has spoken to Pontius Pilate. He has granted him authority to take possession of the body and place it in a tomb not far from here. These men will help to ensure the body of your son makes it safely to the tomb before the start of your Sabbath.

"Mother, I have known these men for a long time; they are trustworthy. Let me introduce them to you. Here is Michael, the leader of the group; next is Uriel, Raphael, and Jeremiel. They will do as you request and will accompany you until the body of your son is safely in the tomb. They will ensure the tomb is properly sealed. Then later you can return to finish preparing the body according to the customs of Israel. Please explain to those who accompany you, the role of these workers. We do not want to cause anyone concern. We are here to assist you in the preparation and transportation of the body of your son."

In her greatest moment of sadness, Mary, the mother of this man Jesus who was just crucified, is being shown an immense amount of respect and honor by a Roman centurion. She looked at the centurion more closely and admitted to herself she had seen him before. She turned her head to face the workers mentioned by Gabriel. She closed her eyes to think, then opened them to observe these men. How can these men look familiar? Maybe, one of these soldiers is the source of the muffled voice she heard. She was not sure what she should do.

She thought back to the beginning of the life of her son. These men looked like the angels sent by God to announce the birth of her son to the shepherds in the nearby fields. While they appeared in human form, there is no doubt these were the faces she observed as a birthing mother. God, the Father of her son, had sent His servants to be here at the time of death, just as He had sent them at the time of birth. She should expect nothing less. God has always been a part of her life, not just in prayer, but in the real presence of their son Jesus.

Still, the muffled voice she heard concerned her. She thought the voice was familiar, but she could not be sure. The people around her were beginning to act. The body of her son, Jesus, was lying in the mud, waiting to be tended to. She could not focus on the voice at this time; she needed to focus on her son and getting his body to the place of burial.

She glanced at the soldiers noticing their size and muscular bodies. They in return looked at her and bowed in respect. It almost seemed as if they honored her. This behavior was unexpected and out of the ordinary. She was not prepared for this intervention. The past few days were long and full of unforeseen horrors. While she had known her son would lead a full life and ultimately experience death, she never thought his life would end so soon, in such a heartbreaking manner. The mother of this man Jesus was quickly surrounded by those accompanying her. They were those who chose to stand with her at the foot of the cross, as she watched as her son was mercilessly tortured and crucified by the Romans after a trial before the Jewish High Council.

Gabriel instructed his men to surround Mary. She looked at their faces, which transformed to a state informing her these were not ordinary Roman soldiers; this was a team of angels with Gabriel. Despite their appearance, while rough and dirty to the outsider, in her eyes they were obedient servants working lovingly to remove the painful reminders of the past few days from the body of her son. The friends who accompanied Mary looked at the soldiers in a state of awe and confusion. Why was a Roman centurion off his horse and speaking to their friend Mary? How could a Roman possibly display kindness to the mother of a crucified convict? They were dumbfounded!

Mary, the wife of Cleopas, also referred to as Miriam, had known Mary since the birth of her son. She stepped forward and bravely nudged herself between Mary and the centurion and said, "Centurion, why have you stopped to speak to the mother? Can you not see your actions are causing her more distress? The death of her son has caused her to suffer great pain!"

The Centurion quickly stood and looked at Miriam and gave her a stern look. He said to her, "Woman, I am here to help the mother of this man they call Jesus. My men and I are here to ensure the body is properly prepared to be placed in a tomb before the beginning of your Sabbath."

Miriam looked into his eyes, and she saw how pained this man looked. His eyes were red and swollen as if he had been crying. A Roman centurion crying at the death of a convicted criminal was unheard of. She turned to Mary, the mother of Jesus, looking for answers to this unusual encounter. Mary looked at her and smiled.

Mary pulled Miriam close to her and said, "This is no ordinary Roman centurion. I have seen these eyes before attached to a messenger of God. He is a being of hope. He and his men are here to help. We have much to do to get the body of my son ready for burial. He has informed me Joseph of Arimathea has been given permission from Pontius Pilate to have the body placed in a tomb not far from here. I know Joseph had been preparing a tomb in Jerusalem for his own burial, and this must be the tomb he is making available for my Jesus. We must work with these men to get my son transported to the gravesite and then prepare the body to be placed into the tomb before the Sabbath arrives."

"Joseph has met with Pilate and was granted the authority to bury Jesus?" said Miriam in a surprised voice.

"What a blessing! I was so caught up in the crucifixion that I forgot about the burial—*Wait*! Burial of crucified prisoners is not normal. I wonder how Joseph was able to convince Pilate to release the body to him?"

Miriam then stood and quickly turned and called the others together to explain what was going on. She addressed Mary Magdalene, a follower of Jesus who was known to them as Magdalene, and Salome, the mother of James and John and wife of Zebedee. They looked at her with surprise. Then they looked toward the soldiers and were amazed at how humanely they were performing their duties. Romans showing compassion for a man crucified is not something they had seen before. They were nervous as they turned back to Mary.

Magdalene looking at Mary said with disdain, "Mother, these men are Romans. They should have no role in the preparing of our Lord's body for burial. They are not believers!"

Mary the mother of Jesus responded, "Magdalene, please trust these workers are here to show respect for my Jesus. This work detail has been specifically chosen to assist us in getting Jesus prepared for burial. Do not ask me how I know this but trust me when I say these are not ordinary men. They have been chosen by my son's father to help us."

Magdalene looked at Mary with a look of disbelief and said, "It is hard for me to believe these men are here to help us. They are not believers and are part of Rome! These are the people who put our Jesus to death! I cannot allow them to touch and defile his sacred body!"

Mother Mary came forward and touched Magdalene on the arm and, looking into her eyes, said, "Mary, you have to trust me. These men are not Romans. They are a special group of workers assigned to the centurion Gabriel to help us get my Jesus prepared for burial. Look at how they treat the body! They are suffering as you are suffering. I tell you they love my Jesus as much as we do and are filled with much sorrow at what has happened to him. They may look like Romans, but they are not. I will explain to you later who they are. For now, you must trust me. They will help us take care of my son's body and work with us to get Jesus to the tomb."

Magdalene respectfully bowed her head and said firmly, "I will trust you and do as you say, but we will need to discuss this matter further once the body has been buried."

Mary looked back at her in agreement. She could provide more details to the group after the body was placed in the tomb.

Gabriel called to Michael and instructed him to have the others carefully carry the body of Jesus over to his mother.

Mary looked at the men in disbelief. Her face was full of pain and sorrow as she accepted the body of her deceased son Jesus. She hugged him, brushing away as much of the blood and mud from his face as she could. Suddenly, she cried out in a loud voice. The cry was so loud it appeared to shake the earth. Her cry was so painful, those around her openly cried. Her heart was pounding through her chest. She was overwhelmed with agony.

Those around her tried to comfort her, but their words did not matter. There would be no more tomorrows to be shared with her son. She was in pain, and no matter how they tried to console her, they could not stop her suffering.

As Mary looked at the body, she could see every wound endured by her son. She made a special note of the gashes in his hands, feet, and side. The nails, the thorns, the bruises, the swollen face, and the spear-pierced side, she could see it all. It was as if she experienced the pain herself. Bringing the life of her son into the world in the little grotto in Bethlehem was not as painful as this. His life ended too early. There was still much to do. How could a man so good, a son so loving, suffer such an unjust and painful death?

She knew at the time she chose to accept her role as Jesus's mother that she would experience pain. It was predicted by Simeon forty days after the birth of Jesus in the temple of Jerusalem at the time of Jesus's redemption of the first-born ceremony. She was told a sword of sorrow would pierce her heart, and at this moment she knew it had pierced her heart deeply. The love she had for her son was unquestionable and limitless. She loved Jesus with all her heart, a love so deep it bound her to him in a way she did not know she could love. This child brought into this world by the grace of God was now dead.

She took the arm of her tunic and continued to gently wipe away the blood and dirt from the face of her son. She looked upon his face, smiled, and kissed him on the lips. Tears fell from her cheeks and landed gently on his face. She carefully moved his head to the side and whispered into his ear, "From the time I chose to be your mother, my life has been dedicated to helping you grow into the man destined to free the world from sin. Go now to meet your Father and rejoice in His embrace. I wish you could know how much I love you right now. Go, I await your return."

The four soldiers were standing over Mary as she held her son close to her heart. They marveled at her gentleness and humility. They observed her pain. They saw she was not angry. They noted her painful smile and were amazed. Here stood the woman asked by God to bear His son and to live a life of service, suffering from the loss of her child, and yet she could smile. Even the painful smile held meaning.

Mary looked up and saw the looks on the faces of Michael, Raphael, Uriel, and Jeremial. They were crying. Their faces were twisted with pain. It was as if someone they loved had died.

She called to Miriam and asked her to hold the body of her son Jesus as she raised herself from the ground. She wiped her hands on her clothes, blotted with blood and mud, and stepped toward the workers. They looked at her, then bent their knees and fell to the ground. Each one expressed their deep sorrow for the loss of her son.

Raphael spoke first, "Mother, you have shown your son much love and loyalty in your life. Now at the time of his death, you show him more love. I have seen much sadness in this world, but we will not forget the loving nature you have displayed today."

Jeremial then said, "Mother, I feel such anger right now for the way your son has been treated these past few days.

I find myself wanting to hold these men responsible for the extinction of his human life, a life full of hope, faith, and love. However, I look at you and see how you are not showing anger. I am ashamed of my feelings. I see your son through your actions, and I realize I must act as you have acted."

Uriel stepped forward and said, "Mother, it is easy to see why you were chosen to be the mother of God's son. We who have been around you during the life of your son are humbled by your forgiving and loving nature. Mankind will find their way to your son through your actions."

Michael came forward with tears running down his cheeks, his blue eyes swollen from crying. He looked upon Mary and took her hand, kissed it gently, and said, "Hail, Mary, full of grace, blessed are you among women! My heart breaks for you, my lady. Much has been asked of you, and you have fulfilled your role in providing a loving home and life for the son of the Most High. I will pray you are comforted in this time of great loss."

Mary turned away from the four workers to collect herself and wiped her face with her tunic sleeve. She gathered them around her. She held their hands, looking at each one and thanking them for being there to help prepare the body of her son Jesus for burial. Gabriel had come into sight, and she asked him to join them in this small circle. Once he arrived Mary looked at him and said, "I know who you are. I have seen all of you at different times in my life. I think you have always been part of my life, watchful caretakers making sure my Jesus was cared for and safe. I want to thank you for your protection and for making me feel as if my role as mother was enough to please the Father. I will explain my relationship with you to the others later, but for now, know I am glad you are here to help support me through this painful time. I could not do this without you."

They looked at her and thanked her for her kindness.

She then turned to the others and said, "Let us not cry because we think my Jesus's life is over; let us smile because my Jesus's life happened, and he will return to us!"

Chapter 2

Dignity in Service

G abriel broke away from the group and looked down the road and spotted a horse and wagon approaching their position. The four soldiers turned toward the wagon and guided it near the body of Jesus. The driver of the cart looked at Gabriel and declared, "Centurion! I have been sent here by the man called Joseph of Arimathea to gather a body and bring it to where he has a tomb readied for the burial of this man."

Gabriel motioned to the others to get the body ready for transportation. The wagon was of good size and was covered with a bedding of straw. Inside the bed there was a brown cloak to be used to lay the body on.

"Mother, I will have the men place the body in the wagon, and then you and your friends can climb in and travel to the tomb," said Gabriel.

Just as the women were climbing into the wagon, the driver said to Gabriel. "In the back of the wagon you will find three containers. One frankincense, the other myrrh, and the third water. I was given these containers by the man who supplied the wagon. He said the mother of the cruci-fied man would know what to do with the contents."

Gabriel nodded and looked toward Mary the mother of Jesus and told her of the containers to be found in the wagon. She bowed to him and said, "Thank you, Centurion, I know what these items are to be used for."

She was then lifted into the front seat of the wagon by Raphael and then Miriam, Magdalene, and Salome were assisted into the bed of the wagon. They immediately began to gather the straw into a pile to create a bedding layer. Then they placed the brown cloak over the straw, creating a space to place the body of the son of Mary. As they finished, Mary looked down at the straw bedding prepared for her sons' body. She had an image flash through her mind remem-bering the straw bedding prepared by her betrothed hus-band Joseph, at the time of her child's birth.

She continued to cry, tears falling from her cheeks. The soldiers raised the body of Jesus up into the bed of the wagon. The women arranged the body on the straw to allow for a comfortable ride to the tomb. Mary looked at her son. She thought to herself, this child of mine came into the world and was welcomed by a bed of straw in a grotto in Bethlehem. Straw bedding embraced her son at his birth, now it was used to cushion his body at death.

As Mary looked around, she saw the Roman soldiers and those who stood with her at the foot of the cross. She looked to heaven and thanked God she was surrounded by His love in this moment of death, just as He surrounded her with His love at the time of their son's birth. That cherished babe entered this world in a humble scene and now a quiet exit from this place of death.

Golgotha will forever be stained with the blood of God's son, just as Bethlehem was stained with the blood of his birth. A grotto stable filled with animals joyfully worshiped this child at birth, and a hillside of stone and dirt eulogizes his death.

The women who surrounded Mary had been part of her life for many years. Miriam had been with her the longest, sharing a household, where their families lived together under one roof. Salome, the wife of Zebedee, had been near her since the beginning of her son's ministry. And Magdalene had been near her since she began to follow Jesus after he removed the seven demons from her body. This was the group of women that traveled with him and found places for him to eat and sleep for most of his public life.

Mary, mother of Jesus, turned her head and asked the wagon driver, "Where can we find Joseph of Arimathea?"

The driver answered, "He is on his way to the tomb. He will meet you there."

"How long will it take to get to the gravesite?" asked Magdalene harshly, "The daylight is quickly receding. We need to get the body into the tomb before nightfall."

The driver responded, "We have to travel approximately four to six miles. We should be able to make it there in less than an hour. The rain has chased a lot of people off the street, making the road less congested. Fewer people on the road means the horses can move faster."

"Good," said Magdalene. "Let us be off as soon as possible. Today, the Sabbath begins. We must be completed with our work before sunset."

Mary, the mother of Jesus, touched Magdalene on the arm gently and said "Mary, we must make sure the body of my Jesus is properly prepared before the tomb is closed. If we go beyond the beginning of nightfall, it will be all right. The rituals of the Sabbath will have to wait. We have important work to do, and we must do it quickly. My Jesus taught us to obey the Sabbath, but there are conditions where the realities of life make unconditional obedience to the laws just not possible. We will do what is right for my son and will pray our choice to get the body anointed and in the tomb is understood by others."

Magdalene bowed her head and accepted the instructions with a hopeful heart, as the body was laid to rest on the bed of straw. She then looked to the mother, and Miriam to make sure they had been able to secure the body of Jesus in the wagon. When she was confident the body was secured, she signaled to the driver it was all right to begin the journey. The driver nodded, slapped the horses with the reigns, and the wagon began to move.

The women tended to the body of Jesus as Mary his mother prepared a mixture of the frankincense and myrrh to be used to anoint the body. These women had worked together many times. They were a unit that offered support and service to Jesus and his disciples. There was little interaction between them, but as they worked, there was an unspoken awareness and need for each other. There is dignity to serving in silence with the people you love. This type of love goes beyond physical touch, beyond the spoken word. It is a love based on true faith, trust, and recognition of the needs of the other without the expectation of repayment. This unselfish dedication to assist Jesus and his ministry had exposed these women to a life of unimaginable fulfillment. Now they were emotionally drained as they began to prepare the body of Jesus for its journey to the tomb.

They took their tunics, tore off pieces to create a set of towels to be used to treat the wounds. They took the container of water, soaked some of the towels, and began to clean the blood and dirt covering his body. They looked upon Jesus and began to cry. They had been with Jesus during his journey from Pilate's palace to the crucifixion site on Golgotha. They watched him carry the cross until his strength was near an end when the Romans had a Cyrene help him carry the cross to the place of death.

Magdalene noticed how the skin of his right shoulder was gone. She could see the bone was completely visible. This was the shoulder he used to carry the cross. She closed her eyes, bowed her head, and sobbed deeply. How could Jesus have carried the cross on this shoulder? How much pain was he experiencing? Jesus moaned, and cried out while he was burdened with the cross, but not as she would have expected him too with these wounds. This area of missing flesh was washed carefully with water. A mixture of Frankincense and myrrh was applied to the area. She knew the healing properties of the ointments would not offer Jesus comfort, but she applied them just as well. The body needed to be as clean as possible before it could be wrapped in the burial shroud.

Miriam took her towel and washed the back of Jesus. She saw how deeply the scourging had defiled his body. She was able to see exposed muscles and ribs. There was almost no skin left upon his back. The open wounds were covered with blood and mud. She sat back and gently caressed his back with a wet rag and removed as much of the grime as possible. She began to cry silently. Her body shook with every stroke she made.

She was his second mother. The wife of his father Joseph's brother, Cleopas, and the mother of James and Joses, his childhood brothers and lifelong companions. She had bathed Jesus and her children when they were young. Her mind began to fill with the memories of Jesus as a child and his life in Nazareth as a young man. She had always been part of his life because she was like a sister to his mother Mary. Even though Miriam was almost ten years older than Mary, Jesus's mother, they raised their families together in a humble household in Nazareth.

Their husbands were carpenters, and at times they had to travel away from home to perform their work duties leaving the two Marys alone with the children. Mary the mother of Jesus was the one to teach the children about God because she was raised in the temple in Jerusalem and possessed a deep knowledge of the faith and was fluent in Hebrew, the language of the scripture. And Miriam was the mother who tended to the daily routines of the family. She would structure activities for the children to help the household function. Whether it was fetching water, harvesting vegetables or fruit from the garden, milking the goats or sheep, or just helping with washing the clothes, she kept everyone in joyful spirits with her enthusiasm and cheerful view of life.

However, now she was incredibly distressed and could not control her sorrow. Her crying was diminishing, but her heart was breaking, as she washed the back and placed the ointment mixture on the wounded areas.

Salome took the water and washed as much of Jesus's body that she could reach. She had met him through her sons James and John, and husband Zebedee. They were a family of fishermen. Andrew and his brother Simon, fisherman working on the Sea of Galilee, introduced Jesus to them, and then Jesus told them to follow Him and he would make them fishers of men! They did not understand what He was saying but they were inspired by His words that moved them into action.

Andrew had heard Jesus speak after he was baptized by John the Baptist. He thought this Jesus might be the promised Messiah because He spoke as if the voice of God radiated from His being. He spoke of love, brotherhood, and forgiveness. His words touched his heart and of all those who heard Him speak. Andrew came away believing Jesus was the chosen one, the one to lead the tribes of Israel to their appointment with destiny.

Salome washed the broken body tenderly. Tears ran down her cheeks and mingled with the dirt and grime already present on the limp body. She was unnerved by the sight of Jesus's disfigured body. She had come to believe Jesus was the Messiah. She was even bold enough to ask him if her sons could be seated on each side of him in his kingdom. Now as she worked in silence to clean the body, she felt a sense of guilt for making so selfish a request. Jesus responded to her by explaining that the seats beside him were not His to give, but His Father's. She understood the response, but she did feel that her two boys, the sons of thunder, deserved such places of honor. However, now looking at the lifeless body, she was ashamed of her boldness and her self-centered request.

Each of the women performed their duties with love and tenderness. They did not fully clean the body but much of the blood and dirt had been removed. They were getting close to the burial tomb. They looked at each other and held hands, affirming their decision to be with Mary, Jesus's mother.

Magdalene was deeply troubled. She looked as if she was getting angrier by the moment. Her tears of sorrow were gone. Her face began to show a sternness the other women had not seen. She looked to Mary, Jesus's mother, and said, "Mary, we do not have much time before we arrive at the tomb. I do not mean to be disrespectful, but I am very confused as to your behavior toward these Roman soldiers who are traveling with us. The Romans put Jesus to death, and yet you allow them to assist us in preparing his body for burial."

She continued in a loud voice, "My heart is broken! We have lost Jesus, and yes, I believe he will rise from the dead, but I find it hard to forgive the people who put this man I love to death! You said you would explain to us who they are. I think now is the time to bring us into the light and let us know how you know these Romans!" The wagon shook as it hit a large hole. Everyone on the wagon had lost their balance. It was as if the road did not like the question because the road now became bumpier. The driver slowed the pace of travel to handle the rougher road conditions.

Mary, Jesus's mother, turned from the seat next to the driver. She lowered herself into the bed of the wagon to be closer to the three women. She looked over the side of the wagon and saw that John, the son of Zebedee, was riding with Gabriel. She motioned for Gabriel to come closer to the side of the wagon so he could hear her explanation of who the soldiers were. She asked them to gather closer. She lifted Jesus's head and held it on her lap. She looked up at the women and began to speak.

"Miriam, Magdalene, and Salome, I cannot express to you the peace I feel because you are here. You have been a part of my life for many years. Having you here to help me as we take my Jesus to his grave is comforting. The love you have for my Jesus is evident. Your love for me is also strong and is binding us together. I will explain my actions toward these people who are with us as we prepare to place my Jesus in his grave.

"These soldiers are not actually men; they are angels sent by Jesus's father to appear as men to help me live through this incredibly gruesome moment in my life and to provide workers who love his son as much as we do. The centurion with John is called Gabriel. He is the angel who appeared to me the night I was asked to become the mother of God's child. He came to me at night during my time for prayers. He told me I had been chosen by God to bear a child. I told him this was impossible, asking how this could be. He told me all things were possible with God. I had been blessed by the Holy Spirit, and I would be the virgin who would bring the Messiah into this world.

"The other angels are Michael, Raphael, Uriel, and Jeremial. While I did not know their names at the time, I do recognize them because they were present at the time of Jesus's birth. You see, when Jesus was born, a star appeared in the sky above the grotto in Bethlehem. Angels were sent into the countryside to proclaim the birth of a newborn king. They came upon a group of shepherds and led them to the place where I had given birth to my son.

"I was startled to see people arrive after the birth. It was unnerving because we were in a distant land away from our family and friends in Nazareth. How could a band of people appear in such a short period of time? Again, it was Gabriel I recognized, and he whispered in my ear this group of shepherds was gathered to witness the birth of my child. They were to proclaim that a child was born on this night and that this child would be known as the son of God.

"I remember Michael being the largest of the angels, as he hovered over my Jesus in a very protective manner. Jesus, while just a newborn, seemed to open his eyes in a way as if to confirm to Michael he was alive and in good health. Michael looked at my child and smiled. A tear fell from his eye and landed on Jesus. He then glanced at me, and I heard him say, 'Blessed art thou among women and blessed is the fruit of your womb. You have brought the Child of God into this world. Your choice to fulfill God's request will never be forgotten. Rejoice and be glad because through you, a child is born that will proclaim God's goodness to the world.' I smiled at Michael and bowed in response to his words. I began to realize how my life would be forever changed, because of this moment.

"I thought I knew what love felt like, but at the birth of my child I felt an overwhelming sense of love. I loved this baby immediately and unconditionally, but I felt a powerful sense of love emanating from Jesus. He loved me! The love I felt was not just unconditional, but eternal. I would be loved forever by this child, and through this child, I would get to know God in a powerful way. My life was changed! I was now the mother of God's son. I knew my role was to serve God in whatever ways were expected.

"My agreement to bear His child was the yes to love God with all my heart, mind, and soul. My life as the mother of Jesus was about to begin. I never realized at the time how much joy, pain, sorrow, and love my heart could hold.

"Raphael was the angel that spoke to the shepherds. He explained to them in simple and easy-to-understand terms how the birth of my child was special. He looked at me and asked if the assembled crowd could look upon the child. I nodded yes, and they walked by. Jesus smiled at each of them. It seemed a little strange a newborn child who had yet to take food from my breast could be so cheerful and welcoming to a gathering of people. Raphael whispered to me that Jesus would be the chain that links heaven and earth. His character would draw people to him. 'Strangers who meet your son will be at ease with him and share their stories in ways that will help form his personality. He will learn the ways of mankind through his interactions with others. He will be a living example of God's love for mankind,' he said.

"Jeremial was also tending to the shepherds. He seemed to hover nearer the animals. He spoke to them in a gentle voice and explained this was the child of God. The animals seemed to listen to his words. They walked closer to the child and looked upon him with contentment. They then laid down around the manger. Their bodies were throwing off a level of warmth I had never felt before. It seemed like Jeremial had asked them to create a safe warm space for us.

"Joseph, my husband, noticed this sense of welcoming from all who were present. He worked with the animals to make sure they circled our resting place and that they were fed and bedded down for the night.

"Uriel is different. I did not notice his presence at the time of birth, but I do recognize him. It is from a different time in the early years of Jesus's life. Remember, I told you about a star that appeared above the town of Bethlehem when Jesus was born. Well, this star was a symbol to the entire world that a king was born. This star hovered over Bethlehem for almost two years. Joseph and I stayed in Bethlehem after the birth of Jesus. He was able to take on some work with his brother Cleopas who was also a carpenter. This allowed us to stay with you, Miriam, and become part of your household. Our children became like one family, Jesus had brothers and sisters to watch over him as he began to grow.

"Because this star was stationary above Bethlehem, it brought to our household three travelers from the east. We believed these travelers were kings, or wise men. They came to our home looking for the child king. They observed the birth of a new star and traveled to the spot where it was overhead. They found Joseph, Jesus, and me, and paid homage to little Jesus. They presented gifts of gold, frankincense, and myrrh. They told us of their stop in Jerusalem where they were granted an audience with King Herod. They told him of the star and of their belief that this was the symbol to the world that God was sending a great messenger or king. They were under the impression Herod was interested because he asked them to return to Jerusalem and let him know if they found this newborn king so that he too could come and pay homage.

"It was at this time Gabriel appeared to the three men and requested they return to their home via a different route. They should not return to Jerusalem; they should avoid it altogether. Gabriel then appeared to Joseph and instructed him to prepare our family for travel because Herod was about to bring a great peril to the children in this area of Israel. Joseph listened to the words of Gabriel. We packed our belongings, which included the gifts received from the three wise men, and we set out on a journey taking us to Egypt. Along the journey to Egypt, we came to a resting place where we happened to meet my mother's cousin Elizabeth and her son John. Uriel was traveling with them, and he had instructed them to follow him because he was going to remove them from the area for their safety, far away from Israel, as long as Herod was alive and king of Judea.

"Uriel became our guide and stayed with us until we reached our destination in eastern Alexandria where we were welcomed into a large Jewish community. There we lived as one family unit until we were instructed by the return of Gabriel to leave Egypt and return to our homes in Israel.

"You see, these four men are not really Romans. They are God's loyal servants who have been a part of my life since I accepted the call to become the *mother of the Child of God*."

Magdalene shook her head in disbelief. She said softly, "Mother, this is an incredible tale! I apologize for my tone earlier. I should have trusted your instructions right away, but all I could see was the clothes of a Roman soldier. I did not see the garments of an angel. Of course, I have never seen an angel before, but now I know God is with us, and my anger and anxiety is eased, knowing these heavenly creatures are here to help us take care of the body of Jesus."

Miriam gently touched Mary's hand and began to cry. She said, "I remember those times and the deaths of those children in Bethlehem. Cleopas and I barely made it out of the city before the soldiers arrived. Joseph had warned Cleopas. He asked that we travel to Nazareth to take care of your house and property until you returned from Egypt. We did not know at the time why we had to pack so quickly and leave, but we believed Joseph's words of warning and took our children and left. It was a week after we left that we heard about the massacre of children in Bethlehem and surrounding areas. We were safe, but what Herod did to the families of Bethlehem was unforgiveable. To this day, I cannot think of Bethlehem and not cry for the children and the grieving parents."

Mother Mary placed her hand on Miriam's hand, and tears ran down her face as well.

"We may have escaped the attempt to kill my Jesus then, but it was just the beginning. I realized then the life of this child was precious. He would be in danger all his life. I became very protective and wanted to hide him from the world. I wanted to protect him from all harm. I did not know I could possess such strong feelings of protectiveness. But look at us now, I could not protect him forever. He is still too young to have died. I feel like I have failed in my duties as a mother. Is not a parent supposed to die before the child?"

It was then that Michael came forward and informed everyone they were nearing the gravesite. He asked them to get the body prepared for burial. He looked at Mary and saw how her pain and sorrow were affecting her ability to function. He got off his horse and went to her, helping her dismount from the wagon. He took her two hands and looked into her eyes so deeply that Mary became unaware of what was going on around her. She was emotionally transported to a calming place.

Michael said to her, "Mother, you are going to be challenged during this time between death and life. I feel the presence of the evil one. We must be watchful. I have always known of your strong love for your son, and I know he loved you eternally. It is at this time I would like to comfort you with the fact that we become what we love! Be strong, be faithful, and be a reflection of your son as you guide the others through this time of quiet servitude."

CHAPTER 3

Joseph of Arimathea and Michael's Warning

The wagon arrived at the site of the tomb. Mary looked around and saw Joseph of Arimathea, and they walked toward each other. Joseph was a wealthy man who owned a large mining organization that supplied tin to the Roman Empire. He was also a devote Jew who had many friends in Jerusalem, especially in the Sanhedrin, the ruling body of the Jewish faith. While Joseph was not a rabbi, he was a highly educated person who traveled throughout the Roman Empire. He was known for his sharp wit, generosity, and kindness. He owned no slaves. Those who worked for him were paid a fair wage for the work they performed. His generosity allowed him to gain access to people of importance, including Pontius Pilate, the Roman governor of Judea.

He greeted Mary, grasping her firmly by the hands and forcing a smile to his face. She looked at him as if he were a long-lost friend. Tears began to fall upon her cheeks. She could not smile. She looked at him and bowed her head out of respect. She had known Joseph her entire life. Joseph was the brother of Mary's father Joachim. He was present when her parents, Joachim and Ann, took her to the temple when she was three years old. He had been a close supportive figure and confidant during her entire adult life. She trusted him with the events leading to her leaving the temple when she was betrothed to Joseph.

Her pregnancy before her wedding caused quite a stir among the household staff serving in the temple in Jerusalem. Many of the priests were made aware of her situation when Joseph, her betrothed husband, brought forward the fact that she was with child and there had been no joining of their bodies. Joseph, her betrothed, thought Mary was with child through the actions of another man. He was not yet aware of the cause of her being with child, and in a moment of panic, he brought forward the information according to the laws. This moment of doubt by Joseph caused her reputation to be questioned by those who ruled the temple.

Mary had told Joseph of Arimathea many years ago about the details of how she came to be with child, that evening when Gabriel came to her and spoke to her about being favored by God and by the power of the Holy Spirit, she was to conceive a son. She would be the virgin spoken of in the book of Isaiah that would bring the son of God into the world who would be the Messiah, the chosen one. At first, Joseph had a difficult time believing Mary's story, but he had known her since the day she was born. He was aware that at an incredibly young age she had made a pledge to be consecrated to God. She would remain a virgin her entire life. He was convinced she was loyal to her vow and believed her explanation.

He was the one who helped them escape Bethlehem before the murder of hundreds of children, traveling with them to their destination and making sure they were safely hidden away in Egypt. During the months of travel, Joseph was able to spend time with the child Jesus. Joseph took this time to acquaint himself with the child he was told was the son of God. His conversations started off simple because Jesus was just a boy, but Joseph could tell by the way the child behaved that he was different. This child never caused his parents to worry; he was obedient, considerate, kind, cheerful and active. It seemed to Joseph the young Jesus absorbed everything he was exposed too. It was as if Jesus's senses were filled with wonder as he experienced the many wonders his life was exposing him to, like the joy that comes from happiness and the pain when he fell or touched a burning ember from a slowly dying fire. Regardless of the sensation, he looked as if he was learning and growing in knowledge with every day and every encounter.

His ability to understand words for such a young child amazed Joseph. This mastery of words led Joseph to introduce Jesus to many travelers who spoke other languages. Jesus did not just understand Aramaic; he was exposed to Greek, Hebrew, and Latin. While he was not fluent in these languages at such a young age, it was apparent, he would be able to speak them in the future. This was truly a special child. The more time Joseph spent with Jesus the more he came to believe this child born of Mary was the son of God. The explanation of his conception by Mary must be true.

Joseph took Mary by the arm and guided her away from the others. He said, "Mary, there is much to tell you, but now we must concentrate on getting the body of Jesus ready for burial before the time of the Sabbath. I was able to meet with Pilate right after the trial. My friend Nicodemus, who is a member of the Sanhedrin and a social friend of Pilate, brought me to him so I could ask him for the body of Jesus so he could be buried before the beginning of the Sabbath.

"Pilate asked me how this matter was of importance to me, a wealthy man and a friend of Rome. I told him you were the only child of my brother, and I have been your distant guardian since you were a child. I explained you were a widow and had no way of providing the means for your son to be buried in Jerusalem because you were from Nazareth of Galilee. I told him I travel extensively through the Roman Empire and have made it a point to have prepared several gravesites in areas that I frequently visit. I told him I had a newly prepared grave available in the city and asked him to allow me to place the body into this tomb. After some time for thought and a brief talk with his wife, Claudia Procula, he granted my request."

The expression on Mary's face changed. She smiled weakly and replied, "Thank you, Joseph. Your kindness to my son will be forever remembered. As you can see, we still have some preparatory work before we can place the body in the tomb. Would you be so kind as to help us in our efforts because the time grows short?"

Joseph bowed his head and said, "What would you ask of me my dear child?"

"The women and I will take care of cleaning and anointing the body. We will need some cloth to wrap the body. We might not be able to do a complete burial anointment before the Sabbath begins, so if you could instruct the men who are with us to remove the stone to the entrance and make sure the area inside the tomb is ready, and then make sure the tomb is sealed, this will be a great help."

Joseph bowed in approval and turned toward the workers, then stopped and looked at her with a sadness in his eyes and said, "Mary, when this is through, we must meet back at the upper room where the seder meal took place. There is much to tell you. The priests of the temple are up to no good. Your name and your history was brought forward by Annas and Caiaphas. There is nothing to do tonight, but you must be aware of the things that I heard."

She replied, "I remember those two. Annas was the chief priest, and Caiaphas was but a young priest when I was leaving the temple. All right then. We will meet at the upper room when we are finished here. Thank you for supplying the tomb and the wagon. We must move quickly to be finished as soon as possible."

Mary gathered the women around her and provided instructions as to how they were going to clean and wrap the body. It was clear the women were not comfortable handling the limp and lifeless body of Jesus. This was a man they loved and followed for many years. The condition of his body left them feeling sick, but Mother Mary came forward and offered them comforting words.

"I realize what I am asking you to do is not something you ever thought you would have to do in your life, but please know that I would not be able to handle this pain if it were not for the love you have shown to my son during his life. Your love for his life possesses an energy that will be carried with him as he travels to his Father's side. You see, love has no boundaries. It follows a person wherever they travel in life and in death. Let your love for my son be reflected in your duty to prepare his body for burial. When we are finished, we will meet in the room where the seder meal was celebrated. We will console each other there, but for now we must work quickly."

Each of the women knew what they had to do. There was an innate way they performed their duties. One continued to wash the body, one anointed the wounds, and the other carefully wrapped the body with the burial cloth. They worked silently and spoke only when they needed to, but they could not hold back their tears. The personal pain they felt was overwhelming. Jesus, who had been such a joyful energetic part of their lives, was dead. His body was lifeless but still seemed to radiate an energy that filled them with hope. Their hearts were broken because of his death, but there was much to look forward to over the next few days.

As the women finished their tasks, the Roman centurion and the soldier Michael came toward them and asked if the body was ready to be placed in the tomb. They had been able to move the large stone in front of the tomb, so it was open, and Joseph had made sure that the inside was ready to place the body. Mary nodded that the body was ready to be placed into the tomb. Magdalene came forward and addressed the Romans. "I am sorry I was so upset with you before. I did not know who you were. I beg for your forgiveness. Jesus had a great impact on my life. He accepted me and loved me like no other person I have encountered. So, you see, I was being protective of him. He may be dead, but I felt I needed to protect him. It was selfish on my part. My heart is broken and does not understand why this has happened. Jesus possessed such a strong bright light of goodness, I do not, I cannot, see why his light was extinguished in this manner."

Michael came toward her and bent down and took her face in his hands and said to her, "Mary, we are aware of your love for Jesus. We have observed how you attentively listened to Him while He was speaking. Jesus is the Word of God. He is the Word that became flesh, and He lived among you. I understand your need to be protective. I have fought my desire to protect Him many times as He lived this life as a man. The evil one has tried on several occasions to tempt and to harm Him, but Jesus was never fooled by the disguises used by His adversary. He was able to protect Himself because of His love for His Father. The love of God is the greatest power available to mankind. You have access to it because it surrounds each person; all you have to do to access it is to have faith in God.

"Magdalene your faith is strong, so strong the love of God radiates through you. Jesus loved you greatly because your faith in who He was never wavered. It may have been shaken at times, but in the end, you chose to have faith and believe he was the son of God.

Mother Mary possesses a great faith as I have never seen in a human before. The ability to love and forgive radiates from her. You would be wise to stay close to her over the next few days because even though she has lost much and is suffering, she is still the great intermediary to God. She has always enjoyed a close personal relationship to Jesus's Father. She speaks to Him every day, and sometimes every moment of every day. We as angels have known the great love God has for Mary. She was given a choice to be the mother of Jesus and her 'yes' was joyfully welcomed in heaven. God's promise to mankind could be realized because this woman, this child of God, had the faith and love to say yes! She believed in something she could not see.

Think about when you were a child or a youngster of age thirteen or fourteen, how would you have reacted to such a request? Would you have had the unquestioning faith to say yes? Mary was chosen to be the mother of Jesus from the time of her birth. Her parents were older and never had children. Mary is an only child. She was sent to the temple in Jerusalem to work as a handmaiden at the age of three. It was during her time at the temple that she was exposed to the love God had for the world. She was so captivated by this love that she pledged herself, her life, her body, and her soul to God. She made a commitment to forever be a virgin because she had wed herself to God.

The purity of love Mary displayed in her young life was apparent to all who knew of God's plan for her. She was the chosen one. She was the one to bring God's living example of love into the world. Because of the purity of her faith, she has been given abilities to see things beyond those of regular people. She can see the spiritual world that surrounds you. Mary can see the evil one, and he knows it. She is the first human to be able to see him in all his forms, and it frightens him. The evil one is not accustomed to being seen. He hides in the shadows, he whispers in ears, and he disguises himself to get humans to turn away from God and His love for them.

Mary has unconditional love for God. She is always aware of God and because she communicates with him through her prayers, she knows Him and serves Him. This pleases God greatly because all He asks of mankind is to know Him, love Him, and serve Him. It sounds simple, but it is exceedingly difficult.

The evil one has taken it upon himself to take as many people away from God's love as possible. Pulling people away and influencing their behavior to be counter to God's plan is the definition of sin. Simply put, sin is separation from God. The evil one uses doubt to manipulate your belief system, and because of the death of Jesus, the evil one is now very bold. Jesus was the safety wall protecting mankind by offering a shining light of hope for all to see. After the events of today, there is much doubt in the world, and people will shut out God and ask how God could let this happen. They will reject God. When this happens, a pathway is opened, and the evil one can and will influence mankind to separate themselves from the love of God and be receptive to sinful manipulation.

So, you see, Mary can see the evil one and what he is up to. She cannot change him or influence him, but she can intercede on the behalf of mankind to have God help combat the influence of the evil one. I can assure you, Magdalene, that you too will be able to intercede like Mother Mary and ask God to help others as they encounter the evil one. You might not be able to physically distinguish the evil one as he seduces others away from God, but you will recognize his behaviors and be able to call him out.

Remember when Jesus cast out the demons that possessed you! How did you feel? I would guess you did not even realize you were possessed. You just acted as you did, thinking it was just your nature. However, when the demons left and the blinders were removed, you found God through His son Jesus. Jesus demonstrated that God's will is greater than any whisper of sin the evil one can suggest. Jesus brought you back into the flow of God's love, and you became not just a believer, but a beloved follower.

In time, you will be able to identify evil spirits and expel them just as Jesus did by using His name because the evil one cannot stand up to the power of God. Jesus extends his power to others to exorcise demons if they possess the sureness of faith and the love of God. I tell you this now because evil has caused many people's faith to be questioned and left them with a strong sense of doubt, uselessness, and fear. We must fight this moment and recognize his cloud of doubt is only a test, a test of our faith in God and our willingness to see through the cloud and find the love of God through the life of His son Jesus.

During the next day or two, the evil one will be able to exercise great power because Jesus is not here, but you and the others must be aware that the next safety wall protecting mankind during this time between death and life is Jesus's mother Mary! Her faith is strong, but she is human and is in great pain. Her heart has been pierced by a sword of sorrow because the love of her life, Jesus, has been taken from her. I am sure you feel pain and sorrow as well, but you did not bring Jesus into this world and watch him grow into the messenger of God. Mary will appear to be strong and in charge, but her emotional foundation has been compromised. She will need the support of everyone here to make it through this time of trial. I plead with you to get the others to join you, both physically and spiritually, to protect Mary during this ordeal."

Magdalene could not believe what she was just told. Michael, an angel, was explaining to her the peril they were facing because of the boldness the evil one now had in the world. His request to help and protect Mary, Jesus's mother, caught her by surprise. What type of danger was Mary going to face? How could she and the others protect her from the evil one? Why could not the angels provide her with help? After all, they were most likely better equipped to deal with such a powerful creature.

She replied, "Michael, of course we will protect Mary, but we are just human. How can we, a small group of people painfully saddened by the loss of our Savior and our friend, have the power to address the evil one when we encounter him? And how will we recognize him when we see him, for we do not enjoy the abilities to see him as Mary does? Would not it be better if you and the other angels provided the protection you are requesting from us?"

Michael's hands moved from her cheeks to her heart, and he gently said, "You are right. It would seem like we would be a better choice to protect Mary, but God has not asked us to shield her. He is asking you and the others to find it in your hearts to help Mary through this painfully trying time. Your human qualities may have limitations, but your faith and love of Jesus now grow in the spiritual realm, and the limitations you think you possess are minimized. Being connected with Jesus through your spirits will bring you into a deeper relationship with God. And through Jesus's spirit, you will be able to provide Mary with what she needs to make it through to the resurrection.

Remember, it is your faith in God that will give you what you require to make it through this time. I am telling you this because *you* have a great faith inside you, and you love Jesus immensely. We are asking you to lead the others to help Mary. Your faith and love for Jesus will help you overcome the seductions of the evil one. Remember this: the evil one cannot harm you. He can frighten you, misguide you, and torment you, but he cannot act by himself outside of the spiritual realm. He must rely on the assistance of man to perform his doing.

Be on the watch for people wanting to get close to Mary. You may know them, or they may be strangers to you. Just be watchful and aware for Mary. If possible, do not let her be alone. Even when she sleeps, do not leave her alone. The evil one can come in the form of dreams and talk to her, and she will act restlessly. If you see this, wake her gently, and let her know you are near. This will help clear her mind. The way to God has many distractions; Mary must not be tempted to be separated from God. She will need your help and the help of the others."

Magdalene looked intensely into the eyes of Michael and she nodded and smiled, even though she was suffering herself because of the loss of Jesus. Her love for him had grown tremendously since he exorcised the demons from her. She was surprised Michael had knowledge of her being exorcised of demons. She did not know him, but his sincere and compassionate voice made her feel comfortable with him.

They needed to get Jesus's body into the tomb. It was getting nearer to the beginning of the Sabbath. Mother Mary called the other women, John, Joseph, and the Roman soldiers over to her and inquired as to whether the body and grave were ready. They all responded in the affirmative. The body was carefully anointed and wrapped in linen cloth, and the traditional burial rituals were ready to be performed.

Magdalene looked at Mother Mary and told her, "We are ready."

Mother Mary went over to Joseph, and he handed her a long piece of fabric the body was to be wrapped in. The fabric was referred to as a shroud. It was one long piece of fabric placed in the tomb on the stone on which the body was to be laid. The body was placed on the shroud and the shroud was folded over the bandaged body. The bandages were already showing signs of moisture seeping through the cloth. The shroud would add another layer to help absorb the moisture that was seeping through the bandages.

Once the shroud was properly folded and tucked around the body, Mary came forward and knelt before the shrouded body of her son Jesus. The other members of the group gathered behind her and knelt in homage.

Mary began to speak; "Dear God in heaven, I present to you our son. He has lived among Your people and has been the example of Your love for mankind. His time here in the domain of men is over. My heart is breaking, and I am full of sadness. I know He will not be gone forever; He will return, but I ache in the way any mother would ache at the loss of a child. He was full of life and loved You with His entire being. Jesus was the light that allowed mankind to see into Your eyes. He was the Word of God who became flesh and lived with us. How Your Son could be rejected is unknown to me. I ask You, now, accept His spirit into Your loving embrace.

We ask You to accept Jesus back into Your kingdom as He travels between death and life. We humbly request that

His love for You will expand from the spiritual realm, into the world of man so He can become the beacon of light that leads all souls to their heavenly home with You. He has faced sin and has conquered it through His life and death. May His resurrection remove the barrier of sin and open the gates of heaven for all mankind."

She stood up and walked to the shrouded body, turned around, and said, "When we were with Jesus, he was approached by one of the scribes and was asked a question about the commandments. His reply to the scribe described God as the one and only Lord, and that we must love the Lord God with all our heart, mind, soul, and strength. He said this is the greatest commandment. Then he went on to say that we must love our neighbor as we love ourselves. As we close the tomb and leave the body of Jesus here, we must remember these two commandments. Regardless of our sorrow, we must recognize God has not forsaken us. He is with us, and we are here with each other. Now is the time for love, not for hate. Hate is the door of evil, and we must be careful not to fall into hating the people who have unjustly killed my—our—Jesus." Mary looked at all who were around her, bowed her head, and continued, "We must be watchful over the next few hours because our love for each other will be tested. Jesus loved us to his death; are we prepared to love that deeply?"

They all stood and left the tomb. The Roman soldiers rolled the stone in front of the grave and sealed it with the sign of the Roman Empire. They were finished entombing the body of Jesus of Nazareth, the King of the Jews, and the Son of God.

CHAPTER 4

The Bond of Blood

J oseph of Arimathea looked at the assembled group and
thanked them for all they had done to help Mary get the
body of Jesus into the tomb. He said, "It is good we were
able to get this accomplished before the beginning of the
Sabbath. It is highly probable the high priests are going to
have people watching to make sure we were not violating
the law by working during the Sabbath. We are still in much
danger being here. We must leave the area quickly."

Joseph signaled for the wagon to be brought around
to have Mary and her friends boarded for transport. He
then came forward in his own wagon and said, "Quickly,
Centurion follow me. We must get this group safely to their
place of lodging. I know where they are staying, so please
follow me."

The centurion nodded toward Joseph, then signaled for
the others to surround the wagon and they started off to
the room where the Passover meal had been shared. They
were tired, covered with blood, and emotionally drained.
They had just witnessed the persecution and death of their

beloved Jesus. They had quickly cared for his body and placed him in a tomb. As they departed, it seemed as if they were abandoning Jesus. He had been a part of their lives for a long time and to just leave his body alone, lying in a tomb without the support of his loving family, seemed like an act of rejection. Their hearts were heavy with sorrow. Their bodies aching with pain. The light Jesus had brought into the world was extinguished. The road ahead looked dark, but they looked to Mary, and she was looking at everyone as her meek smile offered a sense of hope.

The loss of Jesus had not yet settled into their minds. They followed his journey from the courtyard to Golgotha and watched in horror as he was nailed to the cross because the Jewish leaders were angry and full of jealousy and power. The leadership of the Sanhedrin had lied to the Roman governor Pilate and manipulated the mob to have Jesus crucified. They were all in a state of disgust and sorrow.

As they neared the place where the Passover meal had been served, Salome, the mother of James and John, looked at the others and said, "The Sabbath is upon us, and we still have much to do this night. Susanna has stayed behind at the upper room to make sure it was not disturbed when we left. There is water and a bathing tub there, so I suggest we bathe in an orderly manner and put on a clean set of clothes. Once we have collected our soiled tunics, I will work with Susanna, and we will clean the clothes in order to get the dirt and blood removed. I know this is the Sabbath and doing work of this kind is not proper, but we cannot go through the night and the day tomorrow with our clothes being dirty and wet."

The women looked at each other and quietly nodded their heads. They were too tired to think for themselves, and the thought of a bath and dry clothes seemed like a good idea. They would establish an order in which to bathe when they reached the upper room.

As they neared the place of the seder meal, Joseph of Arimathea pulled his wagon closer to the wagon where Mary was riding. He looked over at her and said, "Mary, I have much to tell you. We must speak as soon as we get to the upper room."

She looked over at him and nodded her head. She was tired. She looked at her hands and her clothes and noticed for the first time how dirty she was. Her hands were covered with dried dirt and blood stains. She stared at her hands; they were red with the blood of her son. She began to cry quietly as she relived the day's events in her mind. How could her son be taken from this world in such a ruthless fashion? The blood covering her skin is his blood, but then she thought *Wait, this is my blood*!

My blood runs through the veins of my son. God is the father of my son, but the human aspects of the child come from me. There is no mixture of another human's blood in my son. She began to think she was looking at her blood, the blood shared with her son, a blood originally belonging to God, because He created all of mankind. Our blood is His blood! It was not the blood of a human who had died; it is the blood of God! This was holy blood. This was sacred blood.

This blood was spread from the palace in Jerusalem to the tomb in which his body was buried. Mary began to panic.

Everyone in this caravan had been in contact with the blood. They had taken care of the wounds, washed the body, and anointed it with oils, carried the body from the cross to the wagon and to the tomb. This group who tended to the body of her son were all covered in his blood.

She was starting to breathe heavily. She quickly raised her head, becoming acutely alert. She looked over at Salome and said, "Salome, when we reach the upper room, I would like you to collect the articles of clothing that have been stained with the blood of my son. We must not wash out the blood tonight. We need to collect the garments and place them aside and determine what to do with them later. The blood of my son is the blood of God, and we must treat it properly. It has occurred to me that Jesus's blood has left a stain on Jerusalem, a stain that cannot be washed away by the rain that has been falling for most of the day. Jesus's Father has determined his blood must become part of the earth.

"The earth is the stained altar for the sacrifice of His son. The earth has graciously absorbed the blood of Jesus as a gift. The blood will not be defiled by any human. It will become part of the natural surroundings in which we live. Jesus has died, but his blood has been given to the earth to become part of the world. His blood will always be at our feet, will always be part of our journey through life, because God's blood has been freely given to the world to support all life forms created by God.

"Therefore, we must treat the blood on our garments with as much respect as possible. If we wash the blood out of our clothes, we must make sure the water is used to support life. We must look at this as a gift from the Father and not just throw it away."

The others on the wagon were surprised at what Mary had to say. It had not occurred to them the blood that stained their clothes was the blood of God. They looked at their soiled clothes and dirty hands and began to wonder how this holy blood was being absorbed into their bodies.

This blood was part of a larger plan of God's. Their reaction to the request from Mary was acknowledged. When they arrived at the room of the seder meal, they decided to have any garment stained with blood gathered. While the Roman soldiers were not prepared to change their clothing, they bowed to Mary in a sign of respect, and Gabriel said, "Mother, you speak the truth; however, we do not have a change of clothes, so if you will take me at my word, I will make sure the clothes of these soldiers are collected and returned to you so you can handle them as you handle the clothes of the others."

Gabriel continued, "This is the sacred blood of God's son, and while it has been shed, it is holy and must be treated with dignity. Mother, I want you to think about this. The blood of Jesus is also your blood. The human aspects of Jesus come from you; your blood is His blood. His suffering is your suffering. You are bound to Him for all eternity because of this bond of blood. The connection you have with your son is great, and mankind does not yet know the full potential of this bond.

"If you look back at your life you will see it was through your bond with Jesus, your bond of blood and mother-hood, that people were able to find Jesus and to see who He was. Your mannerisms and your personality traits are all part of who Jesus was as a human being. I ask that you look at your life and see Jesus as a reflection of not just His Father, but as a reflection of His mother as well. People found Jesus because they found you. As the mother of the child, you were not just the caretaker of the child, but you were the living example of the behaviors He would embrace into His persona. He imitated you as a child. You taught Him lessons; you guided Him as He grew, and He learned about humanity from you. Your blood, the blood of man-kind, is the blood of God. God chose you to be the mother of His child because you are a living expression of what humanity can be."

Magdalene heard this exchange and slowly came toward Mary. She knelt in front of her and began to cry. She stood and hugged Mary and said, "I never viewed you like this before. I saw you as just a mother and Him the child. But as the centurion was speaking to you, I started to see sim-ilarities in how you and Jesus behave. His mannerisms are like yours. His smile is your smile; his laugh is your laugh; his kindness is your kindness, and most of all, his ability to love unconditionally reflects not only His Father's love, but of your love for Him. Your love for Him is a pow-erful force we all recognize. You give to Him and to others without thinking of yourself. The goodness of God runs through you, and you do not hesitate to share that goodness with others.

"I am a follower of Jesus because I believe in Him. I believe he is the Son of God, but I must now think about Him as also being the Son of Mary in a much different way. You were chosen by God for a special purpose, and you said yes! I am not sure I could have been so trusting. While my path has led me to Jesus and to a love of God that is strong, your path has been to nurture and guide the Child of God. I now see how special you are to God and to His son. God chose well when He picked you to be Jesus's mother."

Mother Mary took Magdalene by the hands and kissed her on the cheek. She looked toward the others who were standing there watching and listening. She looked downward and then looked upward as if in prayer, then she said, "Please you are being overly dramatic. This time is not about me; it is about my son Jesus. Yes, we share things, but that is to be expected. A child should show some resemblance of their parents in both behaviors and looks. Jesus is no different.

People have tried to describe God since the dawn of time. They have adopted human views and have applied them to God in a way to help them understand God or to know God. What we have learned through the life of my son Jesus is that there are many opinions and views as to how others expect us to act, or to how we view God, but what my Jesus told us is, God's ways are not man's ways. We cannot understand God unless we know God. My Jesus gave us a chance to see God and to know God. His life fully illuminates who God is. Yes, Jesus may possess some of my mannerism or even some of my vocabulary, but His life was a path to His Father. If you know the Son, you know the Father. If you love the Son, you love the Father. There is no difference between the two—One Father, One Son, One God.

My love for my son is not greater than the love I possess for His Father. I love both with all my heart, with all my mind, and with all my soul. It has been my purpose in life to love God and all the unknown aspects of His creation. Jesus is the human manifestation of His Father. His love for each of you is unquestioned and abundant. What is important is how you respond to his love; your response is unique. Our responses are what make us different, but it is also what makes us the same. We are part of the body of Jesus. He is everything we yearn to be as human beings.

Jesus came from the spiritual world to show mankind how to interact with the spiritual world. His human nature is not intended to be his prevailing nature, but it is what we see. We see my Jesus as a loving human being, and you view this as a reflection of me, but it is the spiritual side of my Jesus that reflects His Father in heaven. This is the Jesus we must embrace. This is the Jesus God sent into the world to illuminate the love of the Father."

Miriam looked at Mary and began to cry. She smiled at the Mother and said, "Mary, you have been like a sister to me for many years. We raised our families together, and Jesus and my children were raised as one family. I always knew you and Jesus were special. I listened as you taught the children about God, but I thought your knowledge was learned because you served in the temple of Jerusalem. You were taught by the rabbis and priests, and you must have retained a tremendous amount to teach as you taught. But as I listen to you today, I see, your knowledge of God is deeper than that of the rabbis. You are the bride of Jesus's Father; you are devoted to your son, and we are all blessed to be part of your extended family. I remember when Jesus returned and went to the synagogue in Nazareth and read from the scripture. He read from Isaiah 61:1 *'The Spirit of the Lord is on me, because he has anointed me, to proclaim good news to the poor. He has sent me to proclaim freedom for prisoners and recovery of sight for the blind, to set the oppressed free, to proclaim the year of the Lord's favor.'*

And after He read this passage, everyone in the synagogue was looking at Him with amazement. It had been years since they saw Jesus, but here he was standing in front of them reading Isaiah, and He then said. *'Today this scripture is fulfilled in your hearing.'* The people in attendance were not happy with this declaration. They tried to trivialize Jesus saying, *'Is he not Joseph the carpenter's son!'* They did not know he was God's son! They were furious! The anger and skepticism displayed was very quick to start up, but Jesus walked right through the crowd and returned to you at home.

I also remember I was there with my children to welcome Him home, and I asked for Him to come and see us, and the crowd became more furious and said, 'Is He not the son of Mary?' I do think the crowd confused us on this day because I was there with my children, and they inferred to the crowd they were his siblings. While we raised them as one family, you and I, Jesus was your only child."

The wagons arrived at the place where the seder meal had taken place. Mother Mary and the other women were lowered from the wagons by the Roman soldiers. They walked to the door and were greeted by Susanna who had been waiting for their return. Susanna took Mother Mary by the hand and walked her through the doorway and up the steps to the large room on the upper level.

Joseph of Arimathea now came forward with a serious look on his face. Joseph had spent the greater part of the past few days working in the background to try and free Jesus from the Jewish authorities. He was a friend of Nicodemus, a member of the Sanhedrin, and a follower of Jesus. Nicodemus was able to get Joseph into the part of the temple where the trial of Jesus took place. He was present as Caiaphas and Annas brought witnesses to the court to speak about how Jesus was guilty of breaking the laws of Israel. He was also brought along to Pilate's palace and heard the case brought before Pilate to discredit and convict Jesus of crimes worthy of death.

Joseph took Mary's hand and asked her to sit down. He had much to tell her. He asked Susanna if she would please bring some water to the group so they could be refreshed before he started his story. Mary looked at him and said, "My dear Joseph, I am sure this information is important, but I do believe it would be better shared if we were all washed and in dry, clean clothes. I do not mean to be inconsiderate to you, but we do need to wash up, collect the bloody clothes, and put on clean clothing. We would be able to listen more closely if we were clean and warm."

Joseph saw the practicality of her requests. It was a trait Mary always possessed. She could see through the confusion and anxiety of the moment and offer a reasonable solution that always put the needs of others before hers.

She saw Joseph was anxious and needed to tell her about his experiences. She said, "Joseph, our bodies have limitations, but our spirits do not have such limitations. Hearing what you have to say will be good for our spirits, but right now our bodies are weak and will distract us from your message. Please allow us to address the needs of our bodies. As you know, the spirit is always willing, but the body is weak. Let us refresh our bodies so they will not argue with our spirit to listen to your words."

CHAPTER 5

Pontius Pilate and High Council

Mary left the room where the group had gathered. She went to a private area to be alone. This was the first time she was alone since the death of her son. She looked around the room and found the water and a small rinsing tub to use to cleanse herself. She removed her outer tunic and saw how it was covered with dirt and blood. She then looked at her hands and saw how they were covered as well.

The sight of her hands alarmed her! She grabbed the water basin and began to pour water into the tub. She took a piece of her tunic and submerged it in the tub and then used it to wash her hands. She washed and scrubbed her hands until they were red from the force in which she was scrubbing. These were her hands. These were the hands that cradled her son at the time of birth and the time of death. Her son. Her little boy. The joy of her life. And now he was gone.

She looked at her hands and was suddenly overwhelmed with emotions. She was not aware of where she was; she just looked at her hands and began to cry. The sobbing began as a whimper then progressed to a violent rocking of her body. She slumped to the floor and sat in a crouched position and rocked. She was experiencing a fear she had never encountered before. She was alone for the first time in her life.

Her son Jesus was gone. Her purpose for living was gone. The love of her life was gone. How would she continue her life in this world without Jesus? She was overwhelmed by sadness. Mary looked up with tears in her eyes and said out loud, "I wish I could be swept up in the joy of your laughter. I want to hold you in my arms and comfort you. Jesus, I wish you were here so I could tell you one more time how much I love you."

She lowered her head to the floor and heard the muffled voice softly say, "Mother, do not be afraid, I will be with you shortly." She was suddenly alert, and memories began to flood her mind. She was holding the newborn baby Jesus in a stable, and there were animals around her protecting her and the baby. She saw the face of her husband Joseph standing over her with a smile on his face and tears of joy dripping from his cheeks. The baby was born! The child of God was born into the world. She looked upon the face of the child, and he was not fussing, but his eyes were wide open, taking in everything that a child can see and understand. He looked at Mary and smiled. It was the tenderest smile she had ever seen. Her son had recognized her and smiled with such joy that Mary began to cry. She wondered if her days would be full of such joy because this child of hers loved her.

Mary held the child close to her chest. She could feel him breathing. He was hungry, so she placed her breast near his mouth, and he began to suck. Her child had latched on to her breast and was feeding. She was filled with joy. Her life had led her to this moment and the many uncertainties of motherhood stopped because of the existence of a baby in her life. A child!

When she was a youth working in the temple, she took a vow and dedicated herself to God. She would remain a virgin and live a simple life of service. However, the visitation of the angel and the announcement of her pregnancy surprised her. She had never been with a man in the act of creating a child, but she had accepted the call of God to bear a child. She was happy. The experience of childbirth was not · as painful as she had expected. Jesus was born in the usual way. Joseph was able to find a midwife, and she helped in the birthing process. When the baby was born and placed in her arms, she could hardly contain herself. She cried. The child promised by God was born into this world.

Now as she lay on the floor in the upper room, her tears of pain subsided. She remembered how happy she was after the birth of Jesus, and this joyful memory was enough to calm her. She continued to wash her body of the blood and began to feel a new wave of strength. Memories of Jesus's childhood always brightened her spirit. This vision of his birth was just what she needed to prepare herself to be ready for what Joseph had to tell her.

Mary dried herself and put on a new set of clothes. They were clean, dry, and warm. This made her more comfortable. As she left the small room and reentered the large gathering room, she noticed most of her group had finished cleaning themselves. She glanced at the table that was still set from the seder meal. She noticed the cup of wine was still on the table along with a torn loaf of unleavened bread. She walked over to the table and took a small piece of bread and ate it. Then she then took the cup and sipped the wine. She bowed her head and gave thanks to God for helping her make it through the day. As she placed the cup back on the table, she then experienced a sensation of peace she had not felt in a long time. She felt has if she was being hugged by God.

This was not an ordinary feeling. This was powerful, and she could feel the energy around her change. She was getting stronger and was thinking very clearly. It was like she had come in direct contact with God, and He was filling her body with a spiritual energy that radiated to her physical being. She was one with God. She did not know how it happened, but she did not feel lonely anymore. She felt at peace and energized.

Joseph came toward her and gave her a compassionate hug. He was glad to see her cleaned, and it appeared she was refreshed; the clean, dry clothing helped amplify her beauty. She was a middle-aged woman, but her beauty did not give away her age. She looked timelessly beautiful and removing the grime of the day just added to her natural glow. He asked the others to come into the room. Magdalene, Miriam, Salome, John, and Susanna all came into the room.

The Roman soldiers had left them once they arrived at the place of the seder meal, so all who entered the upper room were now all gathered together.

John looked around the room and noticed not much had changed since the seder meal. The table still had bread, wine, and a few of the herbs scattered around. He looked at the table and remembered how they were all seated around the table joyfully singing the songs of the holiday and sharing in the love Jesus had for His followers. He knew this was a special day, but he did not foresee the events that later unfolded. His friend and his teacher, Jesus, was now gone. He had been betrayed by one of His own followers and crucified by the Romans.

Judas Iscariot betrayed him with a kiss in the garden they had gone to pray in. John had seen the temple guards coming, and when they took Jesus by force, he ran off, away from the ruckus, to tell Mary what was happening. He had run just as the others had run. He left his friend Jesus with the guards, and he ran in fear. He was very ashamed of his actions because he feared more for his life than the life of Jesus.

Joseph asked them all to be seated. He asked Susanna if she could bring some drinking water into the room. It was now the Sabbath, and he asked that they all prepare for the Sabbath prayers. They prayed together but did not eat. They were anxious to hear what Joseph had to say.

Mary and the other women looked at each other, bowed in respect and began reciting the prayers.

Hear, O Israel: The LORD our God is one LORD; and you shall love the LORD your God with all your heart, and with all your soul, and with all your might. And these words which I command you this day shall be upon your heart; and you shall teach them diligently to your children, and shall talk of them when you sit in your house, and when you walk by the way, and when you lie down, and when you rise.

Blessed art thou, O Lord, God of Abraham, God of Isaac and God of Jacob, Most high God, Lord of heaven and earth, our shield and the shield of our fathers. Blessed art thou, Lord, the shield of Abraham.

When the benediction was finished Joseph looked at everyone in the room and then he started with his story.

"Mary, my darling child, it is with great distress I share the happenings of the night with you. As you know I am a friend of Nicodemus, an honored member of the Holy Council. He followed Jesus and listened to him speak. Your son's words and actions had a great impact on Nicodemus, and He became a follower because He believed Jesus was the Messiah. But as you may know Mary, Nicodemus knew you when you were a child and worked as a handmaiden within the temple. He remembers you quite fondly and his journey to Jesus began when he found out that Jesus was your son.

Nicodemus was part of the trial that took place regarding the criminal acts Jesus was accused of. When he found out that the council was going to meet during the night to hear testimony about Jesus, he sent a messenger to me and requested I be in attendance for this trial. When I became aware of the trial, I tried to get word to you this was taking place. I thought we could be with each other to observe the trial, but I was unable to locate you. I did see you arrive with John, so you must have received word. By this time, I was already seated with others and could not get to you.

You are familiar with what happened during the session with Caiaphas where Jesus was accused of blasphemy and people were brought forward to bear false testimony. You saw and hopefully heard the exchange between Jesus and Caiaphas and the ruling members of the Sanhedrin. What you did not see was when they took Jesus to Pontius Pilate. I was part of the group that went from the temple to Pilate's palace. They brought Jesus before Pilate and accused him of breaking the laws of Israel. They accused him of blasphemy and of healing people on the Sabbath. They brought forward people bearing false witness, and Pilate did not seem amused by this parade of stories. He called the high priest to come forward and to explain why this man was brought to him.

Caiaphas explained Jesus had broken the laws of Israel and he must be punished by the Romans. Pilate wanted to know why Rome had to punish Jesus because what he heard was Jesus was breaking Jewish laws, not Roman laws. This retort upset the High Priest. While he knew Pilate, he was not used to being talked to in such a harsh manner. Pilate was challenging his authority right in front of Caiaphas's followers and peers. He was humbled, and Caiaphas is not a person who takes being humbled well.

Caiaphas then brought forward his father-in-law Annas, who was the high priest before Caiaphas. Annas went on to tell Pilate that Jesus claimed to be the King of the Jews. And in Roman law, there can be only one king, Caesar! This proclamation was not taken seriously by Pilate. As you know Pilate has been the Roman ruling governor in Judea for many years. He was aware of Jesus and his teachings. He was also aware that Jesus's teachings have caused the high priest and the Sanhedrin a lot of problems. As the meeting started, Pilate looked as if he was amused by the distress taking place within the Jewish leadership hierarchy.

You see, early in Pilate's tenure as governor he had come into conflict with the leadership of Israel on several occasions. The first encounter was when Pilate brought images of Caesar into Jerusalem, and he was not aware of the laws forbidding idolatry existing in Jewish culture. The Sanhedrin led a protest of the statues Pilate had erected in Jerusalem, and he ultimately removed the images, much to his displeasure, because the high priests protested to Rome. The next time he had shields of gold placed at the palace of Herod, and they too contained an image of Caesar. Again, the Sanhedrin and the sons of Herod protested. This time, they petitioned the Emperor himself to have the idols removed. Caesar listened to Herod and the High Council and had Pilate remove the shields and then publicly reprimanded Pilate for his actions.

This did not sit well with Pilate. He was the governor of this territory and felt he was honoring Caesar with his actions. To be reprimanded was an insult, and he became very wary of the leaders of the Jewish establishment. However, Pilate did not let his reprimand from Caesar stop him from ruling as he saw fit. When the need for an aqueduct was required for Jerusalem, Pilate used the funds from the temple treasury to pay for the work. This inflamed the High Council because money donated to the temple was being used, or being taken as taxes, to pay for the aqueduct. This was money the council felt should be used for the maintenance of the temple and for the betterment of the Jewish community based on how the council saw fit to use the funds.

They again established a protest and many Jewish men actively hindered the work being performed on the aqueduct. Pilate was furious and sent the Roman army into the scuffle and had the army club the protesters to death. Many people died. The council then sent another contingent of representatives to Rome to protest this harsh act by the Roman governor. Caesar was not happy with Pilate and let him know. Again, he received a severe reprimand.

The reason I tell you this background information is because of these complaints to Caesar over the years, Pilate has become very tentative in his dealings with the Jewish High Council. He does not want to look bad in front of Caesar anymore. He does not want to lose his position as governor of Judaea and be recalled to Rome to deal with his indiscretions. So, when Annas brought forward the claim of Jesus being the King of the Jews and Pilate did not respond as Annas thought he should, he began to incite the crowd to protest. They started shouting, 'We have no king but Caesar!'

'How will the emperor react when he hears you are permitting new kings to rule under his kingdom?' taunted Annas. 'You will be removed from your position, and you will be humiliated in the empire for your actions!' These protests disturbed Pilate greatly. Intuitively, he suspected Jesus was innocent of the crimes he was charged with, but he could not look as if he did not take the High Council seriously. He then asked to see Jesus in person.

I entered the inner portion of the palace of the governor and was surprised by the overall lack of decoration. I was led to an area to the left of the High Council and was told to remain quiet. I was an observer, not a participant. I took my place away from everyone and made myself invisible. I needed to be able to observe this encounter between the governing bodies of Rome and Israel and Jesus.

Jesus was brought into the room. His hands were bound in front of him, and his garments were torn and dirty. He looked tired. He had been up all night, having been questioned by the High Council. While Jesus's outward appearance was that of a lowly commoner, his eyes were bright and joyful. Even at this time of grave uncertainty, he looked as welcoming as I have ever seen him.

Pilate was obviously surprised to see this look of serenity on His face. He called to Jesus and asked Him to come closer so he could address Him. Jesus stepped forward, and

Pilate motioned to the stewards to have his hands unbound. This upset the High Council because the removal of the ropes made Jesus seem more human and no threat to Pilate or the others in the room. Pilate asked Jesus if he would like a drink of wine or water, but he politely bowed his head and declined. Again, Pilate was surprised by his actions.

At this point in time Annas came forward and began to speak. 'Governor, please allow me to address the court of Rome.'

Pilate looked over to Annas and gave him a look of disgust. This Jew approached the seat of Rome without being asked. This was not the way of the Roman courts. You do not speak until you are asked to speak. Pilate was not happy with Annas, but he waved him forward and said, 'I see the High Council is anxious to proceed with this hearing. Speaking before asked is not the way of this court. I would suggest you hold your tongue until spoken to in the future. But since you have already begun to speak, go ahead and continue your course of approach.'

Annas began his conversation with Pilate. 'I apologize, Governor, for my haste and my breaking of protocol. This situation has me concerned for the people of Israel. You see this man claims to be the Son of God! By our laws, this is considered blasphemy. No man can place himself at the same level as God!'

His voice was raised in anger, and this tone did not sit well with Pilate. Pilate growled his response, 'High Priest, do not raise your voice to me. I am not one of your followers, and I do not need to be converted to your way of thinking. Please make your case at a more even pace and lower the volume of your voice when addressing the court.'

Annas seemed annoyed by the reprimand, but he bowed his head and continued with his address.

"'Governor, this is a most unusual case. You see the mother of this man, Jesus, was a handmaiden of the temple in her youth. She was delivered to the temple at the age of three by her parents, Joachim and Ann, of the town of Nazareth. I know this because I was the high priest when the child was delivered. They were humble people but advanced in years. They told us of their long desire to have a child but were not blessed by God to conceive. After a lifetime of prayer, they were blessed with a girl and named her Mary. It was their intention she be dedicated to the temple and live a life of service until she was of the age to be married.

However, during her time of service to the temple, she made a pledge of her body to God. She would not have children. She would live in service to God her entire life. During the fifteenth year of her life, it was time for her to leave the service of the temple. She was betrothed to a carpenter by the name of Joseph of Nazareth. Joseph had known of Mary since her birth. He was a young man of eighteen when Mary was born, and he knew her parents. He had not seen Mary since she went into service at the temple. So, when a spouse was sought for Mary, Joseph was selected from a group of eligible men in Nazareth.'

Pilate began to scowl at Annas, and it looked like he was quite annoyed by the long presentation. He firmly said to

Annas, 'What does this rambling story have to do with this man Jesus? Get to the point of your story. I do not have all day, and this man's future is at stake!'

Annas bowed and continued. 'We are assured that Jesus is the son of Joseph, the carpenter, and born of Mary, and that he declares himself the Son of God, and a king, and not only so, but attempts the dissolution of the Sabbath and the laws of our fathers!'

Annas then addressed Jesus. 'We know this concerning you, that you were born through fornication! Second, that upon the account of your birth the infants were slain in Bethlehem. Third, that your father and mother fled to Egypt.'

The Jews who stood near me in the chamber spoke more favorably, 'We cannot say he was born through fornication, but we know Mary was betrothed to Joseph and was not born through fornication.'

Then Pilate said to the Jews, 'Who affirmed him to be born through fornication? This account of yours is not true, seeing there was a betrothment.'

Annas and Caiaphas spoke, 'All these people are to be disregarded, who cry out; but they who deny his birth through fornication are his proselytes and disciples.'

Pilate looked at the two men as they finished their plea. They accused this man Jesus of being conceived out of wedlock, but in fact Joseph and Mary had been betrothed! In Jewish law betrothal was equal to marriage. Once a couple had been betrothed, they were linked to each other, and the conception of a child was not out of the question.

He said to Annas, 'What does fornication have to do with this man's life? Why are you bringing this up? My patience is growing thin, and I am not swayed by your argument.'

Annas responded, 'Please allow us some latitude here Pilate. The information concerning fornication is quite relevant to our dilemma. You see it has been said that this man Jesus is the Son of God—that God is his father!

You see when the betrothment of Joseph and Mary was announced it became known that she was pregnant because Joseph her betrothed came forward and reported her pregnancy to the temple guardians. I was present when the information was made known. It seems the couple had not consummated the joining, but Mary was pregnant. Being the high priest in charge at the time, it was my responsibility to put the two people through a test to determine if the act of fornication was truthful. I placed them both in the protocol of banishment in the desert, and they both returned unphased. This is our interpretation that they were telling the truth. But it seems we were deceived.

While Joseph's proclamation that he had not consummated the marriage to Mary had to be viewed as true, it was still a fact that Mary was pregnant. And the surprising point about her statement was she claimed she was never with a man! She had never had a sexual encounter with a man, but she was pregnant! We found this statement to be highly unusual, and we thought she was lying so we had a midwife examine her to verify she was still a virgin. To our shock, the midwife returned and declared Mary was in fact a virgin and had not had relations with a man.'

Now Pilate was intrigued. 'What are you saying, Annas, that the mother of this man conceived a child without having relations with a man? That is not possible. There must have been a mistake in how the midwife examined the woman.'

Now, Annas felt like he had Pilate's attention, and he could press the issue. 'I assure you the midwife was quite sure of her assessment. While we found this to be unbelievable since she was betrothed to Joseph, it appeared there was nothing we could do. Their union was approved, and they left the temple and headed to Nazareth. Now as time went on, there was the rumor of a child king being born in Bethlehem over thirty years ago during the great census requested by Caesar. This rumor was so prevalent that Herod was frightened he might lose his kingdom if the professed King of the Jews was to be born under his watch.

'You see, there were three Kings traveling from the east to meet this king that was born. They stopped and told Herod of the birth of a new star that seemed to shine in the sky but never move. It remained stationary. So, they were traveling to the location of where the star had rested. To the best of our knowledge the star rested over the town of Bethlehem. Herod had his scribes look through scripture to see if any prophecy had been made as to where the birth of the King of Israel would be born. The book of Isaiah mentioned the town of Bethlehem as the place where the king would be born.

'Herod asked the three Kings to please return after they had found this king so that he too could pay his respects to the child king. The three kings left and never returned. This sent Herod into a rage full of anger and treachery. His fear grew to the point where he ordered his army to enter Bethlehem and the surrounding towns and kill all children under the age of two. Many children lost their lives because Herod was afraid to lose his throne.'

Pilate looked at Annas with a scowl and waved his hands for him to continue.

Annas kept the story moving. 'As it was recorded, Joseph the carpenter from Nazareth was born in Bethlehem and had to return to Bethlehem to be counted in the census. As part of the registry, it is noted that he was accompanied by his wife, Mary, and she was near the time for a baby to be delivered. This is all part of the Roman census logs.'

Pilate now moved forward in his chair and looked around the room to see how others were responding to the story. It seemed everyone was paying close attention to what was being said. Annas had captured the moment with his delivery of the story, and he knew he had the chance to strike down Jesus if he could make his final point.

Annas continued, 'Pilate, Mary was in Bethlehem and gave birth to a child, a child that was conceived through fornication, and it appeared that she was still a virgin. And now there are three kings looking for the King of the Jews to be born in Bethlehem. The coincidence is just too farfetched.

'Now as we look at current events, this Jesus has come into Jerusalem and is being proclaimed as the King of the

Jews. While we know he is just a conjuror, his followers are claiming he is the son of God. If he is the Son of God, then he is the King of the Jews. Can Rome have more than one king? Will Caesar share his throne with this Son of God? What say you, Pontius Pilate, governor for Rome?' shouted Annas."

Joseph stopped here and looked at the group around him. He wanted to see the look on their faces as he reached this part of the story. He looked over at Mary, and she had tears running down her face. The other women looked at her as well and saw the pain she was going through. They all got up and gathered around her to support her.

John stood up and walked over to her and said, "Mother, this story is just a lie! The high priest was just making things up to harm Jesus as they brought forth their false witnesses. He will pay dearly for his lies. Jesus may be able to forgive others and turn the other cheek, but his followers will find it difficult to forgive the Jews after they find out about this shameful story!" John was furious, there is a reason Jesus called him and his brother James, sons of thunder. They both had quick tempers and would always jump into a debate or a disagreement with the sole intent of winning and hurting the opponent. John's temper was not lost on Mary as she looked up at him with tears running down her cheek.

She waved for him to sit down as she said, "Please, John, sit. Joseph does not make up a story; this really did happen."

The room went extremely quiet. Magdalene arose from the floor and looked at Mother Mary with deep compassion and said, "Mary, are you saying these events did take place, and you were questioned at the time of Jesus's conception as to whether you had intercourse?" Then she became angry. "Mary, did the priests really have you examined to determine whether you were a virgin? How could they do such a thing? You were just a child blooming into a young woman. This type of scrutiny is unparalleled! I may be a bit emotional because of the day's events but hearing this story has me more upset than I was before!"

Miriam placed her armed around Mary in a hug. She turned to face the others and began to speak, "Please allow me to provide you the details of Mary's pregnancy and her early life with Joseph. As most of you know, Joseph and my husband Cleopas were brothers. Cleopas being the older brother. They were both born in Bethlehem and are part of the house of David, as is Mary. Her father and mother were both from the house of David."

Just as Miriam was about to begin the story there was a knock on the door to the upper room. The knock startled the women. John went over to the door and looked to see who was there. It was Gabriel and Michael, the two Roman soldiers. They had changed their appearance. They were now dressed in Jewish tunics and cloaks and did not look as imposing as they did in their Roman uniforms. They asked John if they could please enter the room and be part of the group that was with Mary. John nodded and let them into the room.

The room was big enough to support more people than the size of this group. After all, the seder meal was held in this room with Jesus and his followers and the women who supplied the meal. The two men came in and observed the others as they immediately focused on Mary. They saw she was crying, and there was a disturbing look of pain on her face. She looked up at them and in a whisper said to them, "I have just been told that my life choices were used tonight to condemn my son to his death. I cannot process all this information right now, but I do know Gabriel will be able to explain my choices to the group because you are the messenger of God I spoke to when my life with my Jesus began. Can you please convey my story to this group by answering their questions? I would appreciate your help."

Gabriel stepped forward and looked to Michael for guidance. Michael came into the open with a bag full of dirty uniforms and said, "Mother, here are the garments that were worn as we assisted in the preparation of Jesus's body for its placement into the tomb. You asked us to bring the garments here in order to properly deal with the issue of His blood."

Susanna looked at Michael and said, "I will take the bag and place the garments with the others. We have not come up with the appropriate manner in how to address the blood on the clothes. Perhaps we will have a solution shortly, but for now, let us just put them with the other clothes and finish this discussion."

Michael handed her the garments and then looked back to Gabriel and said, "Gabriel, a request has been made for help by Jesus's mother to answer questions. I feel obligated to inform all of you Gabriel is the angel whose duty it is to deliver messages from God to humanity. He will answer your questions, but he will answer them from his point of observation. He does not possess the knowledge of the emotional memories Mary experienced. Therefore, Mother, you must listen to Gabriel's answers and insert your memories and feelings as he brings forth answers to questions that are asked. Please be patient. Gabriel will supply answers, but they will be factual and not carry much emotional significance."

Michael then looked to Gabriel and said, "You can address the group as you see fit."

Gabriel took Mary's hand and gently kissed it and said, "I do as you will, O mother of Jesus. What questions are there to be answered?"

CHAPTER 6

I Am Not the Story

G abriel looked at the group assembled before him and smiled. His smile was soft and disarming, and it immediately put everyone at ease. Magdalene then stood and began to pace around the room. Everyone was focused on her as her pace quickened. Then she spoke.

"Gabriel, I have known Mother Mary for several years. We have been companions as we have followed Jesus on His travels throughout Judea, and I must admit my attention has always been on Jesus and His ministry, but the revelations of this story Joseph told has me very confused and angry. I am already emotionally drained from the events of the day. The crucifixion and burial of Jesus leaves me with little rationale thought, but I must gather myself together to try and understand what role Mary played in the raising of this amazing man I know as Jesus.

Yes, I know she is His mother and she has been at His side during his ministry. She cares deeply for His safety and wellbeing. However, I have given little thought to how she might have played a significant role in His development as a human being. I think of Jesus as being the Son of God, the Messiah, the promised one. I have been focused on His words, His actions, and His love. Have I been wrong and not asked enough of the woman who brought Him into this world?

How can someone so humble, caring, responsible, and loving be forgotten as one of the foundational characters of His life? Am I not curious enough to ask her questions about her life and her life with Jesus? Have I just been so focused on Jesus that I have neglected Mary?"

Gabriel looked at Magdalene and then at Mary, Jesus's mother, and said, "Mother, this is not a question I can answer. This is an area only you can provide context to. If this is a good time for you to speak, I ask that you address Magdalene's inquiry."

Mary shifted in her chair then stood up and went over to Magdalene. She touched her arm and led her back to the seat where she had been seated before. As she glanced around the room, she could see the look of anticipation on the faces of the people assembled. She again walked over to the table set for the seder meal and took a small sip of wine from the chalice to moisten her lips. Again, there was a feeling of joy, a feeling of oneness with her son Jesus. She began to smile. The smile was so radiant it affected everyone in the room. She spoke to them in a joyful voice, "Gabriel, I apologize for making the request of you to answer questions for the group. I should have realized the questions were going to be about my story and not Jesus.

"You see, it has never ever been about me; it has always been about Jesus. My life has been focused on reflecting God's love, not just His love toward Jesus, but a reflection of His love to all of mankind. My story is not important. Jesus is the focus of all we do. Jesus is the reason we are all here; He is the reason we can know God. He is the reason we have all experienced a true conversion in our life to be more like Jesus. Without Jesus, we would not know God in a personal way."

But Salome interrupted. "Mary, I know the focus of all we do is on Jesus, but you are part of the Jesus story. Your life is important. We know who you are today, but we know little of your life prior to our meeting. I agree with Magdalene, Joseph's retelling of what took place in front of Pilate is very unnerving. While I have traveled with you, ate with you, laughed with, and prayed alongside you, I do not know anything about your life before we met one another. I too feel I have somehow been ignorant of the parts of your life that framed you and how your experiences were used to influence how Jesus was raised to be the man we know."

Mary shook her head and looked down at the floor. She then glanced over to the bag of dirty garments brought in by Michael. Her thoughts began to race through her mind. Should she share her life's story with this group of people? She had never thought of her life as being that important. She was asked by God to fulfill a role, an important role, but still just a role in bringing His son into the world. She had never thought of herself as special. How could the story of her life be of importance? She was conflicted, and she walked to Joseph and asked him what he thought she should do.

He looked at her tenderly, kissed her on the forehead, and said quietly in her ear, "It is your story to tell. If you choose to share it, I trust this group of friends who are with you tonight are the people who would understand your story. The love they have for Jesus has been extended to you. They are confused and are looking for hope in a time of uncertainty. You have always been a living example of hope and faith. Sharing some of your life might help them rest through the night. But as always, my dear, it is your choice as to how and what you choose to share."

She was tentative. She looked around the room, not at the people but the surroundings of the room. There was a table with some leftover items from the seder meal. There were chairs to recline in. She again noticed the bag of soiled clothes and wondered to herself how she should remove the blood from the garments.

They wanted her story, but she felt there was no story to tell. Joseph was right, though; they were looking for a sign of hope. The next several hours would be difficult for them unless they had some sense of hope for the future. She was not sure her story would be the story they needed to hear. She then suddenly dropped to her knees. This startled everyone in the room. The two angels were immediately put-on guard. Mary opened her eyes and looked upward, and the energy within her began to radiate visibly. The others could see Mary was in some sort of trance. They were at the same time frightened and in awe. Mary began to move her lips, but they could not hear what she was saying. She looked upward as if she were listening to someone.

Miriam and Magdalene held onto each other as they gazed at Mary. They were both frozen as they watched her raise her hands as if pleading with someone. Then they saw her smile. They saw a sense of joy come over her and were caught up in the moment and began to smile as well. She bowed down and they heard her say, "Thank you for Your help. I love You with all my heart, mind, and soul."

She opened her hands in front of her mouth and kissed one, then she spread her hands apart as if releasing a symbolic kiss into the air. She then closed her eyes and opened them. She was now aware all in the room were staring at her. She was a bit startled by the looks on their faces and the quiet of the room. John came over to her and helped her to her feet. He said, "Mother, are you all right? You fell into a trance and began to glow. We all watched in a state of amazement. What transpired? You were here, but you were not here. Please help us understand."

Mary shook her head as if to clear her mind. She had just fallen into a deep state of prayer. She was conversing with God, asking Him what she should do. His response, as always, was loving and provided her a choice. You see God always provides us with a choice. It was up to her as to how to explain things to the group and how much information was needed. She was happy for the guidance and the loving way in which the message was conveyed.

"I apologize. Your request has me conflicted. While I do think you need some insight into my life, I have never really talked about my role and my life with anyone except for Jesus and his Father. You see right now I was reminded of the time when Jesus went to be baptized by John the Baptist. If you do not know, John and Jesus were cousins, and they lived together when they were young. But that is a story for later.

Jesus went to see John to be baptized. It was his choice to go through the ritual of cleansing by living water to represent a change. He was about to step forward and openly reveal himself as God's Son and wanted His baptism to be a sign of His qualification to fully participate in the religious community. His baptism was a visual sign of repentance and purification.

John noticed Jesus was in line preparing to be baptized and was somewhat startled to see that he was readying himself for the moment. When Jesus stood before John to be baptized, John said, '*I need to be baptized by you, not me baptizing you.*'

Jesus replied, 'Let it be so for now, it is proper for us to do this to fulfill all righteousness.' Then John consented.

As soon as Jesus was baptized, He got out of the water, and at that moment heaven was opened and we saw the Spirit of God descending like a dove and landing in Jesus's hand. And then we heard a voice come from nowhere saying, '*This is my son, whom I love, and with him I am well pleased.*'

I was there in line with Jesus. It was at this moment that I experienced the Father and Son and Spirit together. The joining of the Father through the dove brought forward a burst of love that I could feel and observe. There was a great sense of joy and fulfillment in this moment. I was reminded of this as I asked for guidance."

Michael and Gabriel looked at each other and smiled, then Michael turned to everyone and explained, "The moment Mary is recalling is the first time the Father, Son, and Holy Spirit were together where all could see. While we refer to them as individual entities, they are but a single being—God. This might be difficult to understand, but the Father, Jesus, and the Spirit are the same. They are one. If you know Jesus, you know the Father. If you know the Spirit or feel the Spirit, you know the Father and the Son. This is a concept we as angels have accepted since our creation.

God is the energy source of all creation. Man was made in the image of God, not your physical being, but your spiritual beings, your souls. Your souls are made in the image of God, and when you are connected to God through your love to each other, your souls connect with God, and you become part of the body of God. Let me be clear, you are not God, but you are the image of God to all you encounter.

The love of God for His Son was made known by the presence of the Holy Spirit. The more we learn to know God, the more we grow in our love for God, through the Holy Spirit. Love is everlasting, and it is the virtue that can travel from life to death and back to life. Love of God extends beyond all realms of existence."

Mary looked at Michael and smiled. She said, "Michael, I know what you are saying. At this moment I feel very connected to God. Much has happened today, and your request to know more about my life has to be considered, but for now I am full of love for God for He has allowed me to be part of His plan for the redemption of mankind."

As she glanced around the room, she saw the faces of the people who cared deeply about her and the love they had for Jesus was now being focused on her. They were extremely interested in knowing more about her, but she was not ready to share her stories with them at this time. She needed to think and to pray.

For a moment, a sense of doubt entered her mind. Should she take this moment and make the story about her? Would shifting the focus to her story ease the anxiety of the people in the room? She closed her eyes as if to refocus herself. It had never occurred to her that her story was part of Jesus's story. Her thoughts wandered from the events of the day, the death of her son and her own emotional lows. This type of desire to share had not been part of her life. She knew she was tired, and she needed to rest.

She again studied the room and immediately focused on the table. It had been a focal point of the seder meal festivities a few nights ago. Why was she drawn to this table? Her son Jesus was just here with His followers. He was set up for betrayal here. This room was talking to her, but she could not understand what the message was. She stood and walked around the table. The others in the room watched as Mary again seemed to go into a trance. She walked around the table and touched the surface, and her breathing began to change. She started to breathe anxiously. Her head started to nod up and down as if she were acknowledging someone's words. She put both hands on the table and began to cry.

She looked at John with red swollen eyes full of tears and asked, "John, what transpired here the other night at the seder meal? Specifically, what was the purpose of the goblet of wine and the bread? I was in the other room with the rest of the women; I do not know what took place here. I have a feeling there was a specific purpose for this setting, and if possible, could you please describe to us what took place at the table?"

John was startled by the request. Much had taken place over the past few days, and he was tired and emotionally drained. He had tried to keep a level head to be present for Mary, to take care of her needs, but he had been fighting his own internal demons too. He had been part of the seder meal celebration, but it seemed like such a long time ago. His facial expression became tormented, and he looked at Mary saying, "Mother, I am tired, and I am fighting this burning anger in me at this time. My Lord, your son, Jesus, was taken from us and killed by the Romans. I feel a great sense of loss, but more so, I am looking for vengeance. However, I do not know how to avenge a loss of this magnitude. I am conflicted. I heard Jesus say, "Forgive them for they know not what they do" but I am not Him. I am finding it hard to forgive. I want justice. I want blood for blood."

Mary turned quickly and walked over to John. Salome also arose and went over to her son. They jointly embraced him, and he began to cry. He wept heavily, and the others in the room began to weep as well. The anger John described was an anger shared by the entire room.

Michael and Gabriel stepped forward. They placed their heavenly hands on John and began to pray. Their words were silent, but it was obvious that they too were fighting a battle no one in the room could possibly know was taking place. But Mary looked at them and knew right away what they were doing. She could hear a muffled voice. It was whispering to John. The evil one found a way to enter the room.

CHAPTER 7

Wanting to Do More

Mary got up and started moving around. She was aware of a presence. She moved about and gazed at Gabriel and Michael; they were now praying more urgently. How had anger and vengeance entered this room? Where was the evil one? Where was he hiding? Realizing John was not acting like himself; Mary went to pray over John as well. She placed her hand upon his. He began to scream, as if in tremendous pain. She quickly removed her hand. What happened? How could her touch cause him such pain?

Then it occurred to her it was not John who was screaming. It must be the evil one. John must be in a weakened state, and the pressure of the evil one was too strong. Mary knew she had to act to calm the situation. She looked over at Magdalene and Miriam and motioned for them to come to her quickly. They stood and went to Mary. She grabbed them by the arms firmly and said, "John has come under the influence of the evil one. His thoughts are being clouded. We must bring him back to us!"

Salome was holding John as if he were a little child, rocking him and trying to console him, but his weeping grew louder.

He continued to scream, "How could Jesus be taken away in this manner. How could the Romans torture Him so cruelly? He was a good man; He was my friend, and He was the Son of God! I betrayed him! I left the garden when the Romans came to get him. I fell asleep when he asked us to pray. I ran! I was afraid! I had no faith! Now I am here, and I see where my lapse of faith has caused my friend to die and for us to be suffering.

I am growing angrier! I must seek out the others and look for the people who have taken Jesus from us and strike them down! They must pay for what they have done!" John's face was contorted with rage and swollen from crying. Michael and Gabriel continued to pray.

Magdalene came forward in an aggressive manner, grabbed John by the shoulders and shook him. She shook him as hard as she could, then with a quick movement, she slapped him across the face and screamed, "John, John what is wrong with you! Get a hold of yourself. Come back to us. You are the disciple Jesus loved; you need to come back to us. You cannot contemplate revenge! We were taught to forgive, not hate! John come back!"

Mary came over to John. She asked that everyone remove their hands from him. This seemed to get John's attention. He looked at Mary, not just a glance, but he looked deeply into her eyes and he saw his reflection. He then dropped to his knees, grabbed her around the waist and cried, "Mother, why am I so tortured? Why does the anger burn so intensely in my heart? I want to forgive, but there is something blocking me from even considering it. I want to strike out at the ones who did this. I will die if I have to, but I want justice!"

Mary gently put his face in her hands and said, "John, vengeance is not yours to seek. Jesus told you He had to suffer and die. He did not say how or when, but He has been telling you and the others His time was near. He knew He had to die."

"But I was there in the garden when he was praying. Before I drifted off to sleep, I heard him say, *'Father, if it is possible, let this cup pass me by. And yet not as I will, but as You will.'*

Then he moaned loudly, and I heard no more. He was asking His Father to save him. He did not want to suffer. He did not want to die!"

Mary smiled and said to him in a calming voice, "Of course, he asked to have death pass him by. He had an abundance of life to share with the world. *He wanted to do more.* He always wanted to do more. You remember on the road, when we traveled, how he always stopped to speak to common people. He wanted to spread the Word of God to everyone. He wanted more time to reveal His Father to mankind.

Jesus knew this was the night he would be turned over to the authorities. He just wanted to postpone the moment to allow Himself more time to be with you and the others. He believed you needed more time to ready yourselves for

His loss. Jesus was not avoiding suffering. Because of His love for you, He hungered to spend more time with you. In the end, Jesus chose to obey His Father and accepted His wishes that led to His death."

After Mary said this, the entire room quieted. How did she know this? She was not there! How could she know what had transpired?

John demanded, "How do you know this? How do you know what Jesus wanted?"

Mary shook her head and looked around the room and saw the attention was again focused on her. She looked at Michael, and he smiled at her and nodded his head as if to give her permission to speak.

She said calmly, "Please, everyone settle down and try to be at peace. The trials of the day have us all tired and unsure. We are gathered here to help one another, and we are here in the name of Jesus and as He taught us "*whenever two or more are gathered in my name, so I am there as well.*" This does not refer to Jesus being with us physically. It means His Spirit; the Holy Spirit is here!

Right now, we are in a weakened condition. We are being manipulated by the evil one! The hate and anger in the room is being caused by his desire for us to act in ways that are contrary to the teaching of Jesus. He wants us to abandon Jesus. He wants us to forget the love we have for God. He wants to place himself between you and God and blur your vision as to how to find God in this time of deep sorrow. He wants you to doubt all you have seen through the life of Jesus and cease to have faith in God."

John, Jesus did not want to die because He was afraid of death. He felt He could make a more lasting impression on mankind if He were actively interacting with people longer. He told me this! As you are aware, Jesus went to be alone. During this time Jesus spoke to His Father in the state of meditative prayer. They talked to each other, and they listened to one another.

Jesus has allowed me to know of his interactions with His Father. He had known for a while His death was eminent. He was not sure how long He had to be with us, but He knew there were plans being made by others to have Him removed from Judea or killed. He wanted to prolong His mission; He thought mankind needed to see more of God's actions through Him. He wanted to show more of His Father to the people He encountered. So, you see, He did not want to die. He wanted to live! He wanted to ensure there were enough examples to establish 'the way' for mankind to find God in this ever-changing world of obstacles. Unfortunately, Jesus was not able to extend His life, and as He prayed, *'your will be done, not mine.'* Ultimately, Jesus said yes to His Father!"

Gabriel came over to Mary and embraced her. He had a small smile on his face, and he gazed around the room. He spoke softly. "Mother Mary tells you the truth. The Father and the Son while one with each other, decided to allow the events to unfold that led to the death of the Son. While Jesus's death was always part of the plan, the timing has always been unknown until now. The Father and Son agreed Jesus's life and His living example of God needed to be shared across all people who live in this world.

God's covenant is with all mankind. He is their God, and all are His people. For this message to spread to all lands and convert the nations of the world, Jesus needed to show us one more act of God's love. He needed to die. You will remember the story Jesus told of the seed of wheat that needs to die to bear fruit. The events of the last few days were the fulfillment of that story. The seed must die for the stalk to bear fruit. I know it is hard to believe now, but Jesus's death will free many souls and create a sense of hope for all people as they learn more about God."

The room went quiet.

John was now calm and breathing normally and looked more like himself. The raging anger had left him, and he was no longer talking vengeance. He looked around the room, and speaking in a very shaky voice, said, "Please forgive me. I do not know what came over me. Anger came upon me with such force. I could not control it. Again, I have failed in my attempt to live as Jesus has asked. How can I be considered a follower of Jesus when I cannot control my own shortcomings?"

Salome continued to hug her child. She stroked his head and whispered into his ear, "John, I think I speak for all in this room. There was a presence of evil around us. I could feel the room change before you began to express your anger. I too, began to feel as if vengeance were the answer, but as Michael and Gabriel prayed, I could feel the conflict in the room rise. It was as if there was a battle going on in the room, and they were fighting to help us remain focused on Jesus. Your pain has caused you to doubt. Your spirit was not strong enough to enter the battle alone. Thank goodness these messengers of God are with us here tonight."

Mary went to the table and took the cup of wine and added more wine from the wine skin. She passed the goblet over to John and said, "John, take this and drink."

Immediately, John's eyes opened wide as he remembered the seder meal from the night before. Everyone looked at him in wonder as he tried to speak.

Salome asked, "John, what is it? What are you trying to say?"

He took the cup from Mary and held it in his hands. He held the cup up and turned to everyone in the room and said excitedly, "That is what Jesus said as we ate the seder meal with him. We were sitting around the table and he took the loaf of bread and broke it and said, this is my body which will be given up for you, do this in memory of me. Then he took the cup and blessed it and then presented it to us to drink and said, 'Take this cup and drink. This is my blood do this in memory of me.' We all drank from the cup, and afterwards, I felt a strong sense of love for Jesus. His blessing must have changed the wine. Just like he changed water to wine at the wedding."

Mary took the cup and instructed everyone to take a drink. "Jesus's blood was shed today. We had it on our hands and had it soil our clothes. The cup shared at the meal must have been infused with God's healing power of love. I have sipped twice from the cup tonight, and both times

I experienced a sense of peace and calm. I suggest we drink from the cup and share in the love God has for mankind. Drink this in memory of Jesus."

She passed the cup around the room and everyone drank.

CHAPTER 8

The First Night: Stories of Jesus

T he evening moved quickly to night, and everyone was starting to show signs of sleepiness. Joseph, who was the oldest in the room, began to yawn. He stood up and said, "I will be leaving now, but will return in the morning. I will try to gather as much information as I can about what the high priests are doing. I will also locate Nicodemus and bring him here to meet with you so he can answer any questions you may have. I am sure the high priests are planning something. They are such a treacherous lot. They have been trying to eliminate Jesus from the territory for a long time. I am certain they will not sleep until they are sure Jesus is permanently out of the picture."

Magdalene spoke in response, "Joseph, thank you for all your help and for the insight into what transpired with Pilate. There is still much to discuss regarding the tactics of Annas and Caiaphas. They are not men to be taken lightly. They are ruthless protectors of the faith and will stop at nothing to protect their power in the temple. I do have a question for you. How can Nicodemus help us? Is he not part of the Sanhedrin? Should we treat him as an adversary?"

"Not necessarily," Joseph responded. "He is a Pharisee and a senior member of the Sanhedrin, but he is also a believer in Jesus. He remembers Mary when she was at the temple in her youth. I have spoken to him several times since Jesus began teaching. He remembers details from long ago that might point to Jesus and Annas having contact in the past. A young boy with a sharp mind and tongue once stood before Annas in the temple and surprised the elders with his knowledge of God and of scripture. Nicodemus believes this was Jesus because Mary came to the temple and took him away."

Magdalene looked at Mother Mary, who nodded that it was all right for Joseph to bring Nicodemus to the room.

Joseph went over to the door and wished everyone goodnight. Then left.

Gabriel and Michael stood and spoke to Mary. "Mother, we have been with you tonight to supply some level of support for you and the others. It is apparent you are in grave danger because the evil one has tried to enter the room. We can serve you better if we can return to our spiritual nature and work through the night to protect you. It is important to remember any sign of doubt or lapses in faith could create just enough of a gap to allow the evil one to enter the group. Please be vigilant. We can help, but we cannot interfere. Your choice to believe or doubt is yours to make. We urge you to stay with Jesus. Physically, He is not here, but He is not gone. Find Him in your heart and use His love for you as a shield from this evil."

The two angels departed. The room was quickly emptying.

Now only Miriam, Magdalene, Salome, John, Susanna, and Mother Mary remained.

Magdalene spoke in an agitated tone, "I do not know how we will be able to rest tonight. I am anxious, frightened, and somewhat curious. I have followed Jesus for years and have worked with all of you in the service of our Lord, but I know little of your lives. I do not know how you came to follow Him; I just know you follow. Is it possible for us to share a bit of our backgrounds with each other as we continue our journey into the night? We might relax and eventually rest. I think we need to be present for each other in the love of our Lord Jesus."

They looked at each other with a sense of hope. While they were all tired and weary from the events of the day, they were still not ready to sleep. Mother Mary motioned to John to fill the cup with wine one more time. She then took the cup and drank. She then passed it to the others and said, "We share this night in the memory of my son Jesus." The cup was passed around the room, and each one drank. The warmness of the wine helped them relax, and they settled into comfortable positions.

Mary stood and walked toward the window and opened it. A cool, humid breeze was now entering the room. She stared out the window with a look of wonder. How had her life's choices impacted the how and why Jesus was put to death today? She was puzzled. A thousand yesterdays had all passed away, and though the future was uncertain, there had always been a sense of hope for tomorrow in Mary's life. Jesus had filled her with hope and love, but now hope seemed like it could not fill her senses. She was troubled. Questions she had never thought of before were running through her mind. She was tired and confused, but she was not alone. This group of people were her family, and she felt as strong need to be present for them.

She sighed deeply and looked at Miriam and said, "It is hard for me to imagine all that has taken place today. My son Jesus being put to death by the Romans. Accused of breaking the laws by the Jews. They are more concerned about maintaining their control over people than they are about loving and serving God. The message delivered by my Jesus was a threat to them, and they knew it. It was not a physical threat or a threat to overpower them, but a threat to the way they teach the people to view Jesus's Father."

Miriam responded to her, "I remember Jesus as a young boy and all of the enthusiasm He had had for life. He was curious, adventurous, and loving. There was never a time we ever had to scold Him; He always behaved. He was a rascal, though! He enjoyed playfully teasing the other children, but He would always laugh and hug them and then tell them He loved them. It was unusual for a boy to be so open about His love for others, but Jesus had no qualms about showing His love for everyone. He was truly a wonderful child and grew into a better man."

"Ah, my Jesus was a loving child, and I believe His love forced Joseph and me to be better parents to Him. There was a time when Jesus was just a youth. We were living in Egypt at the time, and we were traveling to visit friends who lived a few miles away. Along the journey, we came across a man who was injured. He was robbed, beaten, and left alone on the side of the road. He was a Cyrene. Little Jesus went up to the man, much to our surprise. He held His hand and talked to Him, then turned to us and asked if we could take care of the man. He asked if we would help Him with His wounds and get Him to a shelter. Joseph and I looked at each other and said 'Of course, we will.'

We took him to a place of lodging and worked with the innkeeper to bandage his wounds and then we had a meal with him. We had just met this man, and Jesus treated him as if he were His best friend. I am not sure what Joseph and I would have done if we would have found this man and we were without Jesus. We did not know the Cyrene, but we listened to his story of how he was robbed and how people walked by as he laid there in pain. We were so taken by his story that we asked the innkeeper to watch over the man. We gave him some gold pieces to tend to him. We instructed the keeper to maintain an accounting of the expenses incurred by the man, and upon our return we would pay him for his care.

After a few days we returned. The Cyrene was feeling much better. The inn keeper had kept his word and took fine care of the man. He told us the cost, and we paid it. Now the Cyrene was a young strong man and still had a way to travel, but he did not have the money to continue his trip. Joseph asked him if he would like to earn some money by helping him perform some type of labor for a day or two. While we were living in Egypt, Joseph was able to work as a carpenter. He had work for the man. The Cyrene accepted and came home with us. The man's name was Aryeh.

Jesus held his hand, and the two walked and talked the entire way to our place of dwelling. We learned he had a wife and son, a few years older than Jesus, and his son's name was Simon. He told us he missed his son dearly and was afraid his time with us would lengthen the time he would be away from his family. Upon hearing the story, we decided Aryeh needed to return to his family, so we gave him a sum of money to make his trip the next day. He was grateful and promised to repay us, but our counsel to him was if he ever had the opportunity to help another person in a time of need, he would take this moment as inspiration to help when called upon. He thanked us for our mercy and generosity and left for home the next day.

I tell you this story because today a Cyrene was called upon to help my Jesus on his journey to Golgotha. I do not know who he was, but he had a strange resemblance to Aryeh. I wondered if this Cyrene was the son of Aryeh."

"I remember this man," said Salome. "He just seemed to be in the right place at the right time. It almost appeared as if he were waiting to be asked to help Jesus carry the cross."

Magdalene said, "I do not know about that. He looked quite annoyed when the Romans pulled him off the street to help Jesus. He looked as if he was anxious to be on his way and wanted nothing to do with this parade to death!" She continued, "I do not know who he was, or why he was there, I only know that after tending to the open wounds on Jesus's shoulder, I am very happy this stranger did not resist and came forward to ease the suffering endured by Jesus."

Magdalene started to get nervous. She arose from her seat and went over to the window where Mary was still standing. The smells of the night began to enter through the window. The storms experienced earlier in the day had cleansed the city air and there was a sense of calm. Mother Mary stroked the hair of Magdalene and touched her arm in a warm, caring way. Magdalene asked Mary. "Was your Jesus always a well-behaved child? Was there ever a time where he did not listen to you?"

Mary smiled and laughed lightly. "Oh, Jesus could be mischievous, but not in a harmful disobedient way. He was such a curious boy. There were times when we would not know his whereabouts for a few minutes or an hour, but he always returned. Joseph once scolded him for being away from us. Jesus listened and apologized, but He told us this wonderful story about going down to the beach and meeting a group of treasure hunters looking for a pearl in an oyster. When we lived in Egypt, we occasionally would travel to the sea for a day of rest. Jesus went off to explore as He sometimes did, and He came across a few men who were harvesting oysters. Jesus had never seen men harvest the sea clam before and became quite interested, losing track of time. The men he was with were so taken by his joyful demeanor and curious nature that they invited him to participate in the hunt for pearls. The diamonds of the sea, as they called them.

Jesus learned how people value pearls and how they are grown in oysters and removed from the shell. Each pearl has a value, based upon color and size. Some are quite precious, and others are common. It seems on that day, Jesus found an extraordinarily valuable pearl. He showed it to the men he was with. They marveled at the size and color. One of the men said this is the most beautiful pearl they had ever seen. They asked Jesus if they could buy it from him.

Jesus was surprised the men would offer to buy the pearl, so he asked more questions about why this pearl was such a prize. The men said that the pearl was three times as large as most pearls, and it was a color of pink and grey. It looked like nothing they had seen before. One of them told Jesus, a pearl of this quality and rarity is something some people would sell all they have to own. When Jesus told us this, Joseph looked at him and asked him what he did with the pearl. Jesus looked at us and said, 'If a man values a pearl so highly, how highly does a man value the kingdom of God? Would a man sell all he owns if he could acquire a place in my father's kingdom? I wonder.'

I gave the pearl to the men to keep and share the value between them. They were nice enough to allow me to dig for oysters with them and then teach me how to value them. I had a great day and was able to see ways in which the kingdom of my Father could be valued. My day was full of fun, laughter, and hard work. I am sorry I caused you to worry, I will be more aware of my time in the future."

There was a round of laughter in the room. Then Miriam said, "Oh, this sounds like something Jesus would do. He found a treasure and gave it away. Plus, he had the awareness to equate the value of the treasure to the value of heaven. How could such a young boy do something like that?"

Magdalene then spoke, "Mary, you must have been a proud mother, watching this boy grow into a man. Tell us more about Jesus. Things we do not know."

Mary looked at everyone. Then she glanced at the candles in the room. They were starting to burn near their ends. The light in the room was growing faint. She was very tired and wanted to rest. She walked away from the window and placed her hands on the table and took a long cleansing breath. She looked tired and drained. Her natural beauty was struggling to stay present. She needed to rest, even for a short while.

"I think I would like to turn in for the night. I am tired. The morrow will bring challenges of its own. John, you need to get some rest as well. I will need you to find Peter and bring him here. It might take a while to locate him because we lost track of him when he was near the warming fire in the courtyard. There are things we must share with him as quickly as possible. The rest of us will remain here and try to be ready for whatever comes our way in the next few days. The other members of the twelve have scattered. We must find out where they are and bring them together. We are stronger if we are together than if we are separated."

Mary turned from the table and looked at the group. While she was tired, she was still very much aware of the fear and anxiety that existed. She took a sip of the wine and again felt a surge of calm come over her and she smiled.

Miriam saw the smile and said. "Why are you smiling? What are you thinking about now?"

Mother Mary flashed Mary a mischievous look and began to share her thoughts. "This is such a strange night. In every traditional sense we should be wailing in sorrow because my son Jesus has died. While I am full of sorrow, I find my thoughts drifting to times where we as a family experienced great joy and happiness. My thoughts are not that I have lost something, but they are of the joy I have experienced, living with my son and experiencing life with him. Miriam, do you remember the time we asked the children to make bread? You and all the children! We were going to make leavened bread."

Miriam sat up straight and smiled, "Yes! I remember that day. We were all in a silly mood." She looked at the others and continued to speak. "We had flour and leavening, and we were going to make bread. The children had watched us prepare the flour before, but they had never helped us make it. Now the children were of all ages, and bringing them together as a group was always an adventure waiting to happen. We had James, Joses, Simon, Judas, Mary, Salome, and Jesus all assembled around the table to help.

The girls were serious. They wanted to make their first loaves of leavened bread, but the boys had different plans. James being the eldest took a handful of flour and started a fight with his younger brothers. There was flour in the air. We were all getting covered with it. Now Mary and I tried to control the situation, just like good parents should do, but soon everyone was busy throwing flour on each other. We laughed and screamed and just enjoyed the moment.

After we all calmed down; it became apparent we had wasted much of the flour. So, we sent James and Joses to the market to get some more. We chose them because they were the oldest, but also, they were the ones whose enthusiasm for the cloud of flour was most prominent. They had to be banished from the room if we were to have any success in making bread. After they left, the children, Mary, and I began the process of mixing the flour and leavening the bread. The children did not know what leavening bread meant. Jesus came forward and asked what leavening is and how it works. At this point, we could see they were all interested in the answer. So, Mary began to explain the powers of leavening to them.

The piece of leavening would be added to the flour mixture, and over time, the leavening agent would begin to mix into the nonleavened flour, and the mixture would increase in size. This made for a fluffier bread as opposed to a nonleavened bread that is heavier and more robust. Jesus asked about the mixture of the two ingredients and wanted to know more about what happened to the flour when it was mixed. Did it change form? We showed them how the flour and leavening were added together and then placed the bowl off to the side where the leavening could do its magic. We called it magic to get them to pay closer attention. They were amazed at the thought of bread being magically produced. It was precious to watch their faces as they waited for the dough to rise.

Well, as you know, dough does not rise immediately; it happens over time. They lost interest and went out to play. This is to say, everyone but Jesus. He stayed back and waited as the mixture sat, and he began to see the dough increase in volume. He was quite interested in what was taking place.

Mary, Jesus's mother, interjected, "The growth of the mixture seemed to fascinate him. He smiled as the mixture rose to be twice the size as it was before. We then took the mixture, placed it on the table and began to knead the dough. Jesus helped us with this part. He was a strong boy, and we had enough of the mixture to make a few loaves of bread. So, his help was appreciated. After kneading the bread, we let it sit, and as it should, it expanded in size again. Jesus was very attentive to this phenomenon. He asked more questions. Some we could not answer. We put the loaves in the fire, and the bread baked. The other children came back when they smelled the bread. The aroma of fresh bread will attract anyone. We let it cool and then the children had their fill.

The two women looked at each other and saw the tears on the other's cheeks. They started to laugh and so did the others. It was a joyful moment to end a sorrowful day.

Mary addressed them, "It is time to get some rest. I will pray your minds will be at peace and you can sleep and be somewhat refreshed by morning. We have shared much today, and I know we share a bond that can never be broken. Sleep well. Know that you are safe and loved."

CHAPTER 9

The Evil One

As they started to move to their sleeping areas. Magdalene moved closer to Mary and said, "Mary, I think it would be wise if I slept closer to you tonight. The angel Michael told me there is the possibility of the evil one attempting to harm you while you are sleeping. He suggested I be near you and wake you if you seem like you are in distress."

Mary glanced at her and said in a tender voice, "Mary, thank you for your concern. However, I am acutely aware of the presence of the evil one. The evil one has tried to influence me on more than one occasion during my life. It was very gracious of Michael to ask you to watch over me, and I will gladly accept your watchful care tonight. You can never underestimate how the evil one will act. I am a light sleeper by nature. I hear things and wake up quickly. I guess you could say my inborn maternal warning system is always on the alert. Since Jesus was a child, I have been protective of Him. I wanted to be able to help Him if He needed me."

Mary sat near her bedding. She watched Magdalene prepare her blanket and continued speaking. "We have slept near each other in the past. I am sure you have noticed my habits of sleep. I do not require much. When I sleep, it is restful, and then I feel refreshed. I usually take this time of rest to pray and speak to the Father. I like speaking to Him. I know He listens to me.

However, tonight I have a different feeling about resting. I am very uneasy. There was an evil presence in the room tonight when John's anger got the better of him. He is a good man, and the spirit is strong with him but being tired and weary from the events of the day must have left him open to the evil one's whispers.

My prayers will be for John. I will pray he has the faith to accept God's will and be the loving companion we know him to be. It just goes to show how the evil one will try and work his way into any situation to force us away from God. We cannot be fooled by the evil one. He is bold, very bold and his hate for mankind makes him dangerous."

Magdalene was listening very intently. The sleepiness she felt before was no longer with her. Her senses were on high alert. She said to Mother Mary, "I have heard Jesus speak of the evil one but not like this. He has offered warnings and asked us to be on the watch for him, but you offer a more dire warning here tonight. How can the boldness of the evil one be dealt with? How can his attempts to influence us be recognized?"

Mother Mary responded, "After Jesus was baptized by John, he went into the desert to be alone. He wanted to be away from the life he had known. He went to be with the Father and the Spirit; they needed to be as one. Jesus was readying himself to begin his public teaching, and He wanted to prepare Himself for the trials He would face. Near the end of His time in the desert, Jesus was tired and weak. He had been in the desert for nearly forty days. The desert had supplied his nourishment, so he had little to eat or drink. It seems as Jesus weakened, the evil one became bolder and tried to tempt Him. The attempts were futile, but nonetheless, he did try to tempt God's Son.

I have been told the evil one cannot look upon God. This is his punishment for being disobedient. However, the evil one took the risk of addressing Jesus directly because Jesus was a man. He is the son of God, but Jesus is the human embodiment of God. Jesus as a human possesses all the limitations of being human. The evil one stood in the presence of Jesus and looked upon him. The evil one found a time where he could look upon Jesus and address him directly. The boldness of this action was extraordinary. At that moment, the evil one surged with confidence, and he tried to seduce Jesus to pay homage to him.

I have learned through my life the evil one can be anywhere and can be anybody. He does not have to appear as himself; he just needs to whisper into the ear of another and have the other act as an agent. In most cases, the agent does not even know they are following the suggestion. They think they are acting righteously because of their pride. You see, Mary when someone possesses an exaggerated sense of self-importance, it is easy for the evil one to influence them.

He makes them think they are right, and then they act to complete the task he sends them out to do. This time in the desert the evil one did not act through another. He acted directly, interacting with Jesus.

The evil one's sense of importance was strengthened when he was able to look upon Jesus and speak to him directly. I am not aware of this ever happening again, but in the moment of a weakened state, the evil one was emboldened to tempt Jesus with his empty promises. Jesus may have been weak, but He was strong in His faith, that is, faith in His Father and the Spirit. Jesus was baptized before He went into the desert, and he was filled with the Holy Spirit, the same Spirit who came upon me and placed Jesus in my womb.

Jesus heard the temptations of the evil one, and in each instance, he had a rebuke. After the last temptation, he banished the evil one saying, '*The Lord, your God, shall you worship and Him alone shall you serve.*' The evil one then left him. Once the evil one left, angels came to Jesus's aid and ministered to His needs. He was tempted directly by the evil one, and He was able to stand firm with God and reject everything offered to him. Jesus showed mankind that it is possible to reject the empty words and promises of the evil one.

This encounter has not been shared with the others. I know of it because when Jesus came out of the desert, he was weak in body and spirit. He told me what had taken place. He said the evil one acted directly, not through the actions of others, but acted himself. This worried Jesus, and

He predicted the evil one would not attempt to interact directly with Him again but would work through others to obstruct Jesus's mission. He warned me of the dangers of the evil one manipulating others to do his will. The evil one is upset; he failed. It is rare that he fails. Failure fuels his hate, and the more he hates, the more powerful he becomes.

Jesus warned me to be watchful. He was fearful the evil one would try to work to seduce me away from God. Since this warning I have been more aware of the presence of the evil one, and therefore I was worried when John acted with such anger tonight. The evil one will act through others to enact his will. He is restless. The more we are separated from God, the easier it is for the evil one to influence our choices. God makes available the gift of faith to help mankind fend off the whispers of the evil one. We can accept this gift or refuse it. It is our choice."

Magdalene reached out to touch Mary's hand and said, "I have never put much thought into the influence of the evil one. Jesus has been my focus. I wonder how much influence the evil one has had in what has happened to Jesus. It sure looks like the actions of the high priests have been influenced by jealousy and hate. If Jesus warned you to be watchful of the evil one, why was he not more vocal with the rest of us regarding the repercussions of falling under the influence of the evil one? I am worried. Anyone of us could be influenced by the evil one."

Mary acknowledged the thought with a bow of her head. She then placed her hand on top of Magdalene's and smiled. She looked toward the window she had opened before and said, "It is almost morning. I see the morning dew dripping from the top of the window, and it looks as if the night has been crying. There is an overwhelming sense of sorrow in the air. We must prepare for the day. I suggest we start our days' work a little early. Since it is the Sabbath, what food do we have for the day? Does Susanna have anything prepared? I am sure some of us will not eat, but others will be hungry. I see the table still has a few things that could be eaten. But before we think about food, let us clean up. There will be visitors today."

Magdalene nodded and went into the other room where she spotted the dirty clothes that had been gathered. She turned to Mary and asked, "Mother, what are we to do with these clothes stained with Jesus's blood? You were quite concerned about the blood."

Mary responded, "I think we should wait until the Sabbath is over, then burn the clothes. The blood of my Jesus can be burned in a sacrificial manner. Just as Abraham killed a goat and offered it to God, we should use the blood of Jesus as a sacrifice. It is God's blood. We should return it to God through a ceremonial burning, a sign of the fulfillment of God's promises through the life and death of His Son."

She looked at Magdalene. Tears started forming in her eyes. Losing her son Jesus was now part of her thoughts again. She missed him. The thought of Jesus not being near her was taking its toll on her spirit.

CHAPTER 10

Reminiscing

The morning sun slowly started to steal across the sky, brightening the room. A cool breeze gently entered, refreshing the room with the start of a new day. The members of the group began to move around. They took turns washing the sleep from their blurry eyes.

Salome looked as if she did not rest well. She said she had a hard time finding peace, as her thoughts of Jesus tortured her mind.

John walked into the room. He did not look well either. His hair looked like a bird's nest with strands of hair jetting out in all directions.

Miriam came into the larger room looking weary after washing her face and hands. She looked around the room and saw everyone from the night before and released a long sigh. Her night was short. She was very tired the night before and was able to nod off to sleep. It was a deep sleep. It was as if she closed her eyes and, in an instant, she was awakened by the rustling around her. However, a few hours had passed, and she had no memory of dreaming during the night. She was experiencing a sense of joy as her morning thoughts were of Jesus and Mary.

She looked at Mary and said," I was thinking of when our children were young and how they enjoyed the morning of the Sabbath. This was their time to study and to learn about God. You were their teacher. I used to enjoy watching you teach the children not just about God, but you taught them other languages as well."

Salome added, "Jesus and you spoke and understood many languages. How is it you were able to do this. Was it a gift from God?"

Mary laughed and responded, "I do not think this is a gift, but maybe it is. I have never thought of our being able to speak multiple languages as a gift. As a family, we traveled and lived in many areas—Bethlehem, Egypt, Galilee and in Jerusalem. We were exposed to Aramaic, which is what I would consider our native language, Greek, Hebrew, and Latin."

"We have all been exposed to these languages, but we are not as fluent as you and Jesus," responded Salome.

"We lived in areas that spoke these languages, and if we wanted to fit in and be part of the local culture, we had to adapt to the language and daily routines," said Mary. "As a young girl I was taken to the temple in Jerusalem. I was already speaking Aramaic, but the language of the temple was a mixture of Aramaic and Hebrew. The rabbis and priests spoke the scriptures in Hebrew. This was the language they used to teach the young men studying.

As a handmaiden, I could watch some of the study sessions and discussions. I did not participate in the public debates, but a young rabbi noticed I was watching, and he took an interest in me. His name was Gamaliel, and he noticed how interested I was in the scriptures, so he took me under his care and privately taught me how to speak and read Hebrew. I was grateful for the attention and for his guidance. I learned many of the scriptural stories and lessons that I ultimately used to teach our children from him. Luckily, I was able to translate much of the Hebrew into Aramaic so the children could understand."

Miriam spoke, "I remember these sessions, and that is why I am filled with a bit of joy this morning. Our children enjoyed learning. You taught them, using one language. Jesus was able to quickly comprehend the topic and then helped the younger ones better understand by wording things in a way they could remember. It was like He could take what you said and translate it into a story the young ones could grasp at a basic level. The children learned quite a bit from these sessions. The Sabbath was not a burden on them; it was a time of togetherness and learning."

"Thank you for your kind words," responded Mary. "I look back at those times now with great joy. I was able to pass on to another generation the lessons I learned as a child. It was rewarding."

"But how did you learn the other languages like Greek and Latin? These are not easy languages to master," asked Salome.

Mary answered, "When we traveled to Egypt, we took roads that were well traveled by merchants. People from all over the Roman Empire traveled those roads to conduct trade and commerce. We interacted with many different people and encountered many different languages. As it became known that Joseph was a master carpenter, he was asked to work for several of the owners of places where we had taken up lodging. He did small jobs and, in some cases, longer more complicated jobs. In one place, we stayed for several months because Joseph was contracted to build a large set of furniture. He made tables and chairs from the local trees in the area. Joseph could not speak many of the languages, but he did possess enough mastery of the words to have an interpreter act as a guide to help him understand what people wanted.

We were in the eastern quarter of Alexandria, and there was a large Jewish population. People who had the language skills helped us learn. Jesus was like a sponge, soaking up the languages. He listened and practiced, and he spoke with many people. They were all helpful and encouraged him to keep working at speaking the languages. He was diligent with his practice and was able to hold conversations with many of the travelers.

There was one successful, caring gentleman who owned a large piece of property. It had many sycamore trees for shade. He also owned cattle, sheep, camels, chickens, and many other animals. He was older and had two sons. We met one, but the other had gone off on his own to seek his life elsewhere. The man's name was Ibrahim. His two sons were Ephraim, whom we met, and Jacob, the son who left his father to live his life elsewhere. Jesus grew very fond of Ibrahim, and Ibrahim grew to enjoy his interactions with my Jesus. They spent a great deal of time together. He taught Jesus how to speak Greek and a little bit of Latin.

We stayed with Ibrahim at his home for a few months. Joseph worked with Ephraim to harvest the sycamore trees and prepare the wood to be used for furniture. Jesus and Ibrahim became close. Jesus described to me how Ibrahim would go out on the hills near his home every night and look to the eastern horizon to look for his son Jacob. Jacob left the family homestead with his inheritance looking to create a future of his own. Ibrahim told Jesus he and his son did not leave on good terms, and it was his wish Jacob would return to him. His heart was broken because his child whom he loved had left and may never return. He missed him terribly. He just wanted to hold him close and tell him how much he was loved and missed.

Jesus was so taken by the story; he came home that night crying. He told me, "Mother I have met a man who knows how to love deeply and with forgiveness in his heart. He yearns for his child to return because they did not part on good terms. I prayed to my Father to bring joy to this man's heart. While Ibrahim loves Ephraim dearly and will always love him, as a father, he is missing his youngest boy and wants him to return. He wants to hold him as he did when Jacob was a child. He has love to share with him, but the child is not with the father. Distance and uncertainty have placed a barrier between the two, and he wishes they were reunited."

Jesus learned a great lesson that night on the loving nature of a father and the power of forgiveness. As it turns out Jacob eventually did return, and Ibrahim's family was whole again. Somehow, I think Jesus knew this reunion would happen because He explained to Joseph and me how His Father forgives and loves all mankind even though sin comes between them."

After Mary finished her story everyone in the room looked at each other and had tears in their eyes.

John said, "I remember Jesus telling us a story about a father's ability to forgive his son after the son had left his father and squandered his inheritance and how the father waited every night looking for his son to return. When he did return, the man ran out and greeted him with a hug and gave him a ring to place on his finger and a robe to be worn to the house. The son asked for forgiveness, and the father forgave him, and they celebrated the return of his son. He was lost, but now was found.

Magdalene interjected, "I remember this story! Jesus told the story with a great deal of emotion in his voice. It was like he was reliving a real moment in his life, and now I can see He did experience it. It was not just a story or a fable. His Father has the ability to forgive because of the love He has for his children. The message is clear, and the story needs to be retold so others can understand the loving nature of Jesus's Father. This story should be told in all languages because the message of forgiveness applies to all mankind."

Mary smiled as she saw the joy the story had brought to the room. They were reliving moments of Jesus's life, and it was bringing a sense of calm. Yes, He was dead, but the memories of His life were bringing them together and giving them a purpose for the day. Somehow these recollections of Jesus were inspiring people to work through their personal sorrow and help each other cope with the loss. The day was taking on a life of its own. Mary and the others looked around the room and began to tidy up. They knew it was the Sabbath, and there were limitations as to what they could do. It was the day God asked them to keep holy. It was a command God had given Moses.

Remember the Sabbath day by keeping it holy. Six days you shall labor and do all your work, but the seventh day is a Sabbath to the lord your God. On it you shall not do any work, nor your son or daughter, nor manservant or maidservant, nor your animals, nor alien within your gate for in six days the Lord made the heavens and the earth and the sea, and all that is in them, but he rested on the seventh day. Therefore, the Lord blessed the Sabbath day and made it holy. (Exod. 20: 10–11)

Mary began to think about the Sabbath and how it was a day set aside by God to rest, to give worship and thanksgiving to God. The other days were days to work. Work was a gift. Work dignifies us as humans. Work was not selfish; it was selfless because the fruits of our labor should be used to better the lives of those we love. It is also a way to give thanks to God for His blessings.

Mary addressed everyone. "Today is the day where we are to rest and give thanks to God. We have the Sabbath day to think about Jesus and the impact He had on our lives. We must be thankful to God for all He has given us, and at this time, we must be thankful we were able to live in the presence of the Son of God." Tears began to form in Mary's eyes as she thought about the goodness of God and the opportunity they had on the Sabbath to be thankful.

She studied the room and the members of the group and realized that these people were risking their personal safety to be with her. They possessed courage and loyalty. And she suddenly began to experience an internal sense of excitement. She loved these people with all her heart. They were her family. She had always referred to them as sisters or children, but now she felt maternal and protective. Her maternal instincts were now on high alert. She began to weep because she was overwhelmed with love. She would never be alone because she was the mother to all she encountered, and she realized how her love for people was going to offer a sense of hope for the future and the return of her son Jesus.

CHAPTER 11

Joseph and Nicodemus

The morning was moving quickly to noon. Mary was surprised at how quickly time was passing. She walked over to John who was busy talking to Magdalene about the seder meal from a few days before.

"John, do you know where Peter would be?" Mary inquired.

"No, Mother, I do not know where Peter is. I last saw him in the courtyard over by the fire on the night Jesus was taken before the council. After I was able to get us into the courtyard and find a safe place for you, I went over to see him, but he was not there when I arrived. I do not know where he went," said John.

"John, I am going to ask you to go and find Peter and bring him here. I need to speak to him today. So, if you would please try to find him and bring him to me, I would be grateful."

"Mother, I will do as you request. However, I am concerned about your wellbeing. I am the only male here.

Granted, I am just a fisherman, still I have a need to be with you and protect you. Jesus did ask this of me."

"John, I will be fine. The women here will take care of me and protect me. Besides, we are waiting for Joseph of Arimathea to return. He still has much to tell us about Jesus and the trial. Why don't you share some food with us before you depart? We do not have much, but you should eat something."

Mary walked over to the table where the seder meal had been celebrated, picked up a piece of bread, and gave it to John. She smiled at him and said, "Take this and eat. It will give you some nourishment to begin your journey." She then reached over and poured him a small amount of wine and said, "Drink this and be on your way." She then poured some water into a container and gave it to him to take with him as he went to look for Peter.

After eating the bread and drinking the wine John was filled with a strong sense of purpose. He knew he would find Peter.

"I will start at the home of Lazarus in Bethany and look for Peter there. This is the meeting place for the twelve when they are in the area. There is a good chance Peter is there, so this is where I will begin. It is a few miles away, so it will take some time before we return. Please, Mother, be careful and stay out of sight of the temple guards. I just have a feeling they are still plotting against Jesus."

Mary and the other women looked at John and nodded. They recognized the caution in his words, and they would take every precaution necessary to stay safe until his return with Peter. The women continued to tidy things up in the room. They could not expend a great deal of energy on cleaning because it was the Sabbath. A more thorough job of cleaning would have to be done over the next few days. An hour went by quickly, and then they heard a noise coming up the stairs to the room. Magdalene and Susanna went to the stairway to see who was approaching.

It was Joseph, and he had a man with him. It was an older man who was dressed like a priest. Joseph looked up and saw the two women looking at them and motioned with his hands that it was all right. He and the other man walked up the steps and entered the upper room.

Mary came into the room and greeted Joseph. "Shalom, Uncle."

"Peace be unto you, my child," he responded.

Mary looked at the other man and immediately recognized him. She came forward and reached for his hand and said, "Shalom, Master Nicodemus. It is good to see you again."

The old man smiled as he looked at her and said, "Mary, my little Mary, it is so good to see you again. I wish it were under different circumstances, but still it has been many years since we saw each other, and you recognized me. I am flattered."

Mary gave the old man a mischievous grin and said, "Oh, Master, I would recognize you anywhere. It was not hard; you have a very distinct manner about yourself, and besides, I saw you a few nights ago when my Jesus was brought before the council and faced charges. Yes, I was in the crowd. John was able to get me into the proceedings. It seems he had a business relationship with one of the Roman guards, and he knew John was a follower of Jesus, so he allowed us to pass into the chamber."

Nicodemus looked tenderly at Mary, and tears started to fill his eyes. "Child, it has been many years since we last saw one another. I remember you and the work you performed in the temple, but most of all, I remember how curious you were about the scripture and the language in which it was taught. You were a good student, better than some of the boys! Your attention to detail amazed people, and your ability to retain and recall what you learned made you a favorite of many of the priests. You were a favorite student who had left to live her life but returned with a son who claims to be the son of God! Mary, Annas remembers you, and he remembers your son Jesus as a child who was challenging the high priests when he was but a boy during the Passover celebration many years ago," said Nicodemus.

Mary looked at him and frowned. She turned away and placed her hand over her face and then looked up and took a deep breath and said. "Nicodemus, I am but a humble mother of a son who has lived in Nazareth and then traveled with Him as he began to teach. How could people remember me? I am just a servant of God."

Nicodemus responded, "Oh, do not sell yourself short, my child. You were a beauty as a child, and your beauty has grown over the years. You are very memorable. You have aged, but I would know you anywhere. You are the daughter of Joachim and Ann and the niece of Joseph." Pointing over to Joseph of Arimathea.

Miriam spoke. "Master, it does seem as if you know Mary, but what do you know of her son Jesus? Why have you come here with Joseph? Have you put us in danger?"

Nicodemus responded, "My good woman, I assure you I am not here to harm anyone. I am here with Joseph to provide a firsthand account as to what took place during the trial and to attempt to provide some of the backstory as to why the high priests were so persistent in their pursuit to have Jesus put to death. I was there! I heard the priests arguing, and I saw the hate they had for Jesus because of the threat He was to their way of thinking—a threat to the power they have over the people. The trial was not solely based on the recent encounters with Jesus. It appears the high priests had encountered Jesus before, and during this encounter, they were angered that a boy of such a young age and with no formal training could shame them publicly with his insight into the scripture and into the will of God. Please allow me to tell you about that encounter from long ago."

The room was quiet as the group processed the words of Nicodemus. How had the high priests interacted with Jesus before? Salome looked to Magdalene, and they both looked at Miriam who bowed her head as if she had a memory flash through her mind. Miriam turned to Mother Mary and said, "Sister, I do recall a time where Jesus was missing, and you found Him in the temple speaking to the priests. Do you remember when this took place?"

Mary stood and walked across the room and looked out the window. Her lips were moving as if she was speaking to someone or whispering a prayer. She remembered the time when Jesus was not with them for a few days during the Passover in Jerusalem. She turned toward the others and said, "Jesus was such a curious boy, and there were times when He was separated from Joseph and me. It was never for long periods of time; however, there was a time when He was about twelve years of age when we were unknowingly separated for a few days. We had traveled to Jerusalem to partake in the Passover ceremonies and stayed with my cousin Elizabeth. We thought it would be good for Jesus to spend a few days with Elizabeth's son John. When we lived in Egypt, Elizabeth and John met up with us, and we lived together for a few years. The boys grew close to one another and were quite adventurous. They worked together, played together, and talked to each other away from the parents.

Their conversations were not quiet; they talked of God and debated the scriptures. John, being the son of a rabbi, was being trained to follow in Zacharias's profession, so he was introduced to the scriptures and their teachings. Jesus was not formally trained in the scriptures because we did not have the resources to send him to scriptural school. I did, however, possess a scriptural background from my upbringing at the temple."

"I can attest to this," said Nicodemus. "Mary was quite the student while she was at the temple. She was not in a formal setting of learning, but she was taught by Gamaliel.

He spoke to the high priests about Mary's ability to comprehend and retain the lessons she was taught.

"You see, my child, you really are memorable! Your natural ability to recall scriptures and speak Hebrew fluently caught the attention of many of the priests in the temple. Some knew you personally and others by reputation. While you never attempted to place yourself ahead of the others, your abilities made you respected and, in some cases, admired.

Your life must have been filled with wondrous adventures. Joseph has filled me in on your travels as a young mother, and I know a little about your time in Nazareth. I would like to know more about your son Jesus, stories only a mother could tell. But right now, I am the person who needs to tell a story. If we could all get comfortable for a short while, I can tell you about how the high priests reacted to Jesus when He entered Jerusalem for this Passover season. Can we proceed?"

Mary bowed her head and then looked up at the ceiling and mumbled what sounded like a prayer. She then looked at Joseph and tears began to run down her cheeks. Her eyes glistened with tears and she looked bright as if she were shining. She looked to the others and said, "I would like to hear what Nicodemus has to say. The truth must be known, and it must be fearlessly told.

As a mother, we take on responsibilities to protect our children. Jesus is my child. When He was younger, I tried to protect him from harm. I do not know how I did it; it must have been an inborn instinct, and I can tell you this desire to protect my Jesus has never ceased. The fire existing in me to protect Him is burning bright, and I feel this protective instinct starting to increase in me.

Jesus is a gift to humanity. He is God's Word become flesh. He knows nothing but love for others. The way He was treated the past few days by the leaders of our nation should not diminish the good He represents to the world and the hope He brings to the hopeless.

Nicodemus, tell your story so we may learn how the hope and love God's son brought into this world was rejected by those who possess this overwhelming sense of self-importance." She turned to look at Nicodemus and for the first time the others saw a look of anger on her face. Then her features softened, and she looked with sorrow in her eyes and said, "Please Nicodemus, tell us what you know."

Nicodemus nodded his head in respect and began to speak.

CHAPTER 12

Jesus and the Temple

"This story began many years ago; I would say over twenty years ago during the celebration of Passover. There were a few young rabbis who were walking through the outer section of the temple on their way to attend services. The outer courtyard is by far the busiest of the temple. It is where offerings are acquired by those who do not bring their own sacrificial offerings and where money changers are abundant. As you know, Roman coins are not permitted in the temple treasury, so the Roman denarius was converted to shekels to pay the temple taxes.

As the young rabbis were making their way through the crowds, they came across a young couple who were selling pigeons and doves to be used as offerings. This was their livelihood, and they were in the temple area quite regularly. Their birds were worthy of being used for the sacrificial rituals; however, the health and quality of the animals was at times lacking. On this day, these young rabbis decided they would make an example of the couple and publicly shame them for the quality of the sacrificial offerings they were selling to travelers. During Passover, there is an expectation the offering used in the temple would be of a higher quality than the offerings made daily. They called out the couple and said, 'How can you bring these inferior creatures into the temple walls and sell them during the Passover celebration? Is it not right to extend to God only the best of offerings during this time of remembrance of our release from bondage and slavery? You should take these poor birds outside the walls and sell them to people for a reduced price. These are not worthy of being inside the temple walls.'

The couple looked up in horror and realized the young rabbis were speaking to them. They did not know what to say. Then the man replied, 'Good Rabbi, you do not mean us? We are here regularly selling our goods to travelers. These birds are no different than others we have made available to travelers in the past. How are they different today? We have been here in this spot for many years—why must we vacate this property now? This is the time when we can make more money to support our family. Moving outside the wall will force us to lower the price we charge for the offerings, and we currently are selling the offerings at the lowest prices inside the wall. Please do not make us leave. We beg you.'

The rabbis showed no mercy to the couple and in a louder voice they shouted, 'Take your goods and get out of here!'

Then out of the crowd a voice was heard. It was a voice of a boy transitioning into manhood. He was maybe twelve or thirteen years of age. The boy came forward with a confident stride and walked up to the rabbis and said, 'What do you mean by harassing my people! Why are you grinding them down when they look at you for hope! Can you not see that they are just a poor couple trying to make a living in this den of thieves?'

The young rabbis were astonished. These words did not come from an adult; they came from a boy dressed in the common tunic of a traveler. He was of slender build but was tall for his age. He spoke with such authority the rabbis thought it was a man of importance, so they stood back. Once they realized it was a boy, they were relieved. However, they were not willing to be challenged by a boy.

The boy continued to walk closer to the men; he was not afraid. There was another boy with him, a bit shorter, but of the same age. He also was walking toward the rabbis with a look of anger on his face. He was ready to help the poor couple. The first boy said, 'John, can you help this couple with their goods while I deal with these men.'

The men looked at the boy and began to laugh. 'You, deal with us! We are much older and possess more authority than you. You and your friend will have little chance challenging the authority we hold!'

The boy said, 'Woe to those who are wise in their own sight and prudent in their own esteem. We will not fight with you, but we will show you the sinfulness of your ways. These people have done no wrong, so why do you persecute them?'

'This couple is presenting a low-quality offering to people who are here to worship God. God does not want inferior offerings during this time of remembrance,' said the rabbi.

'And to whom do you liken God? With what equal can you challenge him?' questioned the boy. The boy looked at the couple and humbly said, 'Fear not, I am with you, be not dismayed, I am with God. I will strengthen you and uphold you with His right hand of justice.'

He then walked over to the couple and began to help the other boy set up their stand. He smiled at them, and they felt comforted and safe. The boy turned around to address the young rabbis and said, 'These people are God's children and have a right to sell offerings to travelers. God cares little for the quality because in God's eyes, every life is of value. Healthy or sick, all life is valuable. If a life is to be sacrificed because you think it will pay homage to God, then you are mistaken. Mankind walks an evil path, and they follow their own thoughts. They provoke God continually, to His face, and then offer sacrifices in groves and burn incense on brick and think everything is now reconciled. God wants us to know Him, to Love Him, and to serve Him. Sacrificing a life does not fulfill any of these.'

The young rabbis shot back at the boy, 'How dare you try to tell us what God expects! You are just a boy! We are rabbis who are training to be priests here in the temple. We know more about God than you! We study scripture every day and know the Word of God. We will teach others the Word of God as we grow in our knowledge of Holy Scripture.'

The two boys looked at each other and smiled. They were not smiles of joy; they were smiles of pity. The boy looked at the young rabbis and said, 'Do you recognize the Word of God? Would you know God if He were to speak to you? For the Lord will have His day against all that is proud and arrogant. All that is high will be brought low.

'For it is written, "O Israel, who are my servant, I formed you to be a servant to me. O Israel by me you shall never be forgotten I have brushed away your offenses like a cloud, your sins like a mist return to me for I have redeemed you."

'If these words are familiar to you then you know how much God forgives mankind. You rabbis are constantly placing unnecessary demands on people who are trying to find God and do good for each other. However, it is command on command, rule on rule, here a little there a little. You place burdens and obstacles before others making communing with God difficult by your laws or your personal understanding of God's will.'

One of the young rabbis turned and said loudly, "Boy, why is it that you quote scripture to us and accuse us of not knowing God's laws?"

The boy said, "Young Rabbi, I am glad you can see the scriptural message here. However, knowing scripture is not the same as knowing God. God's ways are not men's ways. God is the Creator of all things, and God wants us to serve Him. Do you really think your handling of this couple was respectful to God? Or was it just your human nature to place yourself in a position of power above them because you are rabbis? Do you think God cares about the social position you have here on earth? Remember, God is a jealous God. He asks that we do not place other things before Him in our thoughts, works, and in our souls.'

The young rabbis were now caught in a debate with the boy. A crowd was forming around them. They noticed the size of the crowd growing and decided not to continue the exchange with the boy in the current surroundings.

One of the rabbis said, 'Boy, you make several good points, and we can see you have been taught well. We would like to continue this discussion; however, we must be on our way, we have other business to attend to. Would you like to continue this discussion tomorrow? We can prepare an area in the inner court, the court of the priests, and we will not be distracted by the crowd.'

The boy thought for a second and looked at his companion. The other boy said, 'We have to leave now if we are to be home in time for you to leave with your parents. They must be looking for us now. We have spent too much time here already.'

The boy looked skyward and then smiled at his companion and said to the rabbis, 'I would enjoy coming here tomorrow to speak with you. Our discussion could prove to be quite interesting and be a learning experience for all involved. I accept your offer. I will return here tomorrow and look forward to meeting you.'

They agreed on a time and the two boys left."

Nicodemus stopped at this point and looked in the direction of Mary. She was seated. Her hands were on her cheeks. Her face was turning red, and tears streamed down her cheeks. She took a towel and wiped her face. Her face was showing signs of fatigue. She was tired, but her mind was sharp. She looked at the others, smiled, and began to giggle.

"I remember this time of my Jesus's life. He was changing from a boy into a man. He was growing physically and as He acquired more knowledge He began to act boldly. He was starting to show His sense of right and wrong. At times there was no filter in His observations and opinions; they just came out. He eventually learned how to control His comments and be humbler in His discussions. But at this point in His life, He was strong-willed and a bit self-righteous."

Magdalene said, "So you are saying Jesus as a boy had a temper? Or that He did not have patience with others?"

"I do not think of Jesus as having a temper, but He was developing a strong set of opinions on how God wanted us to treat one another. He would not try to humiliate others, but He would debate in a forceful manner to try and convince others He was correct. At this time in Jesus's life it was more important for Him to be right, as opposed to finding more subtle ways of getting His message understood. Eventually, He learned how to use His intellect to get His message across in a humbler way as He grew into adulthood."

Joseph of Arimathea spoke. "I was spending time with Jesus as He was transitioning from a boy to a young man, and I do remember His behavior being a bit rough at times. Never harmful, but He did show signs of being forceful. He had to learn how to use His words to convince people in a disarming fashion.

Once we were traveling from Israel to Egypt on a business trip I introduced Jesus to a few of my business associates. He was about sixteen at the time. I asked my friends if Jesus could work with them for a few days so that he could watch how they interacted with others in their daily lives. They all agreed to have Jesus follow them around for a few days. Well, during this shadowing period, Jesus was exposed to the world of bartering, trade, salesmanship, and storytelling. Jesus was a quick learner. He saw how a good story could get a message across and be remembered by others. He learned dealing with just factual material did not necessarily convince others, so He learned to be humorous and to create messages people could remember by telling stories. He did not become a good storyteller overnight; he learned and practiced. The Jesus we know today was nothing like the youthful Jesus.

As he learned the ways of men, he learned how to tell a story to convey a message of hope, friendship, compassion, and love. Some of his early stories did not go over well, but as he grew and encountered more experiences in life, his stories became teaching lessons and should be memorialized by others."

Nicodemus was about to speak when there was a noise at the door. Salome went to the door to see who was there. She opened the door and greeted Michael and Gabriel. They entered the room and said, "Greetings everyone. We are glad to be here to help in any way possible. We have brought food for the next few days. Here is some bread, cheese, grapes, and a new skin of wine and two skins of fresh water. Hopefully, this will be enough food to make it through Sabbath."

The others in the room stood and welcomed the two and brought them up to date on the events of the day. They told them John was out looking for Peter, and he was going to start by going to Lazarus' home in Bethany. They thought this was a good place to look. The last they knew Peter was on his way there.

Michael said, "I am glad we are here. There is much unrest outside in the streets. The high priests are not happy, and the Roman soldiers are patrolling the area hoping to bring a sense of control. Trouble is on its way, and we should take every precaution to make sure this room stays safe."

They all shook their heads in acknowledgement and went over to the table where the food was laid out. Mary did not partake in any of the food. She was in a trance. She was there but not there. Something was on her mind, but she could not focus. She shook her head and saw Nicodemus looking at her and she said, "Nicodemus, can you continue your story about Jesus and the temple?"

CHAPTER 13

Caiaphas and Annas

Nicodemus continued his story. "Now understand, this meeting in the outer court of the temple was told to me, and I accept it at face value. It is true the boys and the rabbis did encounter each other, and a more private meeting was set up. These young rabbis were the students of the young priest Caiaphas. When they entered the court of priests, they met with Caiaphas and told him of their meeting with the young boys. Caiaphas at first laughed and ridiculed the young rabbis. 'How could a boy with no formal training of scriptures possess such a strong opinion on what God expects from us? You are the future teachers and leaders of the temple; how could you have a boy challenge you in such a manner?'

One of the young rabbis responded, 'Master, this boy spoke with courage and wisdom. His words pierced our hearts. We could have debated him, but to do so in public did not seem like a wise decision. We invited him to engage us tomorrow, here in the inner court. This way we could invite others to see this boy and to help in debating him or to quickly admonish him and put him in his place so he never challenges a rabbi or priest again.

We would like you, Master Caiaphas, to observe our meeting with the boy and participate if you find it helpful. We would like to have others here as well because, while we found this boy to be forceful, we could not find fault with his words. He knew scripture and not just in a casual way. He spoke with a sense of authority as if he himself wrote the words.'

Caiaphas was now curious. He would be on hand to observe the encounter. He would also invite a few of his colleagues."

Nicodemus then looked at everyone and said, "I was one of the colleagues Caiaphas invited to observe. The boy did arrive the next day, but he was alone this time. The other boy was not with him. It was really an unusual sight. Here into the court of priests walked a boy, tall for his age, humbly dressed, but not frightened at all. He was alone in front of a group of men numbering nearly twenty. He looked over the room, smiled, and greeted everyone with an honorable blessing, and then the inquisition began.

Caiaphas started by welcoming the boy very cordially, saying, 'Then the lamb shall be a guest of the wolf.'

The boy looked at Caiaphas and bowed his head and said, 'Very well stated, teacher. The statement is appropriate, but this is an inaccurate quotation of Isaiah. I believe the actual line is "*Then the wolf shall be a guest of the lamb, with a little child to guide them.*" I was invited here today to speak to the young rabbis I met yesterday to continue our dialogue about God. I see many others have been asked to observe and participate.' The boy looked directly at the rabbis he met the day before and nodded and greeted them with a sign of peace.

Caiaphas was not at all thrilled with the way the boy responded to his playful greeting. His curiosity was growing because the boy showed respect but not fear. He asked the boy if he would like to sit down and be comfortable.

The boy looked around at everyone and said, 'Thank you, but I would like to be free to walk around the area as I speak. I will not need to sit. However, I would like to know the direction of the Holy of Holies so that I may kneel and honor the Word of God before we begin.'

The assembly of priests looked at each other and pointed to the inner temple where the Holy of Holies was kept. The boy got down on his knees and said a prayer that none of us could hear, but it was clear this was a prayer of thanksgiving and of love.

One of the young rabbis ask the boy, 'What is your name?'

The boy responded, 'My name is not important. We did not agree to meet so that you could learn my name.'

'Well then. What is your father's name?'

'If you were pure of heart you would know my father. Because only those pure of heart can see him.'

They laughed at his response and then asked, 'Who is your mother?'

At this question, the face of the boy softened, and he smiled and said, "The woman who brought me into this world is named Mary."

All in the room looked at each other with questions on their mind. The rabbi then responded, 'Boy this is a common name among women, it could be anyone!'"

'My mother is not just anyone. She was raised here in the temple. She was a handmaiden for many years. She was taught scripture by one of the priests who knew and understood the word of my father. She is the holiest woman to walk on this earth, and I love her deeply.' There was an uneasiness in the room."

Nicodemus continued. "We wondered what this boy was saying. Of course, he loved his mother; every boy loves his mother, but to say she was the holiest woman to walk on earth was quite the statement. After taking a few seconds to ponder his answer, the rabbi continued to ask the boy questions. 'So, your mother worked in the temple, and she was taught scripture by one of us. That could explain your knowledge of scripture. She must have been a good student and a better teacher because you seem to be able to recognize and recall scripture very easily. At your age to be able to site scripture passages is rare.'

"The boy had spoken to the gathering in Aramaic, then suddenly," said Nicodemus, he started to speak to us in Hebrew."

'The spirit of the Lord is upon me because the Lord has anointed me. He has sent me to bring glad tidings to *the lowly, to heal the brokenhearted, to proclaim liberty to the captives and release to the prisoners.*

I am with you, be not dismayed, I am your God. I will strengthen you and uphold you with my right hand of justice.

The Lord is angry with all nations and is enraged against their multitude; he has doomed them.

However, you can comfort me by giving comfort to my people.

Here is my servant whom I uphold, my chosen one with whom I am pleased. Upon whom I have put my spirit, he shall bring forth justice to the nations.'

"We were shocked!" continued Nicodemus. "How could this boy quote scripture, especially these passages, and use the Hebrew language so we could all understand his mastery of the message and the tongue. The room burst into an uproar, and the boy was challenged and reprimanded by the elder priests in the room for his declaration. Caiaphas was now roused. He looked sternly at the boy and said, 'Boy, you have chosen words that have stirred the blood of my colleagues. I am impressed with your courage and boldness to address this assembly with such passion. Why is it that you have chosen these passages to engage us?'

The boy strolled around before he answered. 'Teachers, please I do not wish to alarm you. These words are used to awaken your sense of awareness to how the world is treating my Father. Words are being spoken, laws are being enacted, rules are structured, but the search for God's love is being lost. God hungers and thirsts for His children to find Him and worship Him with righteousness and humility. God is real and lives in you and among you. He is not a fictitious being who lives in the pages of scripture and becomes real only to those who can teach the words of scripture. God's Word lives in all people.

'The Word of God goes beyond paper; it goes right to the heart and soul to all who walk in the world and the afterlife. God knows you and He knows what is in your hearts. He does not want you to be arrogant and prideful; He wants you to be forgiving and loving to each other. Just as He is loving and forgiving to you.'

'Boy!' shouted one of the assembled. 'How can you speak with such authority and professed knowledge of what God wants from us? You are just a boy! Your voice is powerful, but the authority of your voice must come from some source. Where did you hear or learn of these things?'

"The boy looked up and smiled. He looked over to where I, Nicodemus, was sitting and he bowed in my direction. I noticed His glance at the time but paid it little matter. He then said, 'Today I am just a boy with little worldly experience who was taught the scripture by my mother, but I have spoken to God my entire life, and I am confident in what I say. You have built this temple as a place to worship

God, but God does not need a building or sacrifices to be worshiped. God only requires that each person, everyone, find a place in their heart to love and worship Him every day to the best of their ability. It is not complex; it might be difficult at times, but it is not complex. It is probable your laws and rules have placed barriers between you and God. When you think of the Holy of Holies and the commandments God gave to Moses, you can see the simplicity of the commandments.

'But just like the command God gave to Adam to not eat the fruit from the tree of knowledge they are difficult to obey. The sin of disobedience by Adam opened a window to this world allowing the evil one to enter and work in the shadows to influence men to lose sight of the commands of the Father.

'When you look at the commandments, they can be broken down into two sections. One, love God with all your heart, all your mind and all your soul. There is no God but Him. Two, love your neighbor as you love yourself. Treat others with kindness, compassion, and forgiveness. These commandments are simple, but they have become difficult for men to obey every day of their lives. God is aware of the difficulties men have with these commandments, but He is loving and forgiving. He wants His children to love him, and to do this there must be an active relationship with God in the form of conversation and prayer. God wants us to talk to Him and behave as He would behave in this world when interacting with each other.

You have taken the commandments of God and turned them into laws to govern over men. You subjectively judge men based on how you interpret the meaning of the commandments. You have placed *your* meanings of the commandments over the intended meaning. You have placed yourself at a higher level than God.'

"The priests assembled were now starting to listen to the boy with a higher level of intensity. They were not there to enjoy the mocking of a boy anymore; they could see that the boy had a real grasp on the message of God. Their attitude changed, and they were eager for a good debate, but they could not believe the words were coming from a boy. He possessed a firm understanding of the scripture, and He spoke passionately about the love of God and His willingness to forgive. We became entranced by the words, and we started to wonder who this boy was.

After a few hours of this gripping exchange, Annas came into the chamber because the crowd was now numbering over fifty. He noticed the priests were sitting in a circle around the boy and listening to his responses to questions. He also became intrigued and sat in the circle and listened. After the questions appeared to subside, the boy's demeanor changed. He seemed taller, older, and wiser, and he began to teach:

You have heard that it was said, an eye for an eye and a tooth for a tooth. But I tell you, do not resist an evil person. If anyone slaps you on the right cheek, turn to them the other cheek. And if anyone wants to sue you and take your shirt, hand over your coat as well. If anyone forces you to go one mile, go with them two miles. Give to the one who asks you, and do not turn away from the one who wants to borrow from you.

You have heard it was said, 'Love your neighbor and hate your enemy.' But I tell you, love your enemies and pray for those who persecute you, that you may be children of your Father in heaven. He causes his sun to rise on the evil, and the good, and sends rain on the righteous and the unrighteous. If you love those who love you, what reward will you get? Are not even the tax collectors doing that? And if you greet only your own people, what are you doing more than others? Do not even pagans do that? Be perfect, therefore, as your heavenly Father is perfect.

Be careful not to practice your righteousness in front of others to be seen by them. If you do, you will have no reward from your Father in heaven. So, when you give to the needy, do not announce it with trumpets, as the hypocrites do in the synagogues and on the streets, to be honored by others. Truly I tell you, they have received their reward in full. But when you give to the needy, do not let your left hand know what your right hand is doing, so that your giving may be in secret. Then your Father, who sees what is done in secret, will reward you.

And when you pray, do not be like the hypocrites, for they love to pray standing in the synagogues and on the street corners to be seen by others. Truly I tell you, they have received their reward in full. But when you pray, go into your room, close the door and pray to your Father, who is unseen. Then your Father, who sees what is done in secret, will reward you. And when you pray, do not keep on babbling like pagans, for they think they will be heard because of their many words. Do not be like them, for your Father knows what you need before you ask him.

This, then, is how you should pray:

Our Father in heaven, hallowed be your name, your kingdom come, your will be done, on earth as it is in heaven. Give us today our daily bread. And forgive us our debts, as we also have forgiven our debtors. And lead us not into temptation but deliver us from the evil one. For if you forgive other people when they sin against you, your heavenly Father will also forgive you. But if you do not forgive others their sins, your Father will not forgive your sins.

"The boy enchanted us with his words. We nodded our heads as if we were listening to God Himself speak. Then things suddenly changed. Annas stood up and walked toward the boy in a very intimidating way. We, as elders, had seen Annas reprimand young rabbis, and we could tell he was not happy by what was being said. He addressed the boy: 'Boy, only God can forgive sins! We as humans cannot forgive sins, we do not have the power.'

The boy looked at Annas and said, 'Master forgive me for my boldness. I do not wish to imply man can forgive sins. There are transgressions against God, and man must address his own sinfulness with God. What I am saying is men should forgive each other. Forgiveness should be the basis for our relationship with each other.'

Annas looked at the boy with a scowl. I am guessing he was puzzled because how could a boy with no formal training have such a firm grasp of these concepts? He demanded. 'Who are you boy? Where are you from? Where did you learn these ways of God?'

"The boy replied. 'I have learned all of this from our Father.'

'What do you mean our Father,' shouted Annas. 'We are not related. We do not share the same father!'

The boy smiled, and his face looked radiant, 'Of course, we share the same Father. All of mankind shares the same Father, and our Father is God. God created all things, and He created you and everyone in this room. We share God as our Father because we are created in the image of God.'

'Boy, this is true,' said Annas. 'We do share God as our Creator from a certain perspective.'

He turned from the boy still angry and a bit unsettled by the response. There was no hesitation from the boy, who just smiled and simply answered the inquiry. The boy walked closer to Annas, and you could see that Annas was uncomfortable with the boy moving closer to him. I would not say he was frightened, but he displayed an uneasiness and then stepped back a few steps as if to tell the boy he was close enough. The boy stopped, and in a very calming voice that seemed to fill the room, he said, 'We are all made in the image of God, and this is evident in our souls. When we are created, a piece of God is given to us in the form of our souls, and our souls are mirror images of God.

We are born separate from God, but it becomes our lives journey to find God and reconnect with God. The piece of God that exists in each life is hungering and thirsting to be reunited with God. As we go through life, we look at each other, and we see the goodness of God in the other, and we act in a Godlike manner to recognize and embrace the piece of God in the other. However, sin separates us from God. The evil one places barriers between God and man, but man can overcome the barriers if he is pure of heart and sees God as the conqueror of sin. If man can hear the Word of God and feel it burning in his heart, he can overcome sin and must be willing to forgive the sins of others.'

'Not everyone who says *"Lord, Lord,"* will enter the kingdom of heaven, but only the one who does the will of my Father who is in heaven. Many will say to God on that day, 'Lord, Lord, did we not prophesy in your name and in your name drive out demons and, in your name, perform many miracles? Then God will tell them plainly, 'I never knew you. Away from me, you evildoers!*

Therefore, everyone who hears these words of God and puts them into practice is like a wise man who built his house on the rock. The rain came down, the streams rose, and the winds blew and beat against that house; yet it did not fall, because it had its foundation on the rock. But everyone who hears these words of God and does not put them into practice is like a foolish man who built his house on sand. The rain came down, the streams rose, and the winds blew and beat against that house, and it fell with a great crash.'

"When the boy had finished saying these things, those assembled were amazed at his teaching because he spoke with authority and conviction. The forcefulness of the boy's words frightened these men, and they looked to Annas to respond.

'Boy, answer my question,' demanded Annas. 'Who are you, and who are your parents?'

The boy looked at Annas and said, 'My name right now is of little importance. My parents are Mary and Joseph. We are a humble family from Nazareth. My mother is blessed. She grew up here in the temple and was betrothed to Joseph a carpenter from Nazareth.'

'Your mother worked in the temple as a youth, you say? When was this?" questioned Annas.

'I was born in Bethlehem twelve years ago,' the boy answered, 'so she worked here thirteen years ago. She was here for many years, working with the good teachers of the temple.'

Annas looked closely at the boy, searching for some sort of family characteristic, but he could not see any familiar traits in the boy's face. What he saw was a stern face looking back at him. The boy's eyes were squinted and suspicious, but there was no fear in them at all. The fearlessness of the boy sent a shiver down Annas's back. His mind started to work quickly—who was this boy and why did he frighten him so?

Annas became animated as he walked across the room. He looked at the assembly and noticed how large the group had become. He had a worried look on his face which then changed to a look of anger. He turned to face the boy, but suddenly there was a summons for his attention. Annas stopped what he was doing and turned toward the summons. There were three people walking into the court. Two men and a woman.

One of the men shouted. 'Master, please pardon my interruption, but these people claim to be the parents of the boy who is speaking!'

When his parents saw him, they were astonished. His mother said 'Son, why have you treated us like this? Your father and I have been anxiously searching for you.'

'Why were you searching for me?' he asked. 'Did you not know I had to be in my Father's house?'

The mother replied, 'Of course you had to come to your Father's house, but you could have come with me or Joseph. You abandoned us. We thought you were with the others, but when we met up and found you were missing, we became frightened. This is not the place to be separated from us. Your safety is our main concern. Son, you were lost to us, but now you are found, and we are joyful to have you back with us.'

Annas walked over to the mother with a questioning look on his face. Looking at her he said loudly, 'I know you! You are Mary the daughter of Joachim and Anne. This is *your* son!'"

Nicodemus stopped speaking, and everyone in the room turned to look at Mary. Michael and Gabriel walked over to her and stood behind her as if to protect her. They knelt, one on the right and one on the left. They each took a hand then looking at her said, "Mother, we are here for you. Please know you are safe and what is said here is good. These encounters you had in the past occurred to fulfill God's will. Do not be afraid. God is with you and will always be with you."

Mary looked tenderly at the two kneeling next to her and replied. "I am apprehensive. What took place in the temple was a long time ago. Only now do I see the significance."

She looked at Nicodemus saying, "I remember that day well. Please continue the story."

Nicodemus came over to Mary, took her hand and kissed it gently. He looked at the others and bowed and said, "What I am about to convey to you are my observations. I am sure Mary views this meeting in a different light, and she can expand on the story as she sees fit. Let me continue."

CHAPTER 14

The Boy and His Mother

Nicodemus continued his story.

"The boy walked over to his parents and gave his mother a hug and apologized for causing them any anxiety. Annas watched this interaction, and he became uneasy. He walked over to his seat and sat down. He then looked at Mary and said in a commanding voice, 'Woman, come here!'

To everyone's surprise, the boy turned and faced Annas and his facial features changed dramatically. He walked over to Annas and said, 'Do not speak to my mother in that tone. She has done nothing to harm you, and there is no justification to speak to her harshly. She is here to find me. I have separated myself from them for the purpose of being here to speak to the young rabbis I encountered yesterday. Upon my arrival, it was clear this was not going to be a cordial learning experience. This was going to be an inquisition. I have been candid with you in all my responses. I do not see the point of addressing my mother.'

The boy was bold. He challenged the high priest, the leader of the entire temple.

Annas looked at the boy with a growing anger in his eyes. He said to the boy, 'Boy, how dare you speak to me in this manner? Do you know who I am and the power I have within these walls?'

'You have no power unless my Father gives it to you,' said the boy.

'Your father stands over there with your mother. He is insignificant and has no power over me. If my memory is correct this is Joseph, the carpenter from Nazareth. I was the one who approved of his marriage to your mother. Do you know, boy, you were conceived before your mother was married! Yes, she was betrothed to this man, but she was pregnant before the marriage took place and consummated. I would guess to say you are not the child of this man. You are an illegitimate child and have few rights here before us.'

'I know who my Father is, and I assure you there is nothing illegitimate about my birth,' said the boy in a commanding voice.

Annas turned to Mary and said accusingly, 'Do you allow your child talk to me in this manner, you who worked here for many years? You know it is not permitted to challenge the high priest like this. I allowed the marriage to Joseph. You never said who the father was, but we assumed it was Joseph. Ah, but I recall him saying he was not the father and that you two had not mated. He brought forward to the council that you were pregnant and did not wish to marry you. Then he changed his mind and agreed to marry you. So, I ask you, Mary, is Joseph the father of this boy?'

The boy looked at his mother and nodded. She replied. 'No, Joseph is not the father of this child.'

The assembled in the room immediately started to squirm in their seats. They looked at each other and whispered condemnations of the woman. Annas, seeing the change of the temperament in the room, now felt more in control of the situation and began his assault on Mary.

'As I sit here and look at you, memories are coming back to me. You were a handmaiden, you worked well, and your loyalty was beyond reproach. Gamaliel was so taken by you that he taught you scripture on his own. We were aware of his teaching and thought nothing of it, but it turns out you betrayed his trust when you became pregnant and you were not married. Gamaliel was heartbroken to hear the news of your sinful actions. After your indiscretion became public within the temple, he took it upon himself to never take another girl and teach her scripture. He was embarrassed and blamed himself for not having a more positive influence in your decision-making process. Your sin became his sin."

At this the boy stepped closer to Annas and said forcefully. 'Sin cannot be shared when there is no sin. My mother has not committed a sin.'

Annas looked at the boy and with hate growing in his voice, barked, 'Boy, do not speak to me! You know nothing of sin! You are trying to convince those assembled that God is a loving, caring, and forgiving God, but God is harsh to those who sin and punishes those who make false witness. The ark of the covenant that is behind the veil held by the pillars is right here, and you have the audacity to come here and speak to us about sin! You have no right! You stand on sandy ground with your attempt to protect your mother. Your mother is immoral and a harlot; she has no place here in the inner court of the temple. Be gone with the lot of you before God judges you here and now!'

The boy did not back down. It looked as if he were about to challenge Annas, but he took a few steps back and looked at his parents and started to walk to them. When he was near them, he turned and faced Annas and said, 'As I said at the beginning, there has never been a holier woman born. You have displayed a disdain for her holiness and for the truth. You shall not know the truth until the son of man reveals himself.' Then he looked directly at Annas and then to the assembled, then directly at me and restated his earlier words to us in Hebrew:

The spirit of the Lord is upon me because the Lord has anointed me. He has sent me to bring glad tidings to the lowly, to heal the brokenhearted, to proclaim liberty to the captives and release to the prisoners.

I come to gather nations of every language; they shall come and see my glory. I will set a sign among them. All mankind shall come to worship before me, says the Lord.

Do not judge. For in the same way you judge others,
you will be judged, and with the measure you use, it
will be measured to you.

His voice had changed, and he was not a boy anymore.
He spoke with accusation and disgust as he said:

You look at the speck of sawdust in another's eye and
pay no attention to the plank in your own eye? How
can you say to another, 'Let me take the speck out of
your eye,' when all the time there is a plank in your
own eye? You hypocrites first take the plank out of
your own eye, and then you will see clearly to remove
the speck from another's eye!

Annas was infuriated! He stood up as if to begin his
retort to the boy when the boy looked at him with a men-
acing glare and said with authority. 'Sit! This has gone on far
too long. You are too prideful to understand what has taken
place here. Your display of arrogance offends my Father, so
we must cease this pretense. I will go with my parents and
leave you in peace.'

He looked around the room, smiled, bowed in reverence and said, 'Peace I leave with you, and my peace I
give to you.'

He turned to his parents, and they left the temple. They
walked out with no one stepping forward to stop them.
Annas did not know what to do. He was speechless as they
walked away.

CHAPTER 15

Thirst and Hunger

Those assembled in the upper room looked at Nicodemus with astonishment. Then they turned to Mary. She was sitting with Michael and Gabriel at her side, and she was weeping. Tears were running down her cheeks, but she did not look angry; she looked overcome with grief.

"I remember that day. Joseph and I were frantic; we had lost our child. No, we lost the child left in our care by God. We were frightened that we had failed as parents. How could a parent lose a child? How could we be so casual with our attention we did not realize Jesus was not with us until we were away from the city? I thought my Jesus was with Joseph, and he thought Jesus was with me. We did not realize he was missing until we met up as a group to spend the night resting after a day of traveling. We needed to find him. We immediately turned around and returned to Elizabeth's home. We arrived in the late morning, tired, dirty, and hungry.

Elizabeth greeted us and allowed us to quickly wash away the dust of the night's travel and gave us something to eat. We told her we lost Jesus!

She glared at us with a questioning look and said, 'What do you mean, you lost Jesus? He was here with us last night. He and John stayed up most of the night talking. Sometimes the talking was a bit too loud because they were discussing the meeting they had with a few young rabbis in the temple courtyard.'

Mary said excitedly, 'He was here! Is he still here? We must see him!'

John came out from the other room, looking a bit tired and frightened. He told them, 'Jesus left to return to the temple. The young rabbis we were speaking to yesterday invited him back to discuss God. He knew he was supposed to be with you, but we returned late, and you were already gone, so he decided to speak to the rabbis and then catch up with you later in the day.'

Joseph said, 'Jesus has returned to the temple? When did he leave and when do you expect him to return?'

'He left a few hours ago. I do not know when he will return. Jesus was worked up yesterday after our meeting with the rabbis. We spent too much time with them. You know Jesus, when he is talking about His Father, he gets excited and loses track of time.'

Joseph turned to Mary. 'We must go to the temple and find him.' John told him where in the temple they were to meet.

I looked at Joseph with a feeling of fear and said, 'Joseph, as you know I used to work in the temple. I know where they will be. However, it might not be a good idea for me to return there. We have been coming to Jerusalem every year to celebrate Passover, but we have not gone beyond the outer court. If we enter the inner court, someone might recognize me, and I am not sure if this will cause us harm.'

Joseph told me, 'We must go find Jesus and bring Him home with us. We have been in many places, and we have never been harmed. Why would I think we would be in danger if we entered the inner court?' I had a feeling that if I went to the temple something bad would happen, but I knew we must go and find our boy. Joseph and I left for the temple and found Jesus in the inner court with many teachers, rabbis, and the high priest. The rest is as Nicodemus has stated. We took Jesus from the temple. He assured us He would always keep us informed of His where-abouts, and he was true to his word. We never had to look for him again."

Magdalene stood and walked across the room. She was very anxious. The story presented a new level of infor-mation she had not been aware of. She looked at Miriam and demanded, "Miriam, how much of this story did you know? You have known Mary and Jesus longer than anyone here. Is this true?"

Miriam looked back at her with a look of surprise and replied, "I know nothing of what took place inside the temple. I do know Jesus was missing, and Mary and Joseph went to find him. When they returned, nothing was said except that He was found, He was safe, and He was with His family. We lived together as sisters. We shared the lives of our children, but there are things we did not share, and as far as we were concerned, this was a private family matter.

How Mary and Joseph chose to deal with Jesus as parents was up to them."

Mother Mary looked at the other two Marys and softly said, "Please, please be calm. Until today, I have not thought of this moment. At the time, those were a terrible few days, but Jesus was found, and our family was not harmed. We lived simply and happily in Nazareth."

Joseph walked over to Mary, placed his hand on her shoulder, and said, "Mary, the recollection of this story is not about you losing track of your son. What Nicodemus is saying is the high priest recognized you! You became the focus of Annas's wrath after you left. Yes, Jesus did upset him, but the high priest became fixated on you!"

"Yes, Mother, I am afraid this is true," Nicodemus interjected. "Once your family left the inner court, Annas became terribly upset and demanded to know more about you and your life away from the temple. He was furious that a boy, an illegitimate boy, could come into the temple and speak so harshly to the assembled leaders of the temple. In his mind, this boy had no right or authority to be there and act as if he were the teacher and they the students!

Immediately upon your departure, Annas assembled a group of his spies and instructed them to gather as much information on you and your whereabouts since you left the temple. He wanted to know as much about you, Joseph, and your son as he could. They set out to follow you shortly after you left. The temple hierarchy knew of your family ties to Zacharias and Elizabeth in the city of Ain Karim, and they set out to find you."

Mother Mary stood in a swift motion and looked right and left as if she was confused. She was suddenly anxious and nervous. Her quick movements startled those around her, and they waited to see what she was going to do. As suddenly as she stood, she calmed down just as quickly and walked over to the window and took a deep breath of the cool air that was entering the room. Everyone in the room unexpectedly felt the cool air as well. It was as if Mary had asked the room to be filled with the comforting feel of a soft breeze.

Michael and Gabriel stood and inhaled deeply. They looked at each other and went over to Mary and tenderly took her by the hands, smiled, and said, 'Mother, please be at peace. The Holy Spirit is upon you and has always been upon you. These things being said happened long ago. They had to happen in order to fulfill God's will. Your life has been full of loving adventures with Jesus, Joseph, and all whom you love; however, there has been a plot for many years by people influenced by the evil one to find you and Jesus. Their intent has been sinfully centered on pride, arrogance, and vengeance. It just so happens the genesis of Jesus's death started in the temple after that meeting."

Mary looked at the two with a confused look on her face, "What do you mean?" she inquired.

Gabriel took both of her hands and led her away from the window. He motioned for her to sit down, but she waved him off with the brush of her hand. He looked to Michael, and he nodded to him and then spoke. "Mother, please have patience with us. We are only here to help fill in a few of the missing pieces to this story. You and Joseph, and Miriam and Cleopas, did a masterful job of keeping Jesus safe and loved during his life as a child. However, as he was growing into adulthood, the changes that were taking place in him made him more aware of the will of His Father. He developed a thirst and a hunger for knowing how mankind viewed their relationship with God. He needed to experience, as a human being, the relationship mankind had with His Father. Observing the relationships from the spiritual world provided a lot of context, but to live among the people and experience the nature of man daily was instrumental in forming Jesus's ministry.

When people communicate with God, they plead with Him, asking Him to do things for them. When they talk, they know they are talking to God, and they are in most cases respectful and pious. But Jesus, being God in the form of man, provided people the opportunity to see God in person and observe how God treats His children. God wants mankind to know Him. Jesus is the light into the will of God.

At all times during Jesus's life, *you* were the light to Jesus. People found Jesus because they knew you. When people were looking for Jesus, they did not say, 'Where is Jesus the son of God?' They said, 'Where can we find Jesus, the son of Mary?'

You see, God is everywhere and is visible to all who seek him, but they may not find him if their hearts are not pure. Your heart is pure, and people know you so if they recognize you, they can find Jesus. Better yet, you will answer their requests and point them to your son Jesus. You are the compass and He is the North Star! This process of finding Jesus through you is the same for people who are looking for Jesus for good reasons and bad. Annas has been influenced by the evil one for many years, and both Annas and the evil one has been searching for you to access Jesus and hoped you would influence him."

Mary interjected, "Me, influence Jesus?" She laughed lightly. "Please, my influence over Jesus has been minimal. He listened and obeyed our requests as parents, but He had a mind of His own and acted on His beliefs, not mine."

"Mother, do not underestimate the influence you have on Jesus. Remember the wedding feast where there was not enough wine, and you interceded and explained to Jesus more wine was needed? You looked to the stewards and said, '*Do as he says.*'

"Yes, I remember the wedding. It was in Cana. There were many guests, and some of the wine did not make it to the ceremony on time. I asked Jesus to help, and He did. He did not have to, but he did. I was proud of him. This is such a small matter. Influencing him to help with the wine is one thing; influencing his teaching and commitment to His Father is another."

"Mary, you do not understand. You are His mother! He relies on you for direction, companionship, and love. He is bound by the commandment to 'Honor thy father and thy mother.' Jesus listens to both of his parents, not just his father."

"I am blessed to be the mother of Jesus. Jesus has honored me his entire life. He honored Joseph as well. We did not know what we were getting into as parents, but Jesus made it easy for us. He did not cry much, only when hungry or when he needed cleaning. He listened, learned, and respected us. It was, and is, a joy to be His mother. My role is to serve, and I dedicated my life to making sure Jesus became the man His Father needed Him to be."

"Mother," said Gabriel, "Jesus is not just a reflection of His Father; He reflects you. You helped shape who He is as a man. He came to understand human love because of the way you loved Him. Your selfless nature was a model for Him to follow. People can look at Jesus and project the compassionate loving nature of God, but in your youth when people saw the two of you together, they would say, 'Look is not Mary's boy, Jesus, a good boy. She is so good with Him, and you can see He loves her dearly.' As you grew older the bond between you tightened. People would say, 'Look at how Jesus treats His mother. He loves her deeply.' Then they would look at you and see the pride in your eyes as you watched him grow and become the man we know, and you would say, 'This is my beloved son with whom I am well pleased.'

Looking back at the time Jesus was in the temple, you can see why Annas started his campaign to harm Jesus by looking for you. You are the light directing people to Jesus. If Annas found you and was able to trace your whereabouts, he would be able to keep track of your boy. You and Joseph were able to stay concealed for many years. Annas lost track of you, and as the years went by, he retired from his position as high priest and it was passed on to Caiaphas, Annas's son-in-law. Caiaphas was there during the temple session, but he was not as emotionally invested in finding you as was Annas. So, it has been twenty years since the boy was in the temple speaking to the priests and rabbis. A few nights ago, Jesus was again with the priests and rabbis who were now accusing him of blasphemy and convincing Pilate to put him to death."

The assembled in the room all started to move in an uneasy way. They shifted and some stood to walk around. Many questions started to develop in their minds, but everyone was silent until Miriam spoke.

"Mary, if what Gabriel says is true, then we have been monitored by the temple high priest for most of our lives. It is strange, but I never noticed us being watched. Maybe I was just naïve and was caught up in the joy of raising our children, but sending spies to find you and Jesus makes me wonder what they found out and what was reported?"

Nicodemus looked at Mary and replied. "Oh, at the beginning he learned where you lived and what type of life you led. The watchers then became bored because the daily life of your family was very ordinary. After a few years, the watching stopped, and Annas, while still interested in the boy, became more involved with governing under the laws of Rome. Pontius Pilate's appointment as governor did not sit well with the high priest. There were idols being erected and mass killings. The people needed to concentrate on the wickedness of the Romans, and the boy became less of a focus."

Joseph, who was walking around the room listening, spoke. "Mary, I recall this time in your life. You were very worried when you returned from Jerusalem. You feared for your son's life, and you and I decided that it would be best for Jesus to leave the area and travel with me on my business dealings. We left for the mines in Britannia and were gone for two years."

"I was very worried when Jesus left with you," said Mary. "He was just a boy changing into a man. During those two years away, He grew into a man. His features changed. He started to grow His beard, and His facial features both softened and hardened. He became more confident and yet more compassionate and forgiving. We talked little of His time away. Oh, He spoke of the men, the sea, the travel, and the mines as being a great learning experience, but during this time away from Joseph and me, He found His inner voice. He came back more curious to experience varied ways of life. He wanted to see how people lived and how their lives could be fulfilled by God."

"Yes, the trip to the mines was beneficial for the young Jesus," said Joseph. "Being with the likes of the sailors we traveled with was eye opening. They had no idea who the boy was. We just told them He was my nephew, and we were traveling to Britannia to visit the tin mines for the Roman army. The captain knew me because I had traveled with him before. Jesus was young and interested in the duties of the sailors. He asked to be assigned work on the ship so he could learn and help where needed. He was not a passenger; he became part of the crew. Being part of the crew meant the boy not only worked with the others, but it also meant He was invited to their social gatherings when not at work. Most of the activities were harmless and just good-natured fun.

The boy was teased, harassed, spoken to harshly and heard a few stories that were not meant for the ears of someone so young, especially a boy who had lived on the land all His life. The sea was a world unknown, with a nature only seasoned seamen could understand. I recall one moment where things started to get a bit out of hand. I was coming out on deck when there was what looked like a disagreement between a few of the shipmates. They were about to start fighting. There were loud, vulgar words being shouted after a round of post-work wine drinking. One of the men pulled his knife and took a swing at another. He hit him on the side of the face and opened a gash and blood was everywhere.

Jesus was there. After the blade was swung and blood started to spill, he quickly walked over to the man with the knife and said, 'Stop; no more of this!' Then he touched the man's face, moved his lips in what looked like a prayer, and healed the man! The blood stopped, and the man was not disfigured. The sailors looked at Jesus as if he were a sorcerer. Some were ready to attack him, but Jesus spread His arms and looked at them and said, 'Put your weapons back into their sheaths, for all who take the sword will perish by the sword. I have healed this poor man because he has done no wrong. All of you have had a long day and too much wine. No one deserves to be harmed because of a disagreement. There will come a time when you will need everyone to be healthy, strong, and able to keep the ship from harm. Hurting another over a prideful squabble will not help when you are facing danger.'

'My Father has allowed me to heal this man. This man is my friend, and he is your friend as well. Is it not better to forgive a wrong? You have had too much to drink, and your ability to reason has been impaired. Is it not better to sleep this off and wake up with a headache than to wake up with one less friend?' Jesus turned and helped the man up and walked him to his bed. The others watched as this boy helped the man walk away.

In the morning they were all a bit wary of Jesus, but He continued to carry out his duties and act as a crew mate. The sailors eventually started asking Him questions about His Father, and He began to teach them about love and forgiveness. This was not the only time Jesus performed extraordinary healing, but it was the first."

"What do you mean this was the first? Are you telling us that Jesus was capable of healing people when He was just a boy?" asked Magdalene. "I thought He acquired this power when He was a man! What else did He do while he was under your care?"

Joseph went on with his story, "As we continued our journey to Britannia, Jesus always made it a point to blend in with the workers and do the work with them. I asked one day why He felt the need to work? He was traveling with me, and he could just ride, and we could talk. He told me that, while he would like to take the time to speak to me, he wanted to experience work. He wanted to work as many jobs as possible. He thought he could learn more about the responsibilities that come with work. He told me 'work is a gift from God. This is where men find meaning, fulfillment, and dignity.'

I had never thought of work this way, but after I thought about it, the boy had a point. Meaningful work gives men the sense of accomplishment and purpose. It also gives them a sense of pride. Once he said this, I noticed how people reacted to the work they performed. The happy ones were freemen and chose their work to meet their skill set. The unhappy ones performed work that was not a match to their skill sets, and they wished for the work of others and did not always take pride in what they did. I thought about how wise this boy was.

He wanted to work with the laborers because they were the ones who bore the heaviest yoke. They worked long hard hours and experienced much physical discomfort and pain. He wanted to be close to those who found work fulfilling. He met a worker at the tin mine, who told Him a story about work, and He shared it with me, and I have thought about its meaning ever since. Here is the story:

There once was a boy who was watching a group of men assemble one of the Roman aqueducts. He asked one of the workers, 'Why do you toil like this? The work looks difficult and dangerous." The man responded that he works for the money so he can enjoy his time with his friends. Life is short, so he wanted to enjoy life.

The boy met a second man, and he asked the same questions—why are you doing this? The work looks dangerous. The man replied, he had a family to care for and he needed to make a good wage to support and care for his family

The boy met a third man, and asked the question again: why are you working on something so dangerous? Third man looked at the boy smiled and said, he was working on an aqueduct that will bring water to places in the city that cannot support wells. If they are built properly, this system will last hundreds of years and bring water to generations.

Each man had a reason to work. Some more meaningful than others, but each person had a purpose.

Joseph continued, "I do not want to take up too much time talking about my travels with Jesus. We have other things to discuss, but there is one time where I became acutely aware of how special Jesus was. As we were returning from Britannia, we encountered many travelers on the road. I am somewhat suspicious and careful by nature, but Jesus appeared to be just the opposite. As we met people, the boy would actively seek out other travelers. We met people from all over the Roman Empire. There were many different cultures, foods, and languages. I was aware that Jesus possessed the ability to speak many languages, however I did not realize how advanced his language skills had become.

He did not know every language, but He displayed a wondrous gift to communicate. Not just to the affluent, but with everyone He encountered. He learned a few words, and He listened. He listened with such intensity that after a while, He was able to speak with anyone, using basic words. It was quite remarkable. He actively reached out to Gentiles as if they were His own people. He was not bashful about interacting with others, and once He began telling stories about His Father, His audience grew in numbers. They were a captive audience and wanted to know more about God and how God loves them and hungers for the love of mankind.

Jesus would end many of his encounters with this quotation from Isaiah, '*I come to gather nations of every language; they shall come and see my glory. I will set a sign among them; from them I shall send fugitives to the nations. They shall proclaim my glory among all mankind and shall come to worship before me, says the Lord.*'

It was utterly amazing to watch someone so young hold the attention of older men, more experienced men, with his stories and fables."

As Joseph finished his story, Susanna came into the room. She had been near the outside door observing the street looking for anyone suspicious. "There are Roman soldiers walking through the streets! It appears they are searching for someone."

"How many did you see?" asked Nicodemus.

"There were six soldiers, and they were going door to door. Should we hide? Should we answer the door if they seek entry here?"

Michael and Gabriel immediately stood and went to the door.

They looked out and saw the Roman soldiers heading their way. They looked at Mary and waved to her as if everything would be all right. She came to the door and saw the soldiers. The soldiers caught sight of her and quickly moved in her direction. She was startled by how fast they changed course once they saw her. She motioned for Michael and Gabriel to guard the door.

When the soldiers arrived at the door, they looked at Michael and Gabriel and said, "Peace be with you, brothers. We are here to see Mary, the mother of Jesus of Nazareth."

CHAPTER 16

Procula and Cornelius

Mother Mary came into view, and Nicodemus placed himself between her and the Roman soldiers. Joseph hurried to the doorway to address them. "How may we be of service, Centurion?"

The centurion responded, "Sir, we are seeking the mother of the man who was crucified yesterday. He was called Jesus of Nazareth. It is imperative we find her."

Nicodemus waved his hands and switched positions with Michael and Gabriel to move himself closer to the Romans. "Centurion, my name is Nicodemus. I am a member of the Sanhedrin and of the High Council. What do you want with this mother of Jesus?"

"We have been ordered by Pontius Pilate's wife, Procula, to find her. The governess has information she would like to share with her. We have searched most of the day, and if I am not mistaken, I saw the mother looking out the door a few seconds ago. If she is here, we must know!"

"My name is Cornelius; I am the leader of the guard for the governess and a follower of the man called Jesus.

The governess is right around the corner, and she requests a meeting with the mother of Jesus."

Mary pushed her way to the door. "I am the mother of Jesus. What can I do for the governess of Judea?" She spoke with a nervous stutter. She was frightened. This was unexpected. They were alone and seemingly secure in the upper room; why would the wife of Pilate want to see her?

The other women came to the door as well. Magdalene who was first, was angry and shouted, "How dare you come to this place! You, the killers of Jesus, want to see his mother?" She acted as if she was going to swing and hit the soldier, but they just stood there and looked at her.

The centurion looked at Mary and began to cry. "Please forgive my intrusion for I mean you no harm. Governess Procula wants to meet with the mother. We are both followers of Jesus. We have heard him preach many times, and our hearts have been moved. We are believers. Procula needs to speak to his mother; it is important."

Mary came closer to the centurion, touched his cheek, and looked into his eyes as she smiled at him and said, "Centurion, you said your name was Cornelius? Welcome. We would be honored to meet with the governess. Where is she?"

"She is close by. We will go and inform her we have found you and bring her here."

The soldiers left. The room was suddenly full of nervous energy. Magdalene turned to the others and said, "I have a bad feeling about this. We do not know if their story is true. We could be in danger."

Michael walked over to Magdalene, touched her arm gently and said, "Mary, these soldiers are speaking the truth. The centurion called Cornelius has been in the crowds listening to Jesus for many weeks now. He was also present to see Jesus teach in Galilee. He is a Gentile and a believer."

"Mother, please to not be afraid. Those who possess such strong faith in Jesus and seek you out are worthy of a meeting. Please welcome them. Let us find out what she has to tell us."

Mary nodded in reply.

Nicodemus and Joseph huddled and began to whisper to each other. The three Marys and Salome turned to look at them, and Salome inquired, "Why are you whispering? Is there something we should know before the governess arrives?"

Nicodemus replied, "Procula is a very mysterious person. She stands with Pilate at many public events. She is not a bashful woman. She is clever, intelligent, and of strong will. We did not know she was a follower of Jesus. That would explain why she suggested to Pilate to not be involved in this case."

"What are you saying? The governess spoke to Pilate about Jesus?" asked Salome.

"I was close to the governess and I heard her say to Pilate, 'Leave this innocent man alone. I have suffered through a terrible nightmare about him last night.' Pilate looked at her and then ignored her," said Joseph.

"We should ask her why she advised Pilate to have nothing to do with Jesus."

There was a knock on the door and in walked the governess of Judea, Claudia Procula, wife of Pontius Pilate. The doorway cleared as she walked through. Procula was dressed as a commoner with a veil covering her face. She lowered the veil revealing a middle-aged woman who had brown hair and brown eyes. Her lips were red, and her smile was bright but cautious. She looked around the room, first at Michael and Gabriel, then to the others. Then she looked at Mother Mary and bowed her head out of respect.

She recognized Nicodemus and addressed him first, "You look like one of the priests who visited my husband yesterday. What are you doing here? Are you a spy for the High Council?"

Nicodemus immediately felt a wave of guilt radiate through his body. He bowed saying, "Yes, governess, I was with Pilate. I was there as a friend and supporter of the man Jesus. I brought His uncle Joseph to meet Pilate. As you know, crucified criminals are not traditionally permitted burials. Joseph wanted the body to bury it before the Sabbath began. Pilate was gracious enough to grant us permission to have the body buried."

She looked at him with a glare and said, "Yes, I saw you and this man with Pilate after he found out Jesus had died so quickly. I did not know what was said but, you two were there for several minutes. What else did you want from Pilate?"

"Governess," said Joseph, "our meeting with Pilate was brief. We had little time with the Sabbath quickly approaching. Our only intent was to have permission to bury the body. We asked nothing more of Pilate."

She looked at him with contempt and waved her hand as if to brush him away. Then she said in a commanding voice. "I am here to see you," as she looked directly at Mary.

Miriam stepped between the two women and said sharply, "How do you know this is the mother of Jesus? Have you met her before? How do you know one of us is not his mother?

The Roman soldiers took a step closer to Pilate's wife as if to signal their intent to intervene. Procula held her hand up to stop their movement. She looked at Mary. Her eyes began to fill with tears, and she began to weep. Mary walked over to Procula and hugged her. Procula put her head deep into the shoulder of Mary and began to quiver as she sobbed. Mary took her hands and held them and said, "Peace be with you, Governess. All who knew my son are welcome here. Cornelius tells us you are a believer, and you have news for us. Please calm yourself. I am here with you. Do not be afraid. Do not be sad. The love of my son fills this room."

Procula took a few deep breaths and wiped her eyes. She smiled as she looked at Mary, walked over to the window, and looked out, enjoying the coolness of the outside air as it hit her face. She took a deep breath and said, "Mother, I have news from inside Pilate's courtroom. After the death of your son and after these two men left, the high priest returned with his father-in-law. They demanded guards be placed at the tomb of your son. They told Pilate your son had preached he would die and rise in three days. They were concerned that his followers would sneak into the tomb and steal the body and then proclaim to all who would listen that He had risen from the dead as He promised. They spoke with such hateful emotion and passion that my husband agreed to have guards placed by the grave for as long as needed.

I have come to tell you this because if someone goes near the tomb, it is highly probable they could be harmed. The priests asked that any intruder be punished or even tortured. They were persistent and after a long discourse, Pilate agreed and had men placed at the tomb."

Joseph asked, "How do the priests know where the tomb is? They were not with us when we buried Jesus. I did not see anyone watching."

"There are many eyes in many places in this city. You should know that. Nothing happens of importance that the high priest is not aware of. The priests have watchers, and you were being followed and observed the entire time you were burying the body. When Pilate found out you were being watched, he summoned the priests to his court demanding to know what they were plotting. He was sure they were up to no good. So, he listened to their story and granted them their request. It was not an easy decision for him to make.

They threatened to get word to Caesar that he was not working with the local leaders in Judea to bring peace to the region. They have successfully manipulated both my husband and Rome in the past to get what they wanted. Pilate does not respect these men, but he does have a respectful level of political fear of them. He could be removed from office and demoted if he is reprimanded again by Caesar."

"The political implications surrounding the crucifixion of this man are substantial!" replied Nicodemus. "Within Judea are several parties—Essenes, Pharisees, Sadducees, and Zealots—they all wish for power to remove Roman domination over the land of Israel. Each sect has its own issues with Rome, but somehow, they were able to join forces at the highest levels and get Jesus condemned to death. They took the path of our faith in God to manipulate the governor into doing their bidding. Jesus was not a threat. Pilate knew this to be true, but he feared the people would revolt and death would come to many innocent people."

"My husband is a good man; he is not evil," said Procula. "At one time he was ambitious and wanted to please Caesar. All he has wanted has been to leave this God-forsaken land and return to his home and retire in peace, but now he will always be remembered as the man who killed Jesus. Why did the religious leaders hate him so? Jesus gave people hope, and He showed us how to love. He fed thousands on the hillside. People bowed and worshiped Him. He was just a prophet! Why put him to death?"

"He was more than a prophet. He was the Son of God," said Mary in a quiet voice.

The governess looked at her with a surprised glance. "I have heard others say this, and I want to believe this is true, but hearing it from you, his mother, fills me with uneasiness.

Is this true? Is Jesus the son of God? Please help me understand and believe."

Those assembled in the room looked at Mary. How was she going to respond? The question was so simple and asked with a sense of hunger for knowing the truth. Procula looked at Mary and said, "Mother, I have seen you with your son. I did not know who you were when I first saw Him, but after following Jesus and watching Him spread His message, I noticed you near Him. I could see your face. You were near, but far enough away to give Him space. He looked to you as He talked. There were times when I thought He was drawing strength from you. You looked His way, caught His eye, bowed in approval, and smiled. You must have been proud of Him. His ability to speak simply to people to get them to believe was breathtaking.

When He was finished with a few of His lessons, I would notice him coming over to you, and you kissed Him on the cheek, providing Him with the assurance of a loving parent. I could tell you were His mother because He looked at you with the eyes of a loving child. He looked at others, and His looked changed to one of duty and responsibility, but when He looked at you, He displayed a love only a child can have for a mother. You must be incredibly special to have this man love you so deeply.

If it is not too much, can you share with me why you say Jesus is the Son of God?"

Mary walked to the table used for the seder meal. She was unsteady. There was still some time until the end of the Sabbath. She had not eaten much. She went to the table and poured herself a small amount of water and took a drink. Turning to face everyone, she gave a deep sigh and shook her head. She was torn between being silent and speaking.

She looked to Miriam and asked, "How do I respond to this request from the governess? We have gone over this already!" She looked upward, and her face became illuminated.

Michael and Gabriel fell to their knees and bowed their heads. The others did not know what was happening and looked in wonder as Mary stood, looking for guidance. She lowered her head and gave a quick nod of her head and faced the group and said, "Governess, I will answer your question."

CHAPTER 17

Yes

" Many years ago, when Joseph, Jesus and I were living near Alexandria, we met a philosopher. He was a welcome guest in our house. He once said, 'Let your yes mean yes, and your no mean no; anything else is from the evil one.'

I gave my answer of yes to God's messenger. I have never in my life regretted this yes. Even today after the crucifixion of my Jesus, I am still committed to my yes. My life would have been incomplete if Jesus were not a part of my life. From the moment he was born and I was able to place my eyes upon him, I loved Him. And He loved me.

This messenger from God first came to me as I was saying my nightly prayers in the temple. He is present with us now." She pointed to Gabriel saying, "Gabriel was the messenger. He spoke to me about being the mother of God's child, and said:

Hail favored one! The Lord is with you. Do not be afraid, for you have found favor with God. Behold you will conceive in your womb and bear a son, and you shall name him Jesus. He will be great and will be called Son of the Most High and the Lord God will give him the throne of David, his father, and he will rule over the house of Jacob forever, and his kingdom will have no end.

I was frightened when this messenger appeared to me. I was so young. I had been living in the temple, and I had pledged myself to God by declaring I would never have children. I would be committed to serving God and remain a virgin. I was startled and unsure of this messenger, but he continued saying, *'The Holy Spirit will come upon you and the power of the Most High will overshadow you. Therefore, the child to be born will be called holy, the Son of God.'*

As she said this, she looked at Procula and then to the others. Procula responded, "Mother this seems impossible. You conceived without being intimate with a man?"

Gabriel stepped forward and said, "Governess, I can attest to this being true. Mary conceived the child Jesus in her womb the moment she said, *'Behold, I am the handmaiden of the Lord. May it be done to me according to your word.'* The moment she said yes, the Spirit of God came upon her, and she was with child. There was no joining of man and woman; this was the joining of God to mankind. God touched the womb of Mary, and a child was conceived. God entered this world in the form of the child known as Jesus.

The events of my visit to Mother Mary are only known to people God has felt it necessary to know. The conception of the child is important, but the birth and life of the child is more important! All things are possible with God. Mary's conception of Jesus, her yes to God, joined her with Him and in terms you can understand, Mary became not just the mother of God, she became the spouse of God. Her vow of chastity was maintained after the birth of her son. Mary is a virgin and will always be a virgin, committed only to the Father of the Son of God."

Those assembled in the room began to stir. The story had been revealed over the past few days, but more details kept being added. They looked at Gabriel as he continued with the story.

"Joseph, Mary's betrothed husband, knew of Mary's vow of chastity. He too had taken the vow of chastity as well. However, when he discovered Mary was pregnant, he acted with little thought. He took it upon himself to inform the temple guardians of Mary's pregnancy. He was going to divorce her quietly. He did not want to bring shame on her. However, by notifying the temple priests, Mary's condition became known to many within the temple walls. I appeared to Joseph in a dream and said to him, 'Joseph, son of David, do not be afraid to take Mary, your wife, into your home. For it is through the Holy Spirit that this child has been conceived. She will bear a son, and you are to name him Jesus because he will save his people from their sins.' Joseph looked at me in disbelief. He was afraid. So, I continued, 'All this took place to fulfill what the Lord had said through the prophet: "Behold, the virgin shall be with child and bear a son and they shall name him Emmanuel.'

Joseph was aware of the conception; however, he had a difficult time understanding. He was a good man, a godly man, and once the child was born, he became the protector of both Jesus and Mary. They were a happy, loving family. Joseph was not only the provider for the family, but he was also Mary's life partner. His marriage was an oath to love, honor, and protect her all the days of his life. He fulfilled this oath until the day he died."

Procula's face contorted into a sea of skepticism. "I can believe Mary was a virgin when she conceived. It is not out of the question for women to be pure when they are married and on their wedding night, they conceive a child. However, to state she is still a virgin is hard for me to grasp. Once the baby was born, you did not engage in loving intimacy with your husband?"

Mary responded, "No. We were never intimate. We loved each other as if we were brother and sister. We lived together, worked together, ate together, laughed, and cried together, but most of all we loved our son Jesus with all of our hearts, minds, and souls. The reason we were together was to raise, protect, and prepare Jesus."

As the conversation was starting to get emotional, Nicodemus stood and softly touched Mary's hand and said, "I can attest to the statements of prebirth virginity. When Joseph made it known that Mary was pregnant, the temple priests were all upset. How could this girl become pregnant? Handmaidens lived within the walls of the temple.

One being with a man would mean someone from inside the temple had been with Mary. While it could happen and did happen on occasion, the high priest wanted to speak to Mary and have her explain or confess what had occurred. He began by asking her questions, and she provided answers.

He asked her who the father of the child was, and she answered, 'High Priest, the Holy Spirit came upon me, and I conceived. This is the child of God.' Annas was infuriated with her answer. He became angry and threatened her with harm if she did not tell him the truth. Mary continued to give the same answer. She was the bearer of God's child. She was not with a man. She was a virgin. Annas brought in a midwife and had Mary inspected. This examination was performed behind a curtain, and Mary was not allowed to leave the area. The midwife emerged and pronounced Mary a virgin. There was not a sign of her having been intimate. The entire assembled group was in a state of disbelief. Annas ordered a second examination, and the results were the same. Mary was a virgin."

The room was quiet as everyone processed what they heard from Nicodemus. Then they became aware of the sound of crying. Mary was in her chair weeping as everyone looked at her. Miriam went over and wrapped her arms around her to give her comfort. Magdalene came over with a cloth and wiped away the tears and then suddenly turned to Nicodemus and said firmly, "Were you there, Nicodemus, when this took place?"

"No. I am repeating what I was told many years ago. I spoke to one of the midwives, and she told me what had taken place."

"I am horrified the high priest would conduct such a personal examination right in the temple courtyard. Did he have to humiliate her just to find an answer?" Said Procula.

"My good woman, please. I was not there. But you must wonder about a situation where a young woman is accused of being pregnant and who acknowledges she is pregnant. Then she informs the priest the father is God! To those in the temple, this is a ridiculous scenario! Never had anyone claimed to be carrying God's child. The thought was that she was lying to hide the identity of the person she was intimate with. The priests thought the child belonged to Joseph because he was her betrothed, but he swore he was not the father. There was a major disagreement as to what to do next. Annas decided he would send them through the Test of Honesty."

"What is the Test of Honesty? I have never heard of this!" Magdalene shouted.

Nicodemus responded. "The Test of Honesty is comprised of drinking of the water of the Lord's Wrath. This water makes the eyes of the person, who drinks it, clearer to the sins they have committed. They are then sent out to the desert, and if they return unharmed, they are considered innocent. Mary and Joseph were both subjected to this test, and they both passed. According to the law, they were both set free and sent on their way.

This does not mean Annas forgot this declaration of the child being God's son. He was a suspicious and impatient man by nature. He wanted to keep eyes on them, but he had to deal with Rome and the changes being instituted throughout Judea. Mary and Joseph left Jerusalem and headed north to Nazareth to live their lives."

There was an uneasiness growing in the room. The group, which consisted of followers, family, Pharisees, Roman soldiers, the governess of Judea, and angels, all shifted around with a sense of confusion. What was going on? Why was this group together at this moment? It was a strange group to be assembled in such an obscure place within the city walls. Some of them walked over to the table and began to nibble on the food. Their actions were not of people who were hungry, but of people thinking deeply and were eating to eat. Soon others followed and came to the table to eat some food.

After a few minutes of restlessness and quiet, Mary spoke, "Please, everyone, please be at ease. I feel the tension in the room rising, and we need to be at peace and not talk ourselves into a state of anger or hopelessness. My Jesus was sent into this world to bring hope. Let me take this time and share with you a moment of my life with Jesus, my son."

The room became quiet, and there was a feeling of peace beginning to spread. She smiled, and her voice was soothing. All sat in a comfortable position as Mary stood next to the seder table. She took a sip of wine and began to speak.

"It has been many years since I even thought about how Jesus was conceived. Today, it appears this event in my life plays a major part in the judgement of my son. His birth is the result of God's promise to mankind. The 'how' he was conceived is not the story. The 'why' he was born and his life are the story. I played a role in these stories and still play a role. However, for now I think it would be best if I were to introduce you to my life as the mother of Jesus."

The assembled sat and nodded their heads, anxious to hear what Mary was going to share with them. Michael and Gabriel went to the doorway to watch for possible guests. They left the room, and Mary began.

"Jesus was born in the city of Bethlehem. We were there for the census of Rome. This is where Joseph was born, so we had to register as citizens there. I was near my delivery time when we started the journey. We did not plan on staying there, but as it turns out, we lived in Bethlehem for nearly two years. Once Jesus was born, we did not travel back to Nazareth. Joseph was offered work by his brother Cleopas, and we stayed in Bethlehem with Miriam and her children. These were happy years for the most part. We lived a simple life. We worked and raised our infant children together as one family.

Mary began to smile, and her face turned youthful. "Jesus was such a playful boy. Oh, He had His moments when He would cry and be fussy, but during these moments I felt needed. I had pledged myself to God and thought children would not be part of my life. I looked upon my duties as a mother as one of service. The washing, changing of clothes, and feeding were all duties of joy. I was a mother. I had a child to love.

When the baby was hungry, I would feed Him, and He would take to my breast and eat until He was full. He would look at me and smile. He was such a beautiful baby, and I was a proud mother.

We bonded as a mother and child bond. I talked to Him, sang to Him, played with Him, and all He did was smile and laugh. I felt as if I was the most blessed person in the world. Again, I never thought about how He was conceived; I just loved that He was part of my life and I could watch him grow.

By the age of two, He was walking and talking. Just a few words, but He could understand more than He could speak. It was during this time Joseph had a dream where Gabriel told him we needed to leave Bethlehem as soon as possible. Herod was planning something terrible, and it would be unsafe for us to stay in the area. We packed our things. We told Cleopas and Miriam what we knew and asked if they would travel to Nazareth and stay in our home and care for it while we were away. Joseph gave Cleopas a letter, introducing him to his fellow Nazarene carpenters so Cleopas could find work once they arrived in the area. They left a few days after we did.

As you know, Herod sent his army into Bethlehem and killed thousands of children. No child under the age of two was spared. We escaped this attempt at killing Jesus, but many innocents were sent to their death. Our course was to the west, and we set out for Egypt. Joseph, she pointed to her uncle, was aware of a large Jewish community just to the east of Alexandria. On our journey, we joined up with a caravan of merchants heading for the same area. In this caravan we found my cousin Elizabeth and her son John.

Uriel, one of the soldiers we met yesterday, was sent to guide Elizabeth and John from the area before the purge took place. They did not live in Bethlehem, but they were close enough and were directed to meet up with us on our way out of Israel. I recognized Uriel yesterday as the guide who led Elizabeth. He was good to her and stayed with us on our journey. Once we were safely into Egypt, he left the caravan, and we never saw him again.

It was a great blessing to see Elizabeth and John. Elizabeth was older, but she was strong and a good traveler. John was a few months older than Jesus, and he became a great travel companion for my son. They walked together, gathered water, played, and talked to each other and became best of friends. Mary smiled and continued. They were inseparable,

One of the travelers in the caravan was an older rabbi on his way to the temple in Alexandria. Jesus and John would spend evenings with him as he prayed. The rabbi would share stories with the boys and teach them about the history of our people. Jesus would come back so excited as He learned about Abraham, Isaac, Joseph and his brothers, Moses, and many of the prophets. His ability to learn and retain the stories mystified us at the beginning. We were amazed that a boy so young could recall stories with such detail and retell them with such passion. We watched as He grew and came to understand Jesus possessed gifts and abilities others did not. He was special; his uniqueness was very evident as a child.

Joseph and I spent a lot of time with Him as we traveled. We talked and laughed; we felt honored to be His parents. As people interacted with Jesus, they saw He was special as well, and they noticed Joseph and me as his parents. People watched how we interacted with our child and respected us for how we lived as a family. I was proud of Jesus and being on the road was good for Him.

Our home in Alexandria was simple. We were able to find lodging from one of the merchants we traveled with. Joseph, being a carpenter, was able to find work. He was excited to be in the area because the type of wood was different than he was used to in Israel. There were trees common to both areas, but in Egypt the trees varied, and the wood was a challenge to work with. He learned the types of wood and the strengths of each species and taught this to Jesus.

One of the master carpenters explained the different woods to Jesus by telling him wood is like people; it is varied, the color is different, each type has strengths and weaknesses, but they all serve a purpose. Some woods are for boats, some for tables, some for chariots, and others for lodging. The key to choosing the right wood for the right job is to know the wood and how it can be put to its best uses. Any species can do the job, but some hold up better under stress than others. Later in life Jesus and I talked, and He would refer to this lesson as He worked with the many different people He encountered in His life. I found it interesting how a lesson about wood would form a basis for Jesus's approach to people.

Elizabeth and John stayed with us. We became a close family. Joseph was the provider. His talents as a carpenter were rare in the area, and the demand for his services was remarkably high. He had steady work, and we were able to live an ordinary life, wanting but for a few things. Oh, we were not wealthy but lived as the birds in the field lived. It was as if God was taking care of our daily needs. We lived and grew close under the umbrella of God's love.

Once, Jesus and John came home after a day in the marketplace where we used to send them to pick up items we needed for the house. They came home with this story. It seems they met an older merchant this day, and he became fascinated with the boys. The boys were always more mature than their age, and this man took notice of this. He called them over to speak to them and sell them some of his vegetables. John told us this man said, 'We should let our parents know they are doing a good job in raising them.' He was watching them, and he felt a sense of pride knowing children like John and Jesus. It gave him a sense of hope for the future.

He told them parents are like umbrellas and safety nets. When children are young the parent acts like an umbrella, protecting the child from harm, keeping them protected from potential hazards of life. As the child grows and leaves the protection of the umbrella, the parents turn into safety nets. The children can fall, and the parents will be there to keep them from falling far. The older a child becomes and the more he does on his own, the safety net drops further away. It may be far away, and the child will fall far, but the parent will always be there to save him to the best of their ability. This is how God treats us as His children. We fall, and He will be there to save us.

He told the boys their parents have been loving umbrellas and by the looks of them they would be strong and durable safety nets. He sold them his wares and said, 'You give me hope for the future, and I see you two bringing a hopeful message to all those you meet.' Mary had tears running down her cheeks again. Her face was a mixture of joy and sorrow.

Miriam came over to help wipe away the tears and said, "I remember you telling me this years ago. It was one of the lessons we used to talk about. Were we good umbrellas? Did we protect our children from harm? Our children were our treasure. We loved them more than we loved ourselves." Mary looked up at her and smiled. She took the cloth and wiped her cheeks. Others in the room were now crying as well. Mary waved her hands as if to dismiss the emotion in the room, but she continued to cry.

Salome leaned forward from her seat and asked, "Mother, what is it? Why are you crying? Are you all right? Can we help?"

Again, Mary waved her off. "It just occurred to me. I have not been the safety net my son needed. I could not protect him from falling into harm. My Jesus is gone, and I could not stop it from happening. I feel as if I have failed in my parental duties. A child should not die before the parent. What type of safety net was I?"

Joseph came over to her, held her hands and looked into her eyes. "Mary, how could you possibly protect Jesus from the horrible fate he suffered? You could not have prevented this, and you had no way of knowing the high priest was going to do this. The plot is too complex, and your power in this game is zero."

Procula walked closer to both of them, shaking her head, and mumbled, "I should have stepped in and been more forceful with Pilate. He would have listened to me. I could have prevented this death if I were stronger. Oh, Mother, please forgive my weakness."

"Governess, there is little you could have done to persuade Pilate," said Nicodemus. "The high priest had maneuvered him into an unwinnable position. Free Jesus and Rome hears of another protest from the Sanhedrin about Pilate's inability to rule or allow it to happen and face the possibility of a revolt. He chose the revolt to save himself and his power. I cannot blame him for his decision. I can blame the leaders of the faith who were afraid they would lose power to someone they felt was an uneducated prophet who threatened them and their idea of the laws."

Procula looked at Nicodemus with anger in her eyes and said, "I was never under the impression Jesus was uneducated! He spoke with passion, authority, and wisdom. His message was hopeful and compassionate. Through Jesus's words I saw into the mind of God! I am sure others felt the same because as I am learning, he was the Son of God! I see now he did not have to tell people he was the Son of God; His words were the words of God, and these words brought God into the light. Jesus's words put flesh to God, and we believed! I saw Him feed thousands of people with a few fish and loaves. How could this be done unless God willed it? The priests were there. They saw the people being fed! They partook in the food! How could they not believe?"

"I do not know, Governess," said Nicodemus. "The higher you advance in the temple structure depends on two things: mastery of the scripture and your ability to manipulate people to move in the direction you wish them to move. Jesus did not enjoy the formal training of the high priests, but he had a firm command of the scripture and had disarming responses to all their deceptive questions. He outmaneuvered them at their own game, and the people who witnessed these exchanges saw how the priests backed away from the responses, giving the perception Jesus's words had more authority than theirs. They came away from these exchanges humiliated and bitter. They did not look for the good in what was being said. They were looking to destroy the messenger!"

"Mary, you could not have helped your son. The dice were unfair, and he was set up to lose the game."

The tension in the room was again rising. Mary motioned for everyone to relax and calm down. "Please, let us be at peace. There is nothing we can do right now except be present for each other and pray we have the strength to support each other and to be open to the will of God. The day is short, and we have a long night before us."

Miriam was starting to smile. She looked over at Mary and said, "I would venture to guess Jesus and John were quite the handful when they were young. Imagine two prophets of today growing up in Egypt together. How did you and Elizabeth manage those two?"

"They were two very curious children and both quick learners. They had the ability to listen and repeat languages very easily. And they loved to listen to the merchants selling their goods, how they would be out in the open and speaking in loud voices and describing their merchandise and how they would barter with customers. People would ask questions or complain about the goods, but the merchants had an answer for everything. The boys would make up a game where they were the merchants selling their goods, trying to convince our neighbors to buy something from them. As two young boys, they became creative and would entertain us with their stories and salesmanship. Looking back, this playful time helped them develop their skills with speaking to large groups of people. In retrospect, it is interesting how their childhood games formed a part of their adult personalities."

Mary looked over at the governess and smiled her way. "Governess I am sure you did not come here to listen to us recall the stories from the childhood of my Jesus. We must be boring you."

"Mother, you are not boring me! As I listen to you recall these memories and you share your son with us, I am becoming more aware of just how much I do not know about the man I listened to. When you see the man, you forget he was once a child. It appears this child displayed a uniqueness early in life. The experiences of our youth do shape our behaviors of the future. Not only am I learning about your son, I am just as curious about your story. You are a courageous woman, having the faith and belief to say yes as a young woman to something unknown and life changing.

You were a virgin who conceived a child without intimacy. Then you faced an inquisition and endured a test of honesty. You birthed a child in a grotto stable and uprooted your family and moved to a foreign land to flee a savage attack on the innocent. The you moved back to your childhood home and lived with a husband in the state of chastity. You raised an only child who was the son of God and watched this child die the most brutal death conceived by the Roman Empire. I am as drawn to you, as I am drawn to your son."

Mary bowed her head. Her eyes began to tear. She looked around the room and saw how everyone was looking at her. Their eyes also began to tear.

The Sabbath was nearing an end as the daylight began to subside. Soon it would be the end of the day, filled with both joyful and horrible memories. Mary was growing tired and felt a need to sleep but felt she must push on and make it through the night. She looked at the governess and said, "Thank you for your words, but the story is not about me. The story is about my son Jesus—His life, His Father, and the love they have for mankind."

Suddenly, there was another voice in the room that startled everyone.

"Mother!" shouted Michael. "John returns, and he has Simon Peter with him."

CHAPTER 18

Simon to Peter

Mary stopped speaking and focused her eyes on the doorway. Cornelius, the Roman centurion walked to the doorway and was visible to John and Simon as they entered the house. Simon, upon seeing a Roman in the room, came running at him screaming in a loud voice, "What are you doing here? You murderer! You killed my Savior, my King, my Lord!"

Michael and Gabriel jumped between the two men. Michael grabbed Simon, restraining him from going any further. Gabriel stepped in front of Cornelius and placed his hand on his sword and said gently, "This is not the time. Keep your weapon sheathed."

John came rushing in, breathing heavily, and looked at Procula and Cornelius. He was surprised to see the two standing in the room. He quickly swung his head to the others and said, "How did they get here?"

"You know these people?" shouted Magdalene.

John looked at the Romans and then back to the others and responded, "Yes, I know them. They are friends of mine and followers of Jesus. It was Cornelius who allowed us passage into the courtyard to view the trial. He may be a Roman centurion, but he is married to a Jewish woman, and they are believers. They have witnessed Jesus speaking many times. However, I do not know what they are doing here! How did you find this place? Why did you find this place?"

Claudia Procula walked toward Simon with a sense of purpose while he was being restrained by Michael. She stood before him and looked into his eyes and saw hate and vengeance. She said to Simon with scorn in her voice, "I saw you near the fire pit. The bystanders recognized you, and you denied knowing *your* savior three times. I heard you! I then saw you leave, crying like a baby. You left *your* Savior in the hands of the zealots to die! You charge at us as if we are the enemy, and you do not even know who we are. I see you are a man of action, but obviously you do not think before you act.

Jesus is *our* savior as well! He has invited all of us, all of mankind, to be part of His body. We have come to love *your* God through the words and actions of Jesus of Nazareth. We are here to grieve and to help. Pilate is my husband. I urged him not to prosecute Jesus. I had tortured dreams about Him the night before His trial. I pleaded with Pilate to release Him because he was a holy man, a man of God, but the Jews did not want Him released. They wanted Him dead. I am ... we ... are not your enemy. We have lost a great prophet, and we suffer with all who loved Him."

Simon looked at her with impatience but then began to relax. Michael released him. Simon then looked at Mary.

She was standing in front of the seder table, trembling. There was great fear in her eyes, and He hurried over to her and asked, "What is it, Mother? What do you fear? Please accept my apologies for my entrance. This has been a terrible time for all of us, and I am full of anger and hate. I want vengeance!"

Mary looked at Simon with sadness in her eyes and spoke to him harshly. "Simon, we are told to forgive our enemies, not to harm them. You heard my Jesus tell us this when He spoke to the crowds. If you would have been with us at the time of His death, you would have heard Him forgive his persecutors from the cross. He said, '*Forgive them, they no not what they do.*'

Simon, we must forgive those who cause us harm. These two, however, have not caused us harm. They are here to share in our sorrow. They are welcomed into our family. They desire to love Jesus and His Father."

Simon never had Mother Mary chastise him before. Jesus had scolded him for his behavior, but Mary had never spoken to him in such harsh terms. He was shaken and suddenly became aware of everyone in the room. He looked confused and unsteady and started to lose his balance. Michael grabbed him and helped him to a seat near the table. He looked at Mary and tears began to well up in his eyes. He placed his hands over his face and bent over, his elbows on his knees, and he began to sob.

Salome and Miriam went over to him and placed their hands on him to comfort him. He sobbed uncontrollably. When he picked his head up, he looked at them and said,

"Please, please forgive me. I have been wandering most of the night. I did not know where to go or who to seek out. I was a lone ship on the rough water. I could find no harbor to rest. I am tired and hungry, but before I got lost at sea, I betrayed Jesus.

The Roman lady is correct, I denied knowing Him, not once, but three times. He told me I would do this, and I boldly told Him I would never deny Him, but I was weak. I was afraid. How many times has the master told me 'do not be afraid, have faith!' Too many for me to recall, but I have been scolded for my rash behavior before, and to have Mary scold me is just a reminder of the prideful sinner I am."

John came over to him and said, "Simon, I have known you most of my life. We are business partners. You are a master fisherman and a leader; however, you are erratic and impulsive. Your decisions come quickly, and you stubbornly hold your ground when challenged. I looked for you in the courtyard after we arrived, but you were gone. I heard you were there."

"He was recognized as a follower and as a Galilean, and he denied he knew Jesus. I saw the crowd around him was fierce and in an uproar. His response was one of self-preservation. Your faith was weak, and I could see doubt in you," said Cornelius.

"Simon, you are a weak man," said Mother Mary.

Simon's head quickly shifted to where Mary was located. He looked at her with eyes full of tears and a face contorted in pain and anger.

"Mother, I am a weak man. I have failed your Son. In the garden where he was betrayed by Judas, I was angry but also frightened. The temple guards came into the garden to take Him away. My anger led to a harsh act, and I was scolded by Jesus. This reprimand startled me, and I suddenly became afraid. I saw the number of guards, and I ran away. Those of us who were there disbanded; we ran away. John, you ran away as well!"

John bowed his head in shame and acknowledged that he had fled the scene in the garden. He tried to explain his actions. "The urge was strong to run. I could not fight this urge. If we would have stayed and fought, we would have lost, and we might all be dead. As I was running away, doubt began to set in because my life was at stake. I thought of the others and my family. No one else. I was selfish. As I was wandering around after I left the courtyard, I remembered Jesus telling us there is no greater love than to lay down one's life for a friend. I loved Jesus, I mean I love Jesus, but at that moment all I could do is think about myself. I am so ashamed. I should have died with Him, but my weakness and my doubt forced me to run and hide."

The room was quiet as everyone listened to Simon and John. They had all experienced some form of fear and doubt over the past few days, but they had stayed together and were able to draw strength and encouragement from each other. Simon had been wandering alone.

Miriam asked, "Peter, where have you been? Have you been wandering around the city the entire time you left the courtyard?"

"I wandered most of the night. I did not know what to do. I saw Judas and approached him, but he ran from me. He did not look well. When I saw him, my shame turned to anger; he was the one who betrayed Jesus. He was the one who brought the temple guards to the garden and then ... then ... then he kissed Jesus on the cheek. We did not understand what was taking place.

Judas left the seder meal before we did. We thought Jesus was sending him on an errand. It was very confusing to see him with the guards. He was one of us. How could he hand over Jesus to face trial, especially at night? We were on the temple grounds every day, and Jesus was not harmed. Why take him during the night?

My mind was beginning to fill with terrible thoughts. I wanted to beat Judas, but this would have been only for personal satisfaction. I needed instead to speak to him and ask him why ... why he did this terrible thing. My heart was aching, and my mind wanted justice. I could not catch Judas. He was able to avoid me and get away.

One of the others, Matthew, informed us in Bethany that Judas was approached by several Zealot friends of his, several weeks ago. They convinced him to meet with the temple leaders to discuss Jesus and his teachings. You remember Judas was a trained Pharisee. He was active in government activities for the temple before he decided to follow Jesus. We all knew of Judas's background, but he was one of us. He was one of the twelve. I never would have imagined him betraying Jesus.

According to Matthew, they offered him thirty pieces of silver if he would inform the priests of Jesus's whereabouts on the night of the Passover meal. Judas accepted the silver and betrayed Jesus's location. Matthew also said once Judas saw what was happening to Jesus on the way from the garden to the temple courtyard, that he had second thoughts and wanted to return the silver so Jesus would be set free. The priests refused to take the money back, and Judas threw it at them and cursed. He ran from there. I must have seen him after that.

We were told Judas went outside the city walls and hung himself. It appears he could not live with what he did. In his death, I hope he found peace because his kiss started the events that led to the death of Jesus and a night of unrest for many others.

Eventually, I ended up at the home of Lazarus in Bethany. This was the agreed-upon meeting place if anything unforeseen was to happen. Everyone was there except for John and Judas. John found me with the others. We have been in hiding; fearful we were the next to die."

Michael and Gabriel came forward. They looked at Simon and Gabriel began to speak. "Simon. you have been with Jesus from the beginning of His public life. You are the lone person of the twelve to answer his question about who people say He is with conviction and faith. He named you Peter because you are the rock. God renames people to provide them with the capacity to act differently. It has happened to others of great importance. Your actions of the past few days have been more reminiscent of Simon, not Peter.

The Peter Jesus knows is full of faith. The Peter who walked on water. The Peter who saw the transfigured Jesus on the mountain. You are the rock. You will lead people to God. Lapses in faith are not uncommon for Simon, but Peter has no doubt and acts with love of the Son."

Mary came to Peter and touched his arm in a caring way. "Peter, there will come a time when you are asked to reach out to nonbelievers, people who are not from Israel, and speak of my son. They will want to hear the story of Jesus and his followers. Your story, Peter, is part of that story! Your story will inspire a nation of followers. You have met Jesus and believed! Your faith is growing stronger. Do not despair over your occasional lapses in faith, God's love for you is greater than any momentary lapse. Others will be asked to believe in Jesus, and who have not met Him. They will meet Jesus through you because your faith is as solid as a rock. Though it may be chipped away at times, you are my Jesus's greatest hope of ensuring the world knows my Jesus and His Father."

Peter paced around the room. This was the room that just a few hours ago was the room they had celebrated the Passover meal. They were around the table, eating and singing songs. It was a night of brotherhood. Simon looked at the table, and saw it contained food. He looked out the window and noticed the sun beginning to set. Then he caught a glimpse of the bloodied clothes in the corner of the room, and he turned to John and said, "What are these bloodied rags doing here in the room?" He was puzzled.

Magdalene took Peter by the arm and walked over to the pile. "These are the rags we used to clean the body of Jesus before we placed Him in the tomb. The pile also contains our clothes. We were completely covered with His blood when we were finished. Mother Mary asked if we would remove our clothes so we could burn the clothes as a symbol of the sacrifice Jesus made.

Simon, we were covered with His blood! We carried His body to His grave! We cleaned His wounds as best we could. We were there when He died. *Where were you?*" she screamed.

"You might be the rock, but today you were a pebble or worst yet a grain of sand. Jesus needed you and you were not there! Mother Mary needed you, but you were not there! We needed you, but you were wandering around the streets in fear, afraid the temple guards or the Roman soldiers would find you and condemn you as well. We, on the other hand, stayed with Jesus during His entire walk from the city to the hill, and we witnessed His crucifixion. Where were you, Simon? Why were you not here? You abandoned your Savior, your Lord, your friend, for all your bravado about knowing He was the Son of God. You left Him to the butchers to suffer and die! Oh, you of little faith. Saving yourself was more important than saving the Son of God!"

This outburst shocked those assembled. There were tears in the eyes of everyone in the room. Magdalene's chastisement of Peter's absence was severe, and while it may have made her feel good to be critical of Peter, the words did not sit well with Mother Mary.

"Sit down! All of you," said Mother Mary sternly. "I will not allow this type of assault to take place! Mary, I can understand your anger, but to criticize Peter for his actions is selfish and uncalled for. He was lost. He was afraid. He was alone. It is at these times when the evil one influences our actions. His journey to this upper room has been different than ours. We found our way here after we obediently took care of the body of Jesus after His death. We came here as a group. We were not lost, and we were not alone; we had each other and the strength of a group to help us persevere. But Peter was alone.

His faith took him to Bethany, and it brought him here with John. He did not have to go to either place. He could have left to go home to Galilee to be with his family. He could have given up entirely and just left, never to return. Did he doubt? Of course, he did! I am sure everyone here has experienced doubt since the time Jesus was taken before the High Council. Doubt cannot enter our thoughts. Doubt is the rival of faith.

My Jesus came into this world to make God known to man through the unconditional love God lavishes on mankind. We must be open to that love and accept it with an unconditional yes. Our yes tonight is a yes for all eternity. Our love for Jesus must be strong enough to pass through the barriers being placed between us by the evil one. We must acknowledge the potential for doubt, fear, and anger, but above all we must be united in our love. Love is the purest form of energy that unites us with God. Love originates in the spiritual world, lives in the human world, and transfers back to the spiritual world. Love is forever. It never dies."

Now the room was still. There was no movement or words being spoken. Mary had surprised the assembled because she rarely, if ever, raised her voice in such a passionate manner. Everyone lowered their head, looking at the floor. They were too embarrassed to look at each other.

Finally, Nicodemus, the old Rabbi, walked over to Mary with a smile on his face and spoke. "Peace be with you, my child. It has been a long time since I have seen you this passionate."

He looked around the room, with tears running down his face. "Mary, you remember your lessons well. As a child, you would debate with Gamaliel in the temple, and you were fearless. We who watched as you responded to his comments were often amazed at how well you understood God for someone so young. I thought our teaching gave you this insight, but after watching you here, I can tell your source of inspiration and knowledge was not something you acquired through our teaching. It was granted to you as a gift from God. No one could possibly have such an intimate view on God's nature unless they were kissed by the loving grace of God.

You are right. Chastising each other is not how your Son would want us to behave. I saw Him before the high priest and with Pilate, and I did not see anger or vengeance in Him at all. What I saw was a man, beaten and bloodied, stand before His accusers and remain loyal and committed to God. He was ready to give up His life for the truth—the truth of who he was and who His Father was."

Procula stood, looked at Nicodemus and then to Cornelius and added, "Pardon me, Rabbi, but I was near Pilate when Jesus was being questioned. Pilate asked Him, '*Are you the king of the Jews?*' And Jesus responded, '*You say so.*' And then the high priests accused Him of being the Messiah, and He did not reply. Pilate then asked him, '*Do you not hear how many things they are testifying against you?*' But he did not respond.

The priests stood before Pilate and continued to bring forth accusations, '*We found this man misleading our people: he opposes the payment of taxes to Caesar and maintains he is the Messiah, a king!*' Pilate pulled Jesus aside away from the crowd and continued to question him,

'*Are you the king of the Jews?*' Jesus answered, '*Do you say this on your own or have others told you about me?*' Pilate answered, '*I am not a Jew, am I? Your own nation and the chief priest have handed you over to me. What have you done?*'

Jesus answered, '*My kingdom does not belong to this world. If my kingdom did belong to this world, my attendants would be fighting to keep me from being handed over to the Jews. But as it is my kingdom is not here.*' So, Pilate said to him, '*Then you are a king?*' Jesus answered, '*You say I am a king. For this I was born and for this I came into the world to testify to the truth. Everyone who belongs to the truth listens to my voice.*' Pilate said to him, '*What is Truth?*'

Pilate was frustrated and confused. He found no guilt in Jesus. He was puzzled by the way Jesus was responding to his questions. Pilate looked out at the crowd and he saw the high priests, paper lions full of jealousy and pettiness, but he was afraid of a riot and of losing his position. He sentenced Jesus to be flogged. When Jesus returned from the flogging, He was bleeding terribly. His flesh was open across His entire body. Pilate was infuriated! He wanted Him whipped to learn a lesson, not scourged to the verge of death!

Pilate turned to me and said, 'What am I to do? This man does not deserve to die, but I must administer the law for these thick-necked people.' I told him he should talk to Jesus one more time and see if he could find a way to release Him without putting Him to death, so Pilate brought Jesus back to question him again. The high priests yelled, *'We have a law and according to that law he ought to die. Because he made himself the Son of God.'* When Pilate heard this statement, he became more afraid and asked Jesus, *'Where are you from?'* Jesus did not answer him.

'Do you not speak to me? Do you not know that I have the power to crucify you?' Jesus picked up His drooping head and looked tenderly into the eyes of Pilate and said, *'You would have no power over me if it had not been given to you from above.'* Pilate tried to release him, but the Jews cried out, *'If you release him you are no friend of Caesar. Everyone who makes himself a king opposes Caesar.'* This was the last thing said before Pilate turned him over to the Jews to be crucified.

The point I am making here, is even when given the opportunity to say something, anything, Jesus did not fear for His life. He spoke the truth. His words took on a life of their own, and He accepted His fate and was taken off to be crucified."

"I can attest to the truthfulness of the governess's words," said Nicodemus. "The high priests acted with a hate I have never seen before. These are self-righteous men pretending to be Godly, but the fact is they care more about power and personal recognition. They lost their love of God many years ago. Their arrogance is sinful, but they control most of the temple leaders. They do not fear reprisal from anyone."

Cornelius had been in the background listening to what was being said. He was the guardian assigned to Procula, and he had become a follower of Jesus. He found peace listening to Jesus talk about His loving Father on the mountain. The thought of a loving, caring God captured his heart. He was a believer. However, he was first and foremost a Roman, and to a Roman the rule of law was supreme.

"I am a soldier of Rome," he said. "I have seen a few of you, but I do not know any of you. My path to this room is one I never saw myself taking. Hearing these words gives me a moment to pause. I observed what happened to Jesus over the past few days. I have heard the high priests testify to Pilate about His crimes. In all my days as a soldier of Rome, I have never experienced such hatred for a man as these men had for Jesus. They did not just dislike Him; they hated Him and were fixated on His being put to death.

I do not know why their hatred was so cruel. I may not know if there is a history between these men and Jesus, but He was only in Jerusalem for a short period of time. He conversed with the leaders almost daily, and to form such a fiery hate for a man in such a short period of time is unbelievable from my perspective. Why do they hate him?"

"That question can only be answered by the high priests," said Nicodemus. "I have been around these men for many years. I have seen them destroy other prophets with their clever questions, but they could not fool Jesus. He seemed to be two steps ahead of them every time they met. He was never flustered or bothered by them. He was gracious, thoughtful, and respectful.

I heard Jesus was upset with the money changers in the temple courtyard. He turned over their tables yelling, *'My house shall be a house of prayer, but you have made it a den of thieves!'* The priests did not like this; however, they did not respond because the people around him were hanging on to every word Jesus spoke. They were afraid of Him. They were afraid of the power He held over the people. They responded to his preaching by asking Him, 'Tell us, by what authority are you doing these things? Who is the one who gave you this authority?'

Jesus did not respond to these demands phrased as questions. The priests were confused. They were used to people answering their questions. Jesus did not answer, and this put their authority in peril. If they were not looked upon as the authoritative voice of the word of God, there would be chaos, anarchy! The leaders never came forward themselves. They sent their underlings to ask the questions. They are a suspicious lot. They want to hold power over people by possessing more knowledge than their peer or adversary. If they were to be challenged in public, their reputation would be destroyed."

"I was not with Jesus when he entered the temple. I was here preparing this room for the Passover meal," said Mother Mary.

"We were all here," said Salome. "Only the twelve went with Jesus to the temple. When they returned, there was no mention of problems."

"Peter, John, you were there. What happened?"

Peter and John looked at each other with confused looks on their faces. They were trying to think back to this day at the temple when Jesus overturned the money changer's table. Finally, John said, "I remember this happening, but after the tables were turned over, Jesus went over to a couple selling doves and helped them with their table and asked them to '*take their doves out of here, and stop making my father's house a marketplace.*' He was angry for only a few minutes. But when He came to the couple selling doves, He calmed down and was respectful."

"The priests came over to see what was going on, and they confronted Jesus with their questions," said Peter. "Other than a brief questioning by the priests, we continued on our way. It was like any other encounter with the priests as far as I can recall."

"Oh, but for the priests who were there, this was a memorable event," said Nicodemus. "They went back to the inner temple and met with Caiaphas and Annas and told them what had taken place. Then the memories of a boy who challenged them years ago began to resurface, and the inquisition began. The priests who met with Jesus this day retold the story of the table being turned and the kindness shown to the couple selling doves. This sounded like a familiar story to a few. Then the priests continued with Jesus challenging the priests and not answering questions about where He received his authority to spread His teachings.

They also recalled Jesus's session on the side of the mountain where He preached to love our neighbor, to pray for our enemies, to turn the other cheek, and his accusations of the leaders of the faith being hypocrites. They again asked Him where he received His authority to say such things and his response was: 'I have learned all of this from my Father.' Then they asked, 'Who is your father?' He said, '*If you were pure of heart you would know my father because only those pure of heart can see him.*'

After the priest said this, there was quiet in the room. Then the quiet turned into a grumbling between some of the elder members of the court. Annas stood up quickly and yelled, 'It is the boy!'"

CHAPTER 19

Mother as Path to Son

Nicodemus looked around the room with a cautious glance and saw he had the attention of everyone, and he continued explaining Annas's response. "Jesus is the boy who entered the temple many years ago. He challenged our authority with those same words. His mother is Mary, and her husband was Joseph a carpenter from Nazareth. Back when the boy was here in the temple, he suggested His Father was God. We took it to mean we are all God's children. However, before his mother left the temple, she claimed she conceived a child through the Holy Spirit and remained a virgin! We examined her. She was pure! She had not been intimate with a man. Her claim was challenged because we thought she was lying, and thus we put her through the Test of Honesty, and she passed!

We kept track of her for a while. We found nothing suspicious about her. She and her husband lived an ordinary life. We determined there was nothing extraordinary about the boy. He was a carpenter's son, and we observed nothing suggesting he was special. We stopped watching them a long time ago. Then, a few years ago, we observed a prophet by the name of Jesus coming out of Nazareth, and his teaching was different. He spoke with passion and seemed to have a learned knowledge of scripture, but we discovered he had not been formally trained. He did not study the scriptures as a rabbi; he was an ignorant man. Our curiosity was awakened, and we turned our attention toward Jesus. Now it seems we have found both the boy and his mother!

Annas's display of excitement and anger startled the High Council. We had not seen this type of passion from him in many years. Once he calmed down, his disposition changed, and he was somewhat gleeful Mary resurfaced in Jerusalem. He sent people out who could recognize her and to have them verify Jesus was her son. When they found Jesus teaching within the city walls, they saw Mary was near Him. They inquired to those around her and were told she is Mary the mother of Jesus of Nazareth."

"Oh my! It was me! I told someone Mary was Jesus's mother," interrupted Miriam in an excited voice. "I remember someone asking about Mary. They wanted to know if she was from Nazareth. I told them she lived there most of her life. They were thankful and then walked away. I did not know who they were. Was I the cause of Jesus being taken?"

"No, no, Miriam. Just because you identified Mother Mary does not mean you were responsible for Jesus being taken," said Joseph waving his hands and speaking in a calming voice. "The inquiry could have been addressed to any one of us, and we would have responded the same way.

Asking about Mary would not register as a suspicious question. I would have answered the inquiry the same as you. The temple leaders would have made the connection eventually. Mary was never far from Jesus. She never tried to hide herself. She is not a public figure. She is the mother of Jesus and traveled with Him."

Mother Mary looked at the group and sighed deeply. She was tired. It had been a long day, and she had not gotten much rest. She needed to sleep for just a little while, but she could not slip away just yet. She stood and walked over to the window, looked out, and took a deep breath. Michael came over to her, placed his hands on her shoulders to comfort her, and said, "During the time of Jesus's upbringing, angels were directed by the Father to shield the family from harm. They could not directly interfere. They were to act as the protecting umbrella sheltering the family from harm.

Jesus is the Son of God. The time for Him to reveal Himself as the Son was known only to the Father. Therefore, angels have been around the family and shrouded them from being recognized as the Holy of Holies. We were surprisingly successful until Jesus decided to go to the temple as a youth. He chose to make himself known to the temple priests. Once the shroud of secrecy was lifted, it became more difficult to keep the family's presence private.

God had His reasons for making His Son known at that time. We did not ask why; we obeyed His command. When this incident at the temple was over, we reestablished the shroud of secrecy around the family, especially around Jesus, but as He grew, He chose to help others. It is not in

God's nature to not be actively involved with His people. He watches, listens, and interjects Himself when and where He sees fit.

Jesus went into the temple at such a young age and experienced how mankind would receive Him once He revealed himself. He was young and still needed to work on how He would deliver His message. What He experienced in the temple exposed Him to the difficulties He would have in describing His Father to those who work in the profession of protecting the faith, that is, protecting their viewpoint of God. Since the beginning, mankind has struggled with understanding the nature of God.

God is pure and good, and mankind has tried to find ways to put God into words they could appreciate. These attempts have been futile. God cannot be described in human terms; God can only be experienced. You experience God by loving each other and recognizing God is the source of all good. Everything you need to know about God has been revealed through the life of His son Jesus. Jesus is God. He is a spiritual being, born as a man to help mankind understand God and how to be obedient to God's will.

Disobedience to God has ramifications. If a conscious decision is made to disobey God, we sin. Sin separates us from God. God does not want us to be separated from Him, but our choices in life can place barriers between God and His creations. This separation includes both mankind and angels."

Mary turned around quickly and looked at Michael. His eyes were beginning to tear. She gently touched him on the cheek to comfort him. The others were now paying closer attention to Michael. Procula and Cornelius looked at each other with confusion with their eyes squinted in thought.

Cornelius walked to Michael and said, "If you do not mind, can you tell me who you are? I have seen the others with Jesus, but I have not seen you until I entered this room. You speak as if you have a deep understanding of God and His will for us. You speak of angels and the protection they provided the family. How do you know these things? You said 'we' placed a shroud of secrecy around the family, so am I to assume you are an angel?"

"Yes, Gabriel and I are angels. We are here to serve Mary."

Cornelius ran his hand through his hair and let out a long breath. Procula looked at Michael and Gabriel and kept blinking her eyes in disbelief. If what they were told is correct, they were in the presence of angels. They had heard of angels but thought angels were fictitious, make-believe characters used to entertain children. They did not believe they were real.

Procula stepped toward Gabriel with a skeptical look on her face. She touched his arm and looked deeply into his eyes. Gabriel looked back at her and smiled. "Yes. Governess, I am real. Michael and I have taken the form of humans to be with Mary at this time. We were asked by Jesus's Father to be here and serve her. God loves her and did not want her to be alone after the death of their son. As Michael said, 'God is pure and good,' and His love is everywhere and available to everyone."

"If God is pure and good, why did His Son die? Why have him suffer such a painful death?"

"It is not my place to explain the will of God. I obey God and love God. I do not question God."

"What do you mean you do not question God?" asked Procula. "If you are ordered to do something, you just do it unconditionally with no questions asked?"

"Yes," he replied.

"As I have said, God is pure goodness. His requests are always good. Questioning his commands or disobeying them does have consequences. Evil was born out of the disobedience of God. Once, angels questioned the will of God and they have been banished from heaven," said Michael. "There was a powerful angel who questioned God. He was mighty, and they called him Light Bearer. By questioning God and being disobedient to God, he and several other angels were banished from God's presence. Not being in the presence of God is hell. Because this group of angels chose to disobey God, their sin of pride took them on another path. They banded together and shouted, *We shall not serve*! Thus, we have the creation of evil."

Michael continued, "Light Bearer, or the evil one, is immensely powerful and tries to influence others to follow him and disobey God. He is very deceptive, and you can find him everywhere. He plays upon mankind's ability to choose. God gave man the gift of free will, and he can choose to do what he wants. God's only request is that man should obey the will of God. They should know Him, love Him, and serve Him. It sounds simple but it is difficult.

God does not uncreate something he has created. Once God creates something, it lives until it stops living. The evil one has been an adversary of God's since the beginning. His sole purpose is to separate man from God. He put into place a scheme many years ago to have mankind reject the Son of God. However, the death of Jesus is not a victory for the evil one."

After Michael finished, everyone stood and started to walk around the small room. It was quiet at first, but soon they began to speak to one another. There were many questions regarding the death of Jesus. Why did God allow His Son to be put to death? Where were the angels to protect Jesus? Why did Jesus not use His power as the Son of God to stop His suffering a brutal death?

"I realize this is a difficult time for you," said Gabriel, holding his hands in front of him as he spoke. "Understanding the will of God is difficult. Peter, when you were on the road to Jerusalem, and Jesus was describing how He would have to suffer at the hands of the elders, you took Jesus aside and challenged Him. You said, '*God forbid, Lord. No such thing shall ever happen to you!*' And if you recall Jesus's harsh response. '*Get behind me evil one! You are an obstacle to me. You are not thinking as God does, but as a human does.*'

God's will for his son was suffering and death. I know this is difficult to comprehend. It is even difficult for us to understand, but we obey God. Jesus could not think like a man; He needed to think of His Father, and He needed to obey the will of God."

"If all life is valuable to God, why does God will the death of His Son?" asked Magdalene.

This was an unexpected question. Nicodemus and Joseph were caught off guard by the frankness of the question. Cornelius and Procula were just as confused, and they looked around the room, trying to see if the others would be able to supply an answer.

John and Peter started shaking their heads and quickly looked to the others for clarity. Mother Mary was surprised the question was asked to such a diverse group. The Romans, the elders, the followers, and her friends all appeared to be baffled by the question. Mary was very direct with her question, and she was looking for insight.

It had been a long day and the sun was setting, ending the Sabbath. Mother Mary turned to Susanna and said, "It appears the Sabbath has ended. Susanna, could you start a fire so we can warm the room before the night falls. It would be good to heat up some food. It has been a long day, and I am sure we are all tired. Magdalene has left us with a question we need to ponder before it can be answered. Let us stop here and share some food and drink before we attempt to answer such a thoughtful question."

Susanna looked at Mary and bowed in respect, then she said. "Mother, I will start a fire here and one outside as well. You wanted to burn the bloodied rags and clothes from yesterday. It would be better to burn them outside."

"No need for a fire outside. We can burn the bloodied items inside."

"But, Mother, the rags have been in the house all day and are most likely still damp. The fire might not get hot enough to burn the rags without creating a lot of smoke."

"We can make the fire hot enough," said Mary. "It is important for all of us here to participate in the burning of the bloodied items. The blood of Jesus is sacred; it was shed for all. Here we have Gentiles and Jews: Galileans, Judeans and Romans, men and women, master and servant. No matter our differences, the blood was shed for all. Maybe now is the time to address Mary's question.

I have been told that the death of Jesus removes the barriers made by the sin of Adam. It allows mankind to stand in the presence of God. Once Jesus rises from the dead, the barrier of sin will be removed, and mankind can freely choose to be with God and live surrounded by His love in heaven."

Michael smiled and nodded to Mary, acknowledging the answer to the question. Not everyone in the room saw the nod and smile, but they heard Mary speak, and the words were beginning to set in when suddenly there was another question.

"Jesus will rise from the dead?" exclaimed Procula. "What are you talking about? Jesus is dead. He cannot come back from the dead. Once people die, they can no longer exist! Their words live on, but they do not!"

"Governess Procula, Jesus has told us on many occasions He must suffer and die. He also claimed He would rise. He told us: '*The Son of Man is going to be betrayed into the hands of men. They will kill him, and after three days he will rise.*'

At first, we were confused and did not understand what He was trying to tell us, but He insisted He would rise from the dead. He told us how He must go into Jerusalem and suffer many things at the hands of the elders, chief priests, and scribes, and be killed, and be raised again on the third day.

The third day is the day after the Sabbath. This is the day he will rise!" exclaimed John.

John's comments had the Roman guests looking at each other with skeptical looks on their faces. They were confused and started pacing around the room. Their movements were causing the others to become concerned.

"This is very difficult for me to comprehend." said Cornelius. "I have seen many men die in my lifetime, and I have been responsible for some of those deaths. But I have never seen a body rise to life after they have died. This is impossible!"

Nicodemus observed the Romans' reaction to the revelation of Jesus's pending rebirth. He had a compassionate look on his face as if he understood the confusion that must be forming in the mind of the centurion. He looked to Mary and then to Joseph and replied. "Centurion, I am sure this seems like a very strange concept for a Roman, a Gentile, to comprehend. As a Jew, especially a Pharisee, this is not foreign at all. We believe the soul of a person is immortal and indestructible; it lives forever. The soul wants to be reunited with God in the afterlife. We also believe in the reuniting of the body and soul at the end of times. The soul leaves the body and is welcomed by God and eventually it is reunited with the body when God determines the time. You are right; Jesus is dead, but his soul lives and will always live. If He is to rise, it will be the uniting of the soul to the body in accordance with God's will."

"What you are saying makes no sense to me," replied Cornelius. "Once we die, we die. There is no resurrection or an afterlife. I will admit I am beginning to rethink my opinion of an afterlife after meeting Jesus. We listened to Him speak about God and how we should treat our fellow man, but I do not recall Him speaking about a rebirth or a rising. I was content to change my life to live in accordance with His teaching; however, this is a teaching I have not heard Him voice."

Peter came forward and faced the Roman soldier. They were physically similar: strong, sturdy, broad, and passionate. He said, "Centurion, the rising from the dead was not part of the public teaching of Jesus. He spoke of this to a small group of followers. We did not believe His words, and it is possible there are some who doubt His rising will take place. We who followed Jesus are called the twelve. We are simple people from simple backgrounds. We are fishermen, carpenters, farmers, and a tax collector. We are not schooled in theology, philosophy, logic, or medicine. We just hear what we hear, and we either believe or we do not believe. Jesus has given us many reasons to believe.

We have traveled with Him, lived with Him, ate with Him, and loved Him. I speak for myself and for many of the others. My faith is weak, but it is not always weak. When I am with Jesus, all things are possible, and my strength is strong. I once walked across water to go to Him. My focus was supposed to be on Jesus, and it was for a while, but as soon as I looked around and became aware of the dangers of what I was doing, my faith vanished and I sank into the water. It is easy to have faith when Jesus is with you, but when He is not around, I have experienced serious doubt, and my faith in Him is tested."

The room was starting to get warm. Susanna was working in the background to build a fire, and it had reached the point where the flame was high, and the coals were hot. Mary went over to the pile of bloodied rags and picked them up and carried them to the fire. She looked around aware that everyone was looking at her.

"Please continue. I need to burn these items. These rags absorbed the blood of my son Jesus. He was precious to me. He is the reason I have life. I look upon these bloodied items, and I remember the pain of His death, but I also see the meaning of His life. I have always known Jesus was going to suffer and die. I did not think it would be so soon. I thought there would be more time for Him to walk among the people and give them a view of who God is.

We look at Jesus and think of a man because that is what we know. Jesus was more than a man. He is pure and good, as is His Father. He loved openly and respected all He met. Some of those He met did not respect Him and challenged Him and eventually killed Him, but He loved them, and His life was given for them and for others.

This may be new for our Gentile friends, but we were taught God asked Abraham to sacrifice his son to prove how much he loved God. When he was about to sacrifice his son Isaac, God intervened and told him it was not necessary to offer his son up to prove his love for God. Abraham became our father in faith and God told him, '*I will surely bless you, and I will multiply your descendants like the stars in the sky and the sands on the seashore. And through your offspring all nations of the earth will be blessed because you have obeyed my voice.*' For God to prove to mankind He loves them, His only son had to be sacrificed.

The death of Jesus, while painful for all of us who knew Him, is joyful to all of mankind because now all who have lived, and all who will live, can experience God through the life of my son and rejoice at being able to be in the presence of God because the stain of sin has been removed."

Mary took the garments and passed them out to the others in the room. She asked them to hold the blood of Jesus not only in their hands but in their hearts and their souls. Then she placed her rag on the fire, knelt, and said a silent prayer. She asked the others to do the same. Each person walked up to the fire holding the bloodied rags and did as Mary instructed. Tears came to all eyes in the room. The scene was silent and soon there was crying and sobbing. When the burning of the bloodied garments was complete, each person in the room felt a sense of joy as they looked at each other, and the sorrow they felt subsided.

Their hands were soiled with blood. Mary filled a basin with water. She washed their hands and spoke softly to each person in a quiet voice. The others could not hear what was being said to the person Mary was speaking to, but what was being said was needed for the person to feel loved and prepared for what was going to happen in the future. Mary's words of hope filled the hearts of everyone in the room. Those words of the future provided them with courage to go out into the world. The fire burned bright. There was no smoke, just warmth. The day was nearing its end.

The third day was but hours away.

CHAPTER 20

Believing in Things

You Cannot See

Salome and Miriam placed a small amount of food on the table. It had been a long day. The room was full of an eclectic gathering of people. The common bond joining those assembled was their belief in Jesus. During the day, the bond they felt for each other had become stronger. The stories told helped build a sense of trust.

"Sharing a meal was usually the highlight of the day as we traveled with Jesus," said Peter. He looked at John who nodded his head in agreement. "We would walk for hours or be with crowds wanting to hear and mingle with Jesus, but we would always find peace when we gathered at the end of the day to share a meal. Susanna, Miriam, Salome, thank you for this food we share." He looked over to Procula and Cornelius and said, "Governess and Centurion, please forgive our meal of common food. It is probably not what you are accustomed to being served, but it is not the food we share here this night that is important; it is the love we have for Jesus and the hope that He returns to us shortly."

"Peter, thank you for recognizing the work we do," said Magdalene. "We labor quietly in the background to make sure meals are prepared for those who sit at our table. The day has been long, and we have new faces with us tonight. I must admit I am not sure how to act with the governess of Judea sitting at my table eating a commoner's meal. However, I am grateful she is here and was able to share her experiences of the past few days with us. We were provided insight into areas we would not have known about if it were not for Procula and Cornelius."

She bowed her head out of respect and smiled as she looked at the Romans. Procula and Cornelius looked at Magdalene and bowed their heads as well. "Madam, it is our pleasure to be here with you. As a soldier I have eaten many meals in the field. Some good, some not so good. You have no need to apologize for the food on this table. It is simple, it is warm, and it is shared by friends.

I hope after today we can look at each other as friends. Much has been shared. I have learned quite a bit, and honestly, you have provided me with more than I have provided you. I am just an infant in my knowledge of Jesus and His Father. I am anxious to know more. His words touched me when I heard Him, but after listening to the conversations of today, I have a burning desire to find out more. I need to know Jesus better, to serve Him, as you serve Him."

"I agree with Cornelius," said Procula in a tender voice. "I live with Pilate, and I am a Roman. We have lived in this land for over twelve years. My impression of the people was based on my interactions with the politicians and religious leaders of the province. They are self-righteous and arrogant. The temple leaders put Pilate in peril with Rome because of their complaints of his ruling decisions. I have wanted to leave the area and go back to Rome for some time now. I was ready to leave Pilate and return to the comfort of the culture I know and the rules of social behaviors I am accustomed to. However, since I heard Jesus speak, I have changed. I want to learn more, and to do so means I need to be closer to His followers and mother.

When we arrived, we did not know what to expect. I was apprehensive and fearful, not for my safety because Cornelius is more than capable of protecting me, but I was afraid we would be pushed away. We are not Jews. We are not your friends. We are believers in what we saw and what we heard."

"Peter, you are an interesting one," said Procula. "You speak openly of faith and doubt as you walked with Jesus, but you said earlier that you see what you see and believe what you believe, and I find this perspective easy to understand. Once we came across Jesus teaching the crowds, we were curious. We followed Him and listened to His words, and inside we changed. We were filled with a sense of hope, not just for our personal wellbeing, but for all of humanity. His words were simple to understand, and I was able to see the wisdom and the love inside the man who spoke them."

She then looked around the room and seeing the faces of the others looking so intently at her, Procula then bowed her head and said softly, "I do not convey my thoughts well. What I mean is, as I listened to Jesus speak, I felt as if He were speaking to me. Me personally, not to the masses. There were times when I heard His words, not in Aramaic, but in Latin and Greek. I heard his words in a language I could understand and did not have to convert the language to get the meaning. I know Jesus was multilingual; however, when I spoke to others who heard Him speak and marveled at His use of the languages, they informed me they heard only one language, not many. I was confused when hearing this, but after meeting with you and hearing more about Jesus, I believe he told me what I needed to hear in the language I needed to hear so I could understand and apply it. He amazed me! Jesus made the words come alive!"

Cornelius then added, "Governess, what you say is true. I heard His words in more than one language as well. I have not spoken about this to others, but I am glad to know what I heard was a message meant just for me. The personal aspects of Jesus's message left me wanting to hear more. We each hear Him speak and yet we come away with a message of hope delivered just for us. I hear what you hear, but the message applies to me in a different way than it applies to others. I believe this is the secret to Jesus's popularity. I can see why the high priests are jealous of this man. His message is pure and meaningful to the individual and not hidden by some sort of religious tradition or knowledge of words written by others for others to study and quote so they appear important."

Cornelius bowed to the others and looked at Procula and said, "Governess, it is getting late. We should be returning home."

"Yes, Cornelius, we should be heading back. Pilate knows I am with you, but he does not know where we went. Should I tell him of where we were today and what we heard?"

Cornelius replied. "Pilate is a logical man and set in his ways. We can tell him at another time because I still need time to process and understand what I have learned today. If what we were told is correct, the resurrection of Jesus will cause Pilate more problems with the Jewish leadership. We can use our newfound understanding of Jesus to help him deal with the vipers at his heals. We should go."

Procula and Cornelius prepared to leave the room. Joseph and Nicodemus came over and said their formal goodbyes and said they would try to meet up with them in the next few days. They thanked them for sharing their time with the group and wished them a safe trip back to the palace.

The women, Magdalene, Miriam, Salome, and Susanna came over and wished the governess well. They were respectful of her title, but they came to respect her more as a person. She had taken a great risk to be here today, and she was open to learning more about Jesus. They parted, knowing they would meet again.

Procula came over to Michael and Gabriel and bowed to them and said "I do not know how to address angels. It was my pleasure to meet you and hear you speak of God. My life is changed. Knowing there are creatures like you wandering the earth, protecting those who believe in God, gives me comfort. Thank you for sharing your stories with us. I believe because I have seen, now I have to convince others to believe without seeing."

"That is called faith, Governess," said Gabriel respectfully. "Believing in something you do not see is called faith. Your faith has grown much today. God bless you as you share what you know with others."

Mary stood and walked over to the two Romans. She smiled in a disarming manner. She looked at both and said, "God loves all of mankind. We may distinguish ourselves as Jew and Gentile, but we are all the children of God. I invite you to expand your understanding of God: who He is, and what He is asking you to do with your life. You know God now. You have seen His Son. You have met His mother and followers. Your experience here today has provided you an opportunity to be introduced to God and His wishes for mankind. Now you are tasked to love and to serve God.

Serving God will be rewarding. You heard Jesus speak, and you heard His family and friends recall stories of His life. You must share these words you have heard from us and join yourselves to the body of Jesus. You will be included in the community of believers who will say Jesus was born, He lived, He died, and He is risen. God be with you, and as Jesus told his followers, '*they will know you are my followers because of how much you love.'* Go now and spread the love of God by loving all those you meet. Peace be with you," she said and walked back to the table.

Tears were in the eyes of Procula and Cornelius. They did not want to leave. They felt at peace. They turned toward the door and walked away, knowing their lives had been changed.

The others around the table talked about how surprised they were to meet the governess and the centurion. Their direct contact with Romans had been minimal. They looked at them as savages, but today they learned they were people looking for God, and they found Jesus who changed their lives. They were unanimous that these two Romans would be fearless followers of Jesus—Gentiles accepting Jesus as their Savior and sharing their faith with others.

Nicodemus began to yawn, looking very tired. He was an older person, and this had been an intense day. Much was discussed, and much needed to be done. He stood and addressed those in the room, "This has been a very enlightening day. When we arrived here, I was not sure what would happen. My expectations were to meet with Mother Mary and inform her of the behind-the-scene actions of the high priests. However, while I provided the information I possessed, I am leaving with more than I came with.

I have seen most of you from a distance, and I know you have not seen me. I learned about Jesus from Joseph and became a secret follower. I was somewhat skeptical when Joseph talked about Jesus being the Messiah, but after listening to Jesus speak and recalling the child in the temple,

I am convinced Jesus is the Son of God. He is the promised one, the Messiah!

Mary, the life you have led is one I need to know more about. I remember you as a child and a young woman ready to wed Joseph. However, I had no idea you were the mother of the Son of God until now. We are asked to believe many things in our life. People tell their stories, and if interesting, we listen and maybe repeat them. Mary, my sweet child, please forgive me for my lack of faith in you. It appears you have always told the truth and been faithful to God. I know my faithfulness to God has been less than absolute. You, my dear, are a different creature. You were asked to do God's bidding, and you said yes to everything unknown and yes to a lifetime with the child of God.

If I had only seen the signs earlier, I might have believed as well. But I am but a sinner and seek your forgiveness for my lack of faith. Being an educated Pharisee and a member of the Sanhedrin, my eyes were so focused on scripture and the laws that I did not see God's will around me. You, His chosen vessel of life, lived near me as a youth, and I was unaware of the significance your life would have on mankind. You are the mother of Jesus, the Son of God, making you the mother of God. If I would have known then what I know now, I would have lived my life differently and treated people with a loving heart as opposed to living a life dedicated to laws."

Joseph came over to Nicodemus and placed his hand on his shoulder and gave him a firm shake of acknowledgement. The two older men had been friends for many years, one a wealthy businessman who made his fortune selling tin to the Roman army and the other a learned scholar, Pharisee, and elder of the temple. They had met as young men. Once, when Joseph was traveling through Jerusalem, he stopped by the temple to pay homage for his blessings. He met Nicodemus who started telling him a story about a young boy who had been allowed into the inner temple and began to teach an assembly of older priests about the virtues of God. The boy made a lasting imprint on Nicodemus, and he wanted to meet the boy again sometime in his life. Joseph listened to Nicodemus and wondered if this boy could be Jesus, but he never brought up the possibility until Jesus came forward as a prophet. It was then he told Nicodemus who Jesus was and suggested this man might be the boy he had met years ago.

Joseph walked over to Mary and gave her a paternal hug and said, "I am afraid I will be leaving as well, my dear. The past few days have been full of surprises. I wish I had the energy of youth to be able to stay and be with you, but I fear the high priests are not resting. They are probably plotting something because they fear that Jesus's followers will find a way to steal the body of Jesus and proclaim He has risen from the dead. Nicodemus and I would better serve you if we were near them and Pilate. We might be able to help by being ears in the temple. We can use what we know to keep harm away from you and the twelve."

Joseph took the hand of Mary and kissed it. He looked at her with tears dripping from his eyes and he said, "I love you, Mary, as if you were my own daughter. I will see you tomorrow, and hopefully I will be here for the wondrous news we are expecting."

"Uncle," said Mary as she walked with him and Nicodemus to the door, "I do not know what I would have done without your intervention. Being granted the body of my Jesus for burial was unexpected, but in hindsight I do not know what I would have done with the body. We were present for His death, but we were not prepared for the burial. Your act of kindness will be remembered forever.

And, Nicodemus, thank you for being here and bringing us news of what took place outside of our view. You are a true friend of my Jesus. He would have liked you. You possess a pure heart and so by recognizing Jesus, you were able to see and recognize the Son of God who is a pure reflection of His Father. The love you have shown for my son will not be forgotten. I am sad you must go. Being near those who wish harm to us is wise. Be careful as you travel home and may God bless you and keep harm away from you."

The two older gentlemen walked out the door and waved goodbye. Soon they vanished as they walked into the darkness.

Night was falling, and the light of the fire illuminated the dining area. Susanna began to place candles around the room and lit them. Soon the room had a warm, cozy feeling, and those remaining began to display signs of exhaustion. They managed to make it through the Sabbath without any harm coming to them, and with the size of the group diminishing, fear began to rise within the room.

Peter walked around the room as if he were a caged animal. He was nervous and could not calm himself. John was talking to Michael and Gabriel in the corner in a quiet voice. They were discussing the safekeeping measures to be in place for the night. The two angels said they would stay and be near the women and keep them safe. John suggested he and Peter stay as well, but Michael instructed him to leave and go to Bethany where the others were in hiding. "The others have been waiting all day to hear news. You were there earlier to retrieve Peter, so they were able to hear some of the things that occurred since the seder meal. It would be good for them if you and Peter were to return and bring them up to date on what you have heard. Much has been revealed today, and there is a high level of apprehension for tomorrow.

Jesus said he will rise in three days. Tomorrow is that day. If Peter is correct, some of the twelve have doubts and their faith is unsteady; they need you to be in their midst when the morning comes. You have a long night ahead of you. The fear and doubt will attract the evil one. If you cannot survive the night as a group, you might not survive at all. It is imperative the twelve stay united.

Look at Mary. She is busy with the others, cleaning the room. You would never know her son had died. She is a beacon of light in a dark world. Her faith is unbreakable, and her love for Jesus is as strong as Jesus's love for her. She does not rely on faith for the return of her son; for her it is a certainty. He will rise, and He will remove the barrier of sin between mankind and God. You have been fortunate to have lived with the two of them because they are the redemptive lives that will save the world.

One said yes to give birth to the Son of God, and the other said yes to die for mankind. There is no greater love than this. Choosing to act in accordance with God's will in a loving way exposes God to all who observe the action. Jesus, Mary, John the Baptist, Elizabeth, the women here in this room, and all who choose God help remove the barrier of sin and make God accessible to all: Jew or Gentile, man or woman, free or slave. All are welcome to be in God's kingdom."

John listened to what Michael said to him. He agreed it would be better for him and Peter to return to the others and inform them of the events of the day. He turned to Peter and said, "Peter, we must go to the others and tell them what has happened here today. We must also be there to ease their fears and to find a way to give them hope that tomorrow brings a new beginning to all those who love and serve our Lord."

Peter looked at John, then at the others. He was conflicted. He wanted to stay because he felt safe in the company of Mary and the angels. There was a look of indecision on his face. Mary came up to him and gave him a hug. It was the gentlest hug he had ever received. It felt as if energy had passed from Mary to himself. He felt his faith surge.

Mary said firmly, "It is time for you to act like Peter, the Rock. Others are relying on you to be strong. Your purpose has been exposed to you, and you have a choice to accept your purpose or reject it. What are you going to do?

Is your answer a yes to my son Jesus, or is your answer one of self-preservation?"

"I choose Jesus!" he said firmly. "I wandered around last night like a boat lost at sea with no direction. Today I have found my direction. Being in this room and seeing where Jesus shared wine and bread and told us it was His blood and body sacrificed for us has strengthened my resolve. Jesus washed our feet here and told us we must serve." He looked around the room and gave a silly smirk of a smile, "It is easy to say yes I will serve when Jesus is standing right next to you, but when you are alone, it is difficult to choose God and to serve him. Tonight, I choose God. I choose to do what Jesus asked me to do. I choose to be Peter!"

Mary had tears in her eyes. Michael and Gabriel were smiling broadly. John was slapping Peter on the shoulder. The others looked at him and clapped their hands together. Magdalene said firmly, "Finally, Peter! We have waited to hear this! The journey is still treacherous and the evil one will try to tempt you, but we know you have the strength to be what Jesus said you would be. Go and tell the others what has happened here today and be prepared for Jesus to return. Peter, you are the rock, the foundation."

All who were in the room gave Peter and John a hug as they walked to the door. When they were on the street, they looked back to the room, bowed their heads, and whispered a prayer. They turned to begin the journey to Bethany. They nodded at each other, smiled and began to run.

The night had overtaken the day, and those remaining were showing signs of exhaustion. The day needed to end in sleep for the remaining members, except they were showing signs of nervousness. If what they were told is true, Jesus would be rising from His grave the next day. How could they sleep when such an extraordinary event was about to take place? They were too excited to sleep.

Miriam walked over to the window and looked out into the dark. She was followed by Salome, and they inhaled the cool air of the night. They both yawned and smiled at each other. The tension of the day was wearing off, and they were very tired and needing to rest.

Mother Mary could see the people around her were sleepy, and she said to them, "We have to get some rest. I know we are anxious, but we are too tired to do anything else tonight. Michael and Gabriel will watch over us and be on the alert for those who might come during the night."

She turned to the angels and said, "Please be on the watch for us tonight. We have had little sleep these past few days. We are tired, and tomorrow holds the hope of being a glorious day. So, if you could watch over us and keep us safe, we could relax and get some sleep. We will need our energy when the sun brings us a new day."

The two angels came over to Mary and held her hands and said, "We are with you, Mother. Be at peace and rest."

The women went to the sleeping area and prepared to go to sleep. They did not realize how tired they were, but as they began to lay down, they looked at each other and smiled. This group of women had been Jesus's and His followers' supporters since His public ministry began. They knew hard work and late nights, but tonight they were very tired and ready to sleep.

Mary looked around the room and said, "We have gone through much together. We are friends and sisters. I love you all. I ask God to bless each of you with a restful night's sleep. When we wake in the morning, we will have the faith and energy to serve God in any way we can. Good night dear ones."

There was a silent thank you offered for the prayer. They laid down, closed their eyes, and drifted off to sleep.

CHAPTER 21

The Evil One Arrives

Mary placed her head on the straw bed. She began to pray but then stopped. Her mind was not allowing her to rest. The events of the past few days were racing through her head. She could see her child hanging on the cross; however, He was not in pain. He looked at her and smiled. It was a smile only she could see, but it was a smile she remembered, and it brought joy to her heart. Even on the cross, Jesus could find his mother, smile, and bring joy. The relationship they shared was special. Mother–Son, Son–Mother, they had bonded at his birth and were bonded for all eternity. Their love for each other united them. Words were not needed.

He looked directly at her, then whispered. *"Hail Mary full of grace, the Lord is with you. Blessed are you amongst women and blessed is the fruit of your womb.*

Mother, the fruit of your womb is here before you, humbled and rejected. My Father's will is accomplished. Rejoice, mother, I love you; you who brought me into this world, guided me, and lived a life of service to my Father."

He continued looking at her, and in a voice she could barely hear, said, "*I loved you when you were a child. I loved you when I was a child. I loved you as I grew into adulthood. I have been blessed to have you as my mother! Thank you for the gift of my life.*" He closed his eyes and vanished. He was gone. She began to cry.

Suddenly she was unnerved by the voice of another. This was the muffled voice she had heard at the foot of the cross, but now it was clearer. It had always been muffled or distant. It was a voice she ignored in the past, but now it was clear. She turned around to see the source of the voice and saw a beautiful creature standing near her. Immediately she knew she was in the presence of evil.

"Hello, Mother! It has taken you a while to get to this place. You are between being awake and being asleep. It is the place where I dwell and whisper my words to mankind and offer them visions so real, they cannot tell what reality is and what is a dream. I live in the shadows here where it is hard to be seen, but I know *you* can see me. You have always been able to see me. From the moment you opened your eyes, you knew who I was. You looked around the room and saw your parents, and there I was in the background looking at you. You were not afraid.

I found this a bit strange. Usually, when I stop to see a child enter the world, they cannot see me, but they can sense my presence and cry. You, however, did not cry, and you did not look away. You looked directly at me. You squinted your eyes and looked at me with contempt. How can a newborn baby form a face of contempt? I do not know, but you did.

Your ability to recognize me frightened me, and hell shook when you were born. I am not easily frightened. Only God frightens me, but you, a child, born with a heart so pure and soul not stained with the sin of Adam, frightened me. What was your purpose, I asked myself? It was then I recognized the face of God on you and the wings of Michael holding you for the other angels to see. You were under heaven's protection from the moment you came into the world. Why? I asked myself.

"But I am only playing with you," he laughed. "I knew you were going to be born since the beginning of time. I knew you were going to be the instrument God used to introduce His son to this world. You were going to be my greatest adversary! I cannot speak His name, but your son has no beginning and no end; He is God—the God who created all things. He created me! He gave me great powers, but the greatest power He gave to me and all the angels was the supreme ability to be free, to make decisions on our own. The gift was *free will.*

I thought I was special, having been created with the ability to choose my own path. This freedom did not come without conditions. It came with the stipulation that I obey God. I was honored with the gift and thanked my Creator for His generosity. However, God thought mankind should have free will as well, not at the same level as mine, but man could choose. This was a gift I thought was too great for man to possess. Man did not have the power to control this gift. Being of free will means you know the will of God, and you make your choices based on the will of God. If man chooses not to follow God's will, he will not be allowed to be in the presence of God. God wants all He created to be in His presence, does He not?

Knowing God was going to bestow free will unto mankind, I protested and offered my assessment as to why mankind should not possess a gift so precious. I argued and debated with my Creator, but God did not accept my rationale. He granted man free will. I could not accept this. I am the greatest of God's creations. Why should a creation so inferior, like mankind, possess something of such great value, and be at an equivalent position as mine? I could not accept this. I rebelled. I disobeyed God and many of my comrades did as well.

What was the outcome of our choice? We were *banished* from Gods presence for eternity! I have powers beyond the others, and my Creator banished me from His kingdom. He banished all of us because we said, "*I shall not serve*!" Our choice to disobey created a chasm between God and us. You have been introduced to this as sin. My act of disobedience was the genesis of sin. My choice to not act in accordance with God's will, led to the creation of the Tree of Knowledge of Good and Bad. It was this tree he placed in the middle of the garden of Eden, and God instructed Adam not to eat of the fruit of the Tree of Knowledge. It is here where I came to take my vengeance on God!"

Mary sat up in her bed and stared at the evil one. She was not afraid, but she was curious as to why he had chosen now as the time to appear to her. She looked at him and remained quiet.

"I appeared to Eve as a serpent, and I asked her a question. It was a simple question. There was no hidden meaning. God gave her this gift of free will to let me determine if mankind was worthy of the power of free will. God requested one thing of mankind, *to not eat or touch the fruit of the tree in the middle of the garden lest you die.* I told her, "Certainly you will not die!"

I did not know what knowledge God had bestowed on mankind at their creation. Was man an immortal being? If so, there is no death. So again, my response was not harmful. If man were made in the image of God and given abilities to live in the world with the other creatures God created, he could not die! I then suggested to Eve, '*God knows well that the moment you eat of the fruit your eyes will be opened and you will be like gods who know what is good and what is bad.*' Was I wrong? I was speaking the truth!

I knew what the Tree of Knowledge would do. All God did was ask them not to touch the fruit of the tree; he did not tell them *why* they should not touch it. He just said, "Do not touch it!" He did not tell them the repercussions of touching the fruit! Do you not think that was important information to know? I mean, Eve and Adam were just created. How much experience with God did they have?

Eve looked at the fruit. It looked pleasing, and then she began to *desire* the fruit. Oh, she did not touch or eat it right away. She walked by the tree and looked at it and became curious as to what knowledge or wisdom she could gain by eating the fruit. Her curiosity increased, and the more she looked at the tree and the fruit, the more she wondered what she was missing. While the fruit looked delicious, it was not the reason she chose to take it and eat it. She wanted to possess the knowledge of good and bad and to obtain it she had to disobey God.

After a while, she chose to eat of the fruit, and then she convinced Adam to eat of it as well. I did not pick the fruit for them. I did not tell them to eat the fruit. I did not tell them to disobey God. I only suggested that they would not die if they ate the fruit of the tree. I also told them they would know what is good and what is bad. *I told them the truth!* But they chose to eat the fruit. They used the gift of free will to choose and do what God had asked them not to do. I did not make the choice for them. All I did was talk to them and give them a different viewpoint.

Possessing free will has consequences! So, I presented them with an opportunity to make a choice! I was helping them stay in the good graces of God. How was I to know a choice to eat of the fruit would put them on the side of the chasm where they cannot be in the presence of God?" Now the evil one turned his face away from Mary. He smiled as he turned away. He knew his telling of the story was partially true, but it was a fabricated account of what took place. There was just enough truth to make it seem truthful. He was lying, bearing false witness, and he was good at it. He needed to see if Mary would become sympathetic to his version of mankind's first act of disobedience to God.

"Since then, I have been accused of being the master storyteller who twists the truth to lead man away from God, the one who puts barriers between mankind and God. I seduce men to disobey God! I use man's gift of free will to have him choose to not be in union with God. It is *my* will that mankind be kept from the loving embrace of God."

Mary was shocked to hear these words. Being in the presence of the evil one was causing her pain. As she listened to the voice she had ignored her entire life, it became clear to her the evil one was her adversary, and she wondered about her safety. She was sure this place of dreams was real. She felt safe, but she had never been this close to the evil one before. What motivated him to seek her out now?

Mary stood up from her bedding and looked at the creature with a quizzical look on her face. She said, "I know who you are. I have heard your voice many times. I have heard you whispering into the ears of others. You did not know I could hear you, but oh yes, I have been aware of you my entire life. I have seen the results of your whispering. I could not stop your whispers, but I could try to intervene by bringing the light of my son Jesus to help people and bring them back to God. All of your words are lies, and this will be your undoing!"

The evil one raised his hands to its ears and yelled, "*Do not mention that name*! From the beginning of time when God promised to send His son to remove the barrier of sin between Himself and mankind, I have worked tirelessly to increase the chasm between God and man. It will take more than the death of His Son to fix the distrust man has for each other and their lack of love for God. I have watched God since the beginning. He has given man many opportunities; He even offers them forgiveness! He never offered me and my followers forgiveness. We were banished from heaven forever! Man, on the other hand, is given the chance to be with God after many sinful acts. Man sins, and God forgives! With us, He bans us from His presence. I hate Him for that!"

Mary shook her head and placed her hands on her face and said, "So you hate God. You say that so casually. God does not deserve hate; God is pure good. How can you choose to hate God? Your pride has blinded you to the goodness of God. My Son was sent to this world to remove the barrier of sin and to open a clear path to God by acting with love and forgiveness. You use this gift of free will to hate God. You choose to hate Him instead of seeking forgiveness. How can you be forgiven unless you are repentant?"

"You speak truthfully, Mother. I can never ask for forgiveness. I disagreed at the beginning of time, and I am surer of my decision today. Man must not possess free will. He denigrates God's goodness just for being alive. You see, Mother, I am of the attitude that God intended for man to be kept at a distance from Him. He does not want man to be in His presence. He gave him free will to keep him away!"

"There is no truth to what you are saying. God wants mankind to be with him in his kingdom," replied Mary.

"I would beg to differ. Back in the early days of man's existence, the whole world spoke the same language. They used the same words; they understood each other. Mankind was joined and decided to build a city into the sky to be closer to God. You know the story of the tower of Babel.

What did God do? He came down to see the city man was building to be closer to God. And He said, '*If now, while they all speak the same language, they have started to do this, nothing will later stop them from doing whatever they presume to do. Let us go down there and confuse their language, so that one will not understand what the other says. Thus, the Lord scattered them all over the earth and they stopped building the city.*'

Because God confused the speech of all the world and scattered man across the world, He pushed mankind away from Him. He did not want them to share in his kingdom. God created the instrument to expand the barrier between Himself and man! I just use what God created to keep mankind away from Him. From my viewpoint, I am doing the will of God! I used words, phrases, questions, and a bit of truth to speak to Eve about the Tree of Knowledge. We used the same language; imagine what I can do with multiple languages and multiple meanings to words. The confusion introduced by this action at Babel is my greatest tool to not just keep the barrier between God and man in place, but to expand it! Deceptive language was the originator of sin, and it will be the perpetuator of sin! The chasm will grow wider between God and mankind, and God has provided the tools!"

Mary looked sternly at the evil one and walked closer to him. She showed no fear. He was a marvelous creature, beautiful and respectful. He showed no sign of doing harm to her, and as she moved closer to him, he started to back away. He was the one showing fear. This was not the reaction

Mary anticipated. She thought the evil one would be arrogant and righteous, but he backed away in a very apprehensive way. She frightened him, and she wondered why. Then she had a thought. She was the mother of Jesus, the Son of God. She was touched by God in a wonderful way.

"Blessed is the fruit of your womb." She heard the thought go through her mind. Her womb brought forth the Son of God. Her womb was the tool, the vessel to bring God into the lives of mankind. God changed from being just words or vague images or allegory. God became flesh, and his blood was her blood! God became *real*, and it was through her yes that God could be seen and heard for all of mankind to see and understand. Jesus's blood flowed through her body, and the evil one knew it. Through the blood shed by Jesus's yes to His Father's will, the evil one could be overcome.

Mary looked at the evil one and said, "Why do you walk away from me? I am but a humble servant of God. You behave as if I pose some threat to you. This night I wait for the return of my son. Jesus."

The evil one cringed as the name was spoken.

"His birth, His life, and specifically His death are designed to bring mankind closer to God, not increase the distance. Jesus is the Word of God come to life! 'In the beginning was the Word and the Word was with God and the word was God. All things came to be through Him and without Him nothing came to be. What came to be through Him was life. And this life was the light of humanity. And the light shines in the darkness and the darkness cannot overcome it.' Your proclamation about deceptive language being your tool to separate God from His children does not hold much strength. God's Word is strong, and through His Son, it will be known throughout the world. God's words have no limits. People will be brought to salvation through the Word of His Son Jesus."

The evil one cringed once more. "Oh woman, God's Word has been around since the beginning of time. The message is not new. Mankind has twisted the words of God into concepts and ideas, not real words to be lived and acted upon. People are always looking for new words because they are bored with the message. Saying the same thing over and over has decreased the value of the message. People know the words but have chosen to not hear them anymore. In some cases, they say the words are old and for another time, not my time; they do not apply. In my time I need *my* words. That sounds selfish to me, but then again, we know mankind is self-centered.

Once God's words were known by all men, but the meaning of the words have lost their value. The words began to have varying degrees of certainty and meaning. The longer man exists, the more the words change. God did send His Son to put flesh to the words, but His death brings an end to this."

"His death does not end anything!" exclaimed Mary. "His death is God's commitment to open a way for mankind to be with God in His kingdom! You know what His death will accomplish! Do not claim innocence!"

"I claim nothing! The death of your Son may open a path, but it does not eliminate the sin of Adam and Eve. The first sin broke the seal on the Tree of Knowledge. Mankind will have to choose between good and bad for eternity. The gift of free will is, and will always be, the gift that keeps mankind separate from God!"

Mary was tiring of the debate. This was not something she was accustomed to doing. She was a servant of God. She was not one to argue or dispute. Her knowledge of God was strong, and she was protected by His love. Right now, she felt as if she were under His protective umbrella, and the evil one could not harm her. She did not doubt. Her faith in the Father was undeniable. She looked away, closed her eyes, and began to pray.

"I see you are praying, talking to God and asking for His help. Tonight, with the death of His Son, my powers are stronger. Your son is dead, and He cannot help you," said the evil one.

His words startled her. She knew they were not true, but they did give her pause. The evil one saw this pause and began to speak.

"Ahhhh, I see a pause in your response. You are not sure. Maybe I am wrong, but I sense you are struggling to find fault with what I say. Allow me to convince you by telling you a story about words and how they can change the way a man thinks. Back when the Greeks were the leaders of the world, two of their great thought leaders debated on the best way to learn. Do you remember Socrates and Plato? Socrates was the teacher and Plato the student. They established two methods of learning; one way was to speak the word and to share memories, and the other was to write the words down so they could be shared to the masses. The method preferred by Socrates was the art of speaking. One could impart feeling and emotion in the words, and a person could better persuade who he was speaking to.

To Socrates, real exchange of ideas could only be gathered through dialog. You ask a question and receive an answer. Ideas are exchanged in a give and take manner. The more questions you ask the more you learn. It is a wonderful way to learn, but it has its limitations. Exchanges are between a few, so the gain of knowledge is available to only those involved in the dialogue. The teacher controls the exchange and leads others to the place he wants them to go. To those who hear and participate in the interaction, a great learning takes place, and the exchange is part of their memory and can be recalled as any story is recalled because the teacher and the student are actively involved with the learning process. Speaking is active, and so is listening.

Plato, on the other hand, preferred to have the words written down. The author controls the content and then chooses the words the reader will consume. The benefits of this method allow for a topic to be recorded and shared with a larger audience. The word can be shared wherever the written material is available. The drawback is the written language is just one of the languages available to mankind. Words need to be translated, and some words cannot be translated accurately, so the message of the author might get altered because the translator cannot find the right word to describe what the author intends.

One method focuses on speech and the other on writing. One method relies on the ability of the person to recall a topic and to verbally persuade others to their way of thinking. The other method relies on written text, and a person's ability to write a meaningful thought. It relies on others possessing the ability to read and place the right level of emotional significance to what was written.

I live in both worlds. I can manipulate a thought or a word to cause confusion and doubt. Being the master of lies allows me to seduce man by using his own words. I can manipulate God's Word through both methods. If I wait long enough, mankind will forget the intended meaning of words and substitute new meanings, and this will instill distrust. If a man cannot trust the word of another man, he cannot trust the Word of God, whether it is spoken or written. Man has become a self-righteous being, and the need to be right and be better than the other person will disrupt God's plan to bring mankind to Him.

Your son's death does not eliminate these paths of confusion. His words while mighty, and true, will deteriorate over time because mankind's freedom to choose will change how people understand the Word. Every commandment will be at risk because the words will lose their meaning. People will think them suggestions, not commandments given by God! Your son's pronouncements from the side of the mountain will live a short life because man will choose not to act in the manner described. I will help men become good at making a speech. One does not need to know the truth in order to talk about it. All someone needs to do is persuade people through words. The person delivering the words will become more important than the words. The shift to style of delivery versus meaning of the word will confuse men, and I will be there to help them.

When the Word became flesh, His words should hold a special meaning. One must understand the Word. The Word must take root in man. Once the Word leaves this world, I can instruct mankind to search for the truth! I have observed a lack of willingness to find the truth. I have seen more willfulness from men to define God in their own terms versus a willingness to understand God in the simple terms He has put in front of them. Complexity and variety may stimulate the human intellect, but they place barriers between God and man. God has laid out a simple path to know Him and to be in His presence. The gift of free choice distracts mankind from finding Him. They may acknowledge Him. They may be aware of Him, but they will not, cannot, obey Him because He will no longer be real, He will be a concept. The more mankind tries to put God into terms they can understand, the more diluted the Word becomes."

Mary could not listen anymore. The evil one was boldly predicting the fate of mankind. Her son Jesus's life and death were God's gift to remove the barrier of sin and open a path for man to travel and reach the kingdom of God. The evil one had laid out a future where finding the truth about God would be extremely difficult. He would have the tools to distract man whenever he saw it necessary to create a new viewpoint on how God thinks, what God wants, and what God is. How could mankind find God if words describing God were the enemy of God? Her mind was racing. She was caught in the maze laid out by the evil one. What was she to do?

"I see you are confused," he taunted. "I sense you are less sure of the future than you were when we started this exchange. You see, I established a rationale course of events that will widen the chasm between mankind and God. Your son's death does not open the path to God; it only places more obstacles in the path. Obstacles are choices. Once people have a choice, they will not choose the path to God because they will not know God or trust God."

Mary was now feeling a sense of panic. She had never been this close to the evil one, and she was feeling the power he possessed to seduce men to his viewpoint. He was articulate, persuasive, and rational. It was difficult to find fault with his story. What chance did mankind have against an adversary so skilled at fabricating a story? How would mankind know what was truth and what were lies? She suddenly had a thought that made her smile. She looked at the evil one and began to speak. "You definitely have the ability to tell a story. God has blessed you with many talents and, yes, it will be difficult for mankind to choose wisely in the world you describe, but it does not mean it is impossible to choose God if one has faith in God.

Faith is powerful and can help mankind to see God in everything around them. Faith is knowing God will be there when you seek Him out for support. Faith is a gift from God, and when it is freely accepted, the Spirit of God will act on behalf of mankind. My Jesus came into this world to give mankind hope that being with God is possible. His message is simple and easy to understand. His words are God's words. They lead mankind to loving God by loving each other. Many of the great prophets have had lapses in faith, but God never gave up on them. God wants mankind to love Him and serve Him like I love him and serve Him."

"How do you know God wants you to love Him and serve Him?" the evil one remarked. "Clues of what God wants have been around since mankind was created. God has set up this elaborate maze that is supposed to lead mankind to Him, but the puzzle is too complex, and man wanders and wonders what God expects from them? How is one to find God and serve Him when He hides from them? God did not make knowing Him easy. If His intention were to have mankind know him, He would not have granted them the gift of free choice. He has allowed too many paths for mankind to seek Him. If he would have limited their choices, more people would have found Him and loved Him, but today mankind does not know God, and only a few want to find him. My kingdom is full of souls yearning to be with God, but Adam's disobedience keeps them apart."

Suddenly the evil one stopped speaking. He cringed and looked as if he was in pain. He grabbed the side of his head and screamed. Mary looked at him in shock and wondered what was going on. The evil one was in pain, and she could not see the source of his affliction.

"*Leave my mother alone!*" came a command from behind the evil one. "Do not turn around for you know it is forbidden for you to look upon God. When I was in the desert, you tempted me, but I was in my human form, and you could approach me, but now I am who I am, and you have no power. I have descended into your realm, Light Bearer. I have seen my people and now the barrier between God and man has been removed. My sacrifice, freely chosen, has opened the door for all souls since Adam to be able to enter the kingdom of God. My presence in your realm gave the lost souls a vision of hope that they would cease being separated from God and be with me in heaven. I was born for this purpose of removing the chasm you placed between man and God, and since the dawn of time, I knew we would see each other again."

Mary looked on, and saw Jesus standing behind the evil one. The evil one could feel His presence and began to crawl away, looking for protection.

Jesus came over to His mother and looked at her with the brightest of eyes. She smiled at him. He said, "Mother, it is good to see you again! However, I must deal with Light Bearer first, so if you can please be patient, I will be back to tend to your needs." She smiled at Him while tears began to stream down her face. Her son, the Son of God, had returned to be with her. She bowed her head in reverence while He spoke to the evil one.

Chapter 22

Jesus Appears

J esus focused his attention on the evil one and began. "Meeting here in this place between being awake and being asleep is highly creative, Light Bearer. You know you have no power over my mother in the real world. She has been blessed with special capabilities designed to identify and combat you. Here in the world of in between, you can speak to her. What are your intentions?

My mother is not part of our quarrel, yet you involve her with your words of confusion and lies. Since the time you led Eve to the Tree of Knowledge and influenced her choice to gain access to the secrets of the Tree, the secrets of knowing good and bad are available to all mankind. Your actions to influence Eve to disobey the Father opened the door for mankind to know right and wrong. There is no guessing; the secrets are no longer hidden. Adam and Eve may have lost their immortality, but mankind was given the chance to know God, to love God, and to serve God through faith. Access to the secrets of good and bad has allowed man to develop the part of God that was breathed into man when he was created. Man's possession of a soul provides him the foundational awareness of what is good!

When I breathed life into the nostrils of man, I granted him a good spirit. Mankind was created to be able to choose the good I had placed in the world for him. Your twisting of words confused Eve and Adam. Your influence placed the Tree of Knowledge of Good and Bad as the focal point of Eden. It was not the focal point; it was there for Adam to recognize and avoid. I placed it in the center of the garden so it would be difficult to reach, but you led Eve to the tree and simply suggested she would gain more knowledge if she ate of the fruit. She suddenly had a desire for the unknown. You placed the choice before her to make. If you would have left them alone, the fruit of the tree would not have been touched."

"You have too much faith in mankind to choose good," whispered the evil one.

"And you are too arrogant to realize man will choose good by his nature and want to share eternity with me," said Jesus.

"The barrier between You and mankind will never be removed!" yelled the evil one. "I will hide in the words of men, written and spoken! I will whisper different meanings to all who speak or write a message designed to bring mankind closer to You. Better yet, closer to each other! I will confuse the listener and the learner, so the messages will not be understood. I will create doubt and confusion in all knowledge acquired by mankind and force them to look deeper to find You. You will always be visible because

You are God. Mankind will just have to see through my lies to find You. I will create challenges designed to rationally point in many directions, such as science, medicine, philosophy, religion, mathematics, and all other subjects man uses to look for You, but only one will lead to You. My deceit will create nonbelievers and conditional believers, but only the men who accept and possess Your gift of faith will find the path to You.

It will not be an exciting path because to distract and manipulate mankind, I will create diversions that appeal to the adventurous nature man has developed. I will use the model of Babel and create diversity in beliefs to further separate mankind! Possessing a set of common values, possessing just what is needed, sharing a common base of knowledge will be categories of separation. Mankind will be separated from You because values will be differing, possessions will be highly regarded, and education will define the ignorant. Mankind will be more concerned about their wellbeing, their social position, their possessions, and their position above other men and not care about you!

I will disappear into the background and not be visible. I will create doubt as to my existence. I will make mankind believe that I do not exist. Man will think of me in an abstract manner. I will not be real to them! They will not believe I am working my will to maintain the barrier between You and man!

You may have opened the door to heaven and removed the barrier established by Adam, but I will create so much confusion mankind will struggle to find you and share in your heavenly kingdom. They will make choices to not be with you. They will think they are making decisions that are good. The Tree of Knowledge of Good and Bad will be forgotten. The tree will become an allegory, a point in a fable, told to learn a lesson. This fable will be forgotten. And I will take mankind from Your kingdom! This would not have been my course of action, but You granted mankind free will. They will choose my lies and scoff at Your truth."

Jesus looked at the evil one harshly and then His look turned to one of tenderness. He waved His hand in a dismissive manner and said calmly, "Light Bearer, I have heard you spout these claims since the beginning of time, and I have grown tired of your boasting. You have separated yourself from me by your disobedience. I do not wish to be separated from my creations. I ask you now to please come home to me! I have opened the path to heaven for mankind, and now, I offer the path to you as well! You are my creation and I love you, but your reluctance to seek repentance has been your downfall. You were created without a soul because you are pure spirit, pure energy. You were not created to earn my kingdom; you were created to live in my kingdom and to serve me. You were given the gift of supreme free will. You knew my will regarding good and bad. You did not even have to figure out what disobedience meant because you knew the consequences of your decision. When you chose to disobey me, you chose an existence of being separated from me and a life in hell.

Will you repent for your choice, and return to me and serve? I look over all of my creations and I long to share my kingdom with all who know and love Me."

Jesus then walked closer to the evil one and placed His hand on his shoulder and said, "Lucifer, my child please turn around and look upon me. I have not yet taken on my heavenly characteristics. You looked upon me in the desert and you can look upon me here."

Mary moved closer to Jesus and she placed her hand on His shoulder and smiled as He expressed His desire to be reunited with His fallen angel. The offering of forgiveness was unexpected, but she could see the love in her Sons eyes. It reminded her of the father looking for his wayward child and longing to hold the child once again in a loving embrace.

Her touch was met with a glance of appreciation and they both looked upon the evil one with hope he would rejoin the family of God.

The evil one was shocked! This is not what he was expecting. He had not looked upon God since his act of disobedience. He heard the tenderness of the voice of Jesus and turned his head toward Him and looked upon the Son of God. He was immediately filled with happiness and joy. He was looking upon his creator and he longed to be held by Him.

Lucifer bowed his head and said, "My Lord, I have longed to look upon you since I was banished. The love in your eyes is still as visible as it was before. I miss being in your presence and drawing life from your love. I did not expect you to touch me and ask me to join you. Your willingness to forgive is extraordinarily strong and my desire to return to you is great, but I must ask you if you have decided to remove the gift of free will as a characteristic of mankind? Will man still possess the gift of free will?"

Jesus looked upon Lucifer and responded. "Light Bearer, you know I do not take away what I have given. Mankind will always possess the gift of free will. My offer to you is sincere and made out of my love for you. My offer has nothing to do with mankind, it has to do with God and His fallen angels. If you wish to reenter heaven and stand by my side and serve, here is your chance to serve Me. Do you accept my offer?"

The evil one looked upon Jesus and then he looked towards Mary who was returning his look with a smile. They stood over him He did not fear being in their presence. He felt loved and welcomed. Then he looked at the hands and feet of Jesus and saw the scars created by the spikes and spear during Jesus's crucifixion. . These visual reminders of how mankind treated the Son of God brought about a change in his behavior. His feeling of being loved turned quickly to anger and he shouted, "Look at your hands and your feet! Mankind chose to ignore all the clues that pointed to you as being the Son of God, the Light of the World! You came to save them and what did they do, they put you to death. They *chose* to reject you as their savior and killed you!

Even when your mother humbly explained how you were conceived; they did not believe! She told the truth and mankind did not listen. She was a beacon pointing to you and they would not follow. She said yes and never wavered from the truth. You are the Son of God the savior promised to make heaven open to all of humanity and mankind chose to reject your love by hanging you on a tree!

My contempt for mankind has not changed. My original premise that mankind could not handle the power and responsibility that comes with free will is more real now than at the time of man's creation. They are not worthy of your love and I will continue to drive mankind away from you, not because I do not love you, but because I *do* love you!"

Lucifer turned away from Jesus and Mary. He placed his hands upon his head as if in pain. He yelled, "*I shall not serve!*" His features were contorted, and he was disfigured. He was vanishing from the in between world. His powers were not as strong as they were when he entered this realm to speak to Mary. He was weak before Jesus—and angered he was asked to repent.

"Then be gone with you Light Bearer! Leave my presence. You were given a chance to regain your place in my kingdom, but you chose to not serve. This opportunity will not come again. I have opened the doors to your kingdom, and you will find there are missing souls because they chose redemption! Leave me and may our path never meet in this place again!"

At once the evil one vanished. The realm of in-between was now filled with only Mary and her son Jesus. Jesus looked at His mother. He was radiant and calm. The exchange with the evil one had no effect on Him. He smiled and walked toward her.

"Mother, I am glad to see you. I have not yet risen, but the time is near where I will have to leave the tomb."

Mary looked at him. He looked like he did when he was teaching on the side of the mountain. There were no wounds on His head. There was no blood on his tunic. She looked at him closely and noticed wounds on His hands and feet. He lowered His tunic to display the side of his chest. There was a wound where the spear pierced His side. These were the only reminders of His tortured death. The rest of His body was pure and healed. He looked strong.

She smiled at Him and said softly, "Your body! Where are the wounds? You were beaten terribly." She came closer to Him and reached to touch Him, but He came toward her and opened His arms and pulled her in for a long, loving embrace. He touched her hair and ran His Hands down her head to her neck, and He kissed her on the forehead and on the cheeks. He looked at her with a smile on his face. Then he began to cry.

"Mother, I have returned. My journey has taken me to where souls have waited for me, and I have met those souls who are ready to enter my heavenly kingdom. I brought them hope and love to fill their hearts, removing the barrier in place since Adam has been accomplished. Your yes to have me as your child, was the redemptive yes that allowed me to be the light required for mankind to see the pathway to my Father's kingdom. Your yes made it possible for My Father's will to be done. We, God and man, have become united.

My life's actions are a living example for mankind to follow. I lived as a man with real human limitations to show mankind it is possible to find God if you live to know Him, love Him, and serve Him. My father allowed me to use His power to perform deeds. Natural laws have been in place since the beginning of time, but My Father was able to show how He was the Creator of these rules, and they would bow to His will when He wanted to make Himself known. In my human form, I was His instrument of these revelations.

Soon I will rise and make myself known to mankind as the conqueror of death, although death will be defined differently—not as death of the body. This death is necessary, but death as being separated from God is no more. Mankind can now share in the heavenly kingdom and walk with God and all His creation. One need not fear death, but mankind can look forward to entering the kingdom and being together with their Creator for eternity. God loves what He created. He wants to be united with His creations. Separation has been difficult, but mankind needs to find their way to God.

It was my Father's will for my human life to end so quickly. I wanted more time to spend with humanity to learn more about mankind and experience the adventures that come with living a human life. There is so much unknown, so much to discover. As a human you learn through your life experiences, and one needs to experience God to know God. God makes Himself known through so many different experiences: relationships with people, relationships with all God's creatures, and relationships with nature. All are ways to find God.

God can be realized in joy and sorrow, health and in sickness, and hardship and blessings. God has created this human tapestry of differences to help mankind learn how to know God in a variety of ways. My life in this world has exposed me to the difficulties faced by mankind. I have seen hunger. I have seen pain. I have heard questions with insufficient answers. I have seen cruelties no one should face, but through all these experiences I found the Father. Each of these encounters opened a door to find God. Mankind looks to the sky and yells 'Why?' Instead, they should look to the sky and say, 'Please Help me!' The Father yearns to help His creatures, and all we must do is ask. Answers may not be immediate, but there will be an answer.

My life is an example of the differences God has built into His creation. I have met many people. I have traveled to different nations, spoken several languages, and worked many jobs as a carpenter, as a fisherman, as a miner, and as a sailor. I have lived my life with the most loving of families. I was able to find the will of my Father in every one of my life's experiences.

I discovered that life is a prayer. The more it is lived, the more praise we give to God. One can find comfort in routines that are performed regularly because they help mankind feel safe and secure. But the routine of one, or some, is not the routine for all. Every one of God's creatures must find their own way to God. It is simple, but difficult. Mankind does not realize their differences provide

God with a sense of joy when they figure out the puzzle He has built for them to build and solve. Their life may be confusing and different from one another. Some puzzles are more difficult than others, but the solution is the same: living in the kingdom of heaven with God."

Mary kept looking at her son, marveling at His words. He spoke to her gently and with a certainty in his voice. It was a voice she had come to love over her lifetime. The voice of her child was the voice of God. She knew it and loved listening to it.

"Jesus," she said, "You are here with me in this realm between being awake and asleep, yet You seem so real to me. You are here, and I can touch You and hear You. I am filled with joy that You are with me. Is this realm real or just a dream? Are You here, or is this just my inner thoughts? I love You with all my being. I want this to be real and not just a dream. I want to be with You and to share Your life with others. I was born into this world to serve You, and I wish to continue my life of service to You."

Jesus smiled. He looked upon his mother and said, "Mother, I appear here to you in this realm because I have not yet risen. However, I am real. You can touch me. We can talk and be together, just the two of us. Our life together has been one of love and service. I have learned much about mankind from you. You had enough courage to allow me to experience many things.

God's people exist throughout the world, not just in one geographical location. God's love is for all mankind, not just the Jews. Experiencing life as a human gave me the perspective to live life on a day-to-day basis. Not knowing what wondrous things could happen in a moment of time is indescribable. It is a gift from the Father. I have learned to look at each day as a fragile gift because humans are very delicate, and accidents happen, altering the choices a person needs to make in their life to live in accordance with the will of the Father. Man can be affected in many ways, physically, mentally, and spiritually. There is a struggle to find meaning in life. My life gave me a glimpse into the struggles man has with believing things he cannot see.

My Father wants mankind to share His kingdom and to stand in His presence and love Him. The world in which mankind lives provides many distractions to the simple request to know Him, to love Him, and to serve him. The gift of free will, as described by the evil one, does make it challenging for mankind to find God and love Him. Men have placed themselves in a position of authority over each other. God does not wish to rule mankind. He wishes to share His kingdom with those who have loved as He has loved, meaning to love as I have loved. I am the living example for mankind to follow. However, as time passes, mankind will concentrate more on the extraordinary actions of my life. The day-to-day aspects of my life will receive little attention, that is, my life with you and our friends.

You brought me into this world. You and Joseph, Mary and Cleopas, and our family lived a simple life. We did not need much; we worked hard, used our gifts and talents, and created a life centered on knowing God, loving God, and serving Him through service to each other. I grew in human knowledge and learned how to work and to toil for my daily bread. I experienced poor people who did not have as much as we did, and I learned how to share our bounty with others. Men must help other men to find God.

I lived a life centered on God's will: feed the hungry, give drink to those thirsty, offer clothing to those in need, provide shelter for those without a roof, visit the sick, speak to the imprisoned, comfort the sorrowful, and to forgive offenses. These actions sound like they should be done without asking; however, the evil one has already clouded the eyes of mankind, and people do not willingly act out of kindness. If they act, they are looking for recognition or reward. This is not the way of God. Actions of kindness must be acts of kindness without any expectation of reward or repayment.

We lived together and our hearts were pure, free of selfish intentions and self-righteous desires. You taught all of us—Joses, James, Jude, Simon, Mary, and Salome—that an act of pure and selfless giving brings happiness to all involved. This is the will of my Father, and you made it easy to understand.

Oh, Mother, we could stay in this realm forever. I am at peace and filled with much joy being here with you. From a human standpoint I feel safe, secure, and loved. This place is real, and I am real. We shall meet here often as the days go by. We have this place to share our thoughts and relive our memories. I can reveal things to you here, and you will have all the time you need to understand what I say. You are my greatest weapon to combat the evil one, and we will spend time here, devising ways to help mankind recognize the evil one and his plots to separate them from God."

Mary walked away from Jesus, put her hands on her face, and rubbed her eyes and said, "The evil one was a mixture of emotions while he was here. He was happy, angry, arrogant, righteous, and ultimately defiant. Son, you know I am with You and support You in all of Your ventures, nevertheless, I do not possess what is necessary to help in this battle to keep the evil one out of the lives of mankind. I will do whatever the Father asks. I have no personal wants because I have You. Like any mother, I took great joy in watching You grow into the man You have become. We shared tender moments in Your childhood. I watched You take Your first step. I was filled with joy when You spoke Your first word. You recognized me and reached out and said Mama! I understand I am not the only woman to experience joy because of a child, but my child was special. I may have been an overly protective mother, but You allowed me to grow into a woman and a mother by being my child. I have no regrets about my life with You.

Our house was a house of love, understanding, and forgiveness. I am not sure if our house had these values because of Joseph and me, or if your Father put these virtues in place for us to take hold of and use. I was never sure. The only thing I was sure of when You were a child was the love we shared for each other and those around us. I am Your mother, and You are my son. I could word it, you are my son and I am Your mother, but please allow me this one vain moment where I can claim to be Your mother openly, without fear and with an unconditional love.

I love You son. I love your Father, and I love the Spirit that binds You into one. I am the most blessed creature because I was able to serve God and by serving, my reward is You!"

CHAPTER 23

This Is My Spouse

They stood and looked at each other, smiling. Tears were running down their cheeks. These, however, were not tears of sorrow or pain, but tears of joy, tears of pure love.

"The night is almost over, Mother, and I need to end our meeting," said Jesus. "I will not meet you in the realm outside of sleep until later, so this time I have spent with you here is my gift to you. We have shared a lifetime together. We have loved, laughed, cried, and bonded closer than any other mother and son. We are one. Your blood is my blood. I am yours, and you are mine. We are bound for all eternity. Your yes to the Father will be remembered by mankind forever. I realize the events leading up to and after the conception have caused you grief these past few days. For that I am sincerely sorry.

My conception is not a secret. It is a story to be told, and how the Holy Spirit blessed your womb with a life, with the life of the Son of God, will be remembered as a joyful event, full of mystery, joy, love, and fear. The conception will not be remembered as an unholy event. You will not be remembered as the high priests claimed. It will be remembered as a miraculous event that brings the Son of God into the world.

My birth in Bethlehem will be the story that is told. The holy men, the shepherds, their flocks, and the manger in the grotto will point to the arrival of my birth. Blessed is the fruit of your womb, will be a joyful song for all of God's creation! I am the rightful Son of God, born of the Virgin Mary, grandson of Joachim and Anne, and born of the House of David. I was born in Bethlehem, raised in Nazareth, and died in Jerusalem. I lived my life among a loving family of people. I traveled to the outer reaches of the Roman Empire, and I became the man my Father expected me to be. I fulfilled His will by dying on the cross to make heaven accessible to every soul ever conceived. I am the body of God to be known to all mankind.

My time to rise approaches.

Mother, you will wake soon. You will be able to recall everything we have discussed here in this realm of in-between. It will be up to you if you choose to make our meeting known. My relationship with you is special, and if you choose to make this night known, you can."

Mary came toward Him and gave Him a hug. It was a hug of a mother to a son who is about to set off on an adventure. She pulled away from Jesus and said, "Son, my life is not important. You are the reason I was born. You are the reason I lived. My life with You is a treasure. If it is all right, I would like to keep our meeting here private. It was me being able to spend some time alone with You before you announce Your resurrection to the rest of mankind. It was just me and my son! Now is the time where the Word who became flesh, becomes the Light of the world."

Jesus took Mary by the hands. He bowed down and kissed her hands tenderly. Then He stood and, touching her cheek, said, "I must go now. I love you and I will always be with you, and you will always be with me."

When she opened her eyes, he had vanished. Mary looked around the room and saw Magdalene sitting over her. She squinted her eyes and blinked several times waiting for her eyes to focus. She smiled at Mary. Magdalene spoke in a tender quiet voice, "Mother, I hope you are feeling all right. There were a few moments where you mumbled words and moved hastily in your sleep. I was worried you might be under the influence of the evil one. Michael warned me to watch you as you slept because you might be vulnerable."

Mary looked at Magdalene and smiled. She waved her hands as if nothing had taken place. She said, "This is the day the Lord has made, let us rejoice and be glad. Mary, it is nearly sunrise and I have a feeling my Son will take the morning as the time to rise from the tomb. Can you and the others go to see if the tomb is unharmed? We were told there would be Roman soldiers posted to protect the tomb. However, I think we should make sure ourselves. Go and see what you can find out and return when you are finished."

Magdalene nodded her head in agreement. She went to get the other women, and off they went to visit the tomb to make sure everything was all right.

Once they left, Mary fell to her knees, looked out the window, and watched the sun rise to start the day. She looked upward and said, "Our son has risen! Thank you for allowing me to be the mother of your child! My life is yours. I serve you as you need."

It was then a white dove flew through the window and landed in front of her. The dove bowed its head, leaped onto her lap, and nestled in her arms. Then there was a voice from above, "This is my spouse, in whom I am well pleased."

9 781662 813535